3 1994 01553 7829

STITCHING SNOW

STITCHING SNOW

R.C. LEWIS

HYPERION
LOS ANGELES   NEW YORK

Also by R.C. Lewis
Spinning Starlight

If you purchased this book without a cover, you should be aware
that this book is stolen property. It was reported as "unsold
and destroyed" to the publisher, and neither the author nor the
publisher has received any payment for this "stripped" book.

Copyright © 2014 by R.C. Lewis

All rights reserved. Published by Hyperion, an imprint of Disney Book Group.
No part of this book may be reproduced or transmitted in any form
or by any means, electronic or mechanical, including photocopying,
recording, or by any information storage and retrieval system, without
written permission from the publisher. For information address
Hyperion, 125 West End Avenue, New York, New York 10023.

Printed in the United States of America
First Hardcover Edition, October 2014
First Paperback Edition, October 2015
10 9 8 7 6 5 4 3 2
FAC-025438-15275

Library of Congress Control Number for Hardcover: 2013046571
ISBN 978-1-4231-9468-2

Visit www.hyperionteens.com

SUSTAINABLE
FORESTRY
INITIATIVE
Certified Chain of Custody
Promoting Sustainable Forestry
www.sfiprogram.org
SFI-01054
The SFI label applies to the text stock

FOR PAIGE AND MJ,
AND EVERYONE ELSE
WHO DEFIES THE ODDS

1

IT TOOK ME SEVENTEEN seconds to decide Jarom Thacker's reputation as the sharpest fighter on Thanda had been exaggerated. At twice my size—and age—he was quick, forcing me to move or risk getting pinned against the cage, but he made a rookie mistake. Like everyone else who came through Mining Settlement Forty-Two, he aimed for my gut. So predictable.

Wouldn't want to botch the pretty girl's face, right? Idiot.

I blocked him on the left, but sweat stinging my eyes blinded me to his fist slamming into my right side. Pain flared through my ribs. The fire spurred me on, and I slipped Thacker's grip when he grabbed at my arm.

Unlike him, I had no qualms about uglifying him further. The heel of my palm slammed into his nose with a satisfying crunch despite the cushioning of my shock-fiber hand-wraps, drawing a chorus of sympathetic grunts from the crowd. He staggered back as the coppery smell of blood wove into the usual stench of the cage.

Thacker's broken nose didn't stop him. He lunged blindly, grabbing for any part of me he could reach. An easy dodge, and I took the opening to knee his groin. When he doubled over, I kicked his legs from under him. He dropped and I followed, bracing my legs against his while my upper body pinned his shoulders. The shouts surrounding the cage crested as Thacker pushed against the threadbare mat. Before he could throw me off, I grabbed a fistful of his sweaty hair and slammed his head down.

"Three...two...one..." began Petey. "Fight goes to Forty-Two's own Essie!"

A mix of cheers and groans met Petey's announcement. I liked to think the men in Forty-Two knew better than to bet against me, but it sounded like Thacker's reputation had tempted more than a few. The free-flowing jack-ale probably hadn't helped.

Their problem, not mine.

Once Petey released the gate latch, I swung myself out of the cage and walked straight to one of the washrooms at the back of the tavern. Jeers and shouts followed, but I didn't listen. Petey would offer another glass of jack-ale on the house to ease the pain, and after sleeping it off, they'd remember why it was better all around if they *didn't* throw me down a mine shaft.

Same story as last week.

I threw the lock on the washroom door and started patching myself up. Even with a relatively quick match, I never got away clean. The hand-wraps kept me from breaking a finger, but they were all the safety equipment we got in cage fights. A gash on my upper arm bled freely, thanks to a loose bit of cage wire. I rubbed a sani-swipe over the cut and slapped a smart-plaster on it. It'd probably still leave a scar. Wouldn't be the first.

Next I checked on my ribs. A nice bruise was gearing up, but nothing felt broken. Not like that time two years ago—one of my more memorable losses. Memorable, except for the part where I'd been knocked out.

Knocked out, helpless in a room full of drunk men.

I splashed icy water on my face, forcing deep breaths to keep both the memory and the panic attack at bay. Nothing had happened. Not then, and not today.

"You should stop, Essie," I muttered. "You're not blazing invincible."

Rational talk wouldn't change my mind. It never did. The part of me that liked lashing out in the cage, liked taking down men bigger and stronger than I'd ever be . . . that part always won.

Besides, I needed the winnings.

Once I finished patching, I settled myself on a stack of old boxes in the corner and pulled a digital slate from my coat pocket. I loaded the latest drone program and let it scroll across the screen before noting a few tweaks I wanted to try. My body relaxed as my mind drifted away into schematics and machine code, logic and order, cause and effect.

When I surfaced, the noise outside the washroom was gone. Safe to go.

The Station wasn't empty yet, but the handful of men left were three sniffs from passing out, too far gone to notice me. By the smell of things, nearly as much jack-ale had been spilled as drunk. Petey looked up from polishing the bar and gave me a nod.

"There yeh are. Good fight, that one. Didn't expect Thacker to go down so easy."

"Doubt he expected a girl to give him so much trouble," I countered.

"We'll see how long that lasts. Yer reputation's spreadin', Essie."

A reputation wasn't what I needed—not beyond the one that kept the men in Forty-Two from getting foolish ideas—but there was nothing for it. People would talk.

I tapped the MineNet computer terminal built into the counter, bringing the lights around the touch-panel to life. "My shares?"

Petey logged in and executed the transfer. "There yeh go. Want to put in an order for anythin' while yeh're here? Spare optic lines for the drones, maybe?"

"I'm set with all that. Saving up for some ready-made components so I don't have to stitch every blazing thing from scratch. Maybe a new processing module for my computer so I can get some real work done."

"Well, I'm sure we can't wait to see what magic yeh weave next, once yeh've got everything. Might take the sting out for some of the men who lost tonight."

The frayed edge of my sleeve caught my eye. Maybe I *should* spend a few shares. "A lot of them lost?"

"Fair number thought Thacker'd be a sure thing. Hawkins said you could make it up to them by fixin' the transmission on the old pulverizer."

I grunted. "Aye, well, I assume you reminded him that it's not my job, and I would sooner bring the sun a sniff closer than waste my time on the mining equipment. They have the mech-bots for that."

"Whatever the mechs are doin' gives out after a day or two."

"Fine, I'll download the specs to one of my drones, see what it comes up with. But you can tell Hawkins to stop thinking he'll get me to set foot in that mine."

"That I will. Lemme walk yeh out. Grayson, keep an eye on things." Once his assistant nodded an acknowledgment, Petey took his coat from the hook and turned back to me. "Bundle up, now. It's a cold one."

He said that every time I left the Station. Every second on Thanda was a "cold one." The obviousness never kept him from watching to ensure I followed the advice. I pulled up the hood of my own coat, tucked in my scarf, and accepted his smile as he ushered me out.

An electronic voice greeted me on the other side of the door. "Essie Essie Essie."

I wasn't surprised to see the little robot lurking nearby, but I sighed anyway. "Didn't I tell you to go home?"

"Home Essie home."

"Right, got it."

Petey chuckled. "At least ol' Dimwit's stopped tryin' to follow yeh in."

That was true enough. The men weren't fond of the drone's squealing and squawking throughout the fights.

"I can make it home on my own, Petey," I said.

"I know yeh can. But I have a delivery to make down the way."

"Suit yourself."

We walked to the street, and I enjoyed the quiet while Dim-wit scurried amongst some empty supply crates. The drone's four spider-legs made it faster and more agile than I'd ever be, but it lagged behind like a distracted puppy, its optic lenses swiveling to take in scenery that never changed. Its arms moved endlessly, ready to make mischief, which meant I had to keep half an eye on it. Nothing new there.

Both moons were out, their light glinting off the stark metal structures lining Forty-Two's main drag. The shacks closest to the Station were in high demand, with easier access to supplies, entertainment, and jack-ale; I was more than happy with mine at the edge of the settlement, even if it meant I had a fifteen-minute walk ahead of me.

Fifteen uneventful minutes...usually.

As I turned to tell Dimwit to get moving, a streak of light approached over the eastern edge of the settlement, bringing with it a bone-grinding whine.

"What in blazes...?"

Petey's question was a good one. As the object passed over, I got enough of a look to answer. It was a shuttle of some kind. Not like the usual carriers that took merinium from the mine to a spaceport. No, this was more elegant, carefully designed, with massive engines.

Interplanetary. The kind of shuttle that wasn't supposed to come directly to the settlements.

And judging by the way it careened past, it was completely out of control. Not long after it disappeared beyond the scraggy forest, the ground shuddered.

Petey was on the move before the vibrations stopped, running back to the Station and shouting for Grayson to grab a medical kit and anyone sober enough to see straight. When Petey got back to my side, I was still frozen, staring.

"What do yeh think, Essie?" he asked. "The flats?"

His tone told me we needed to help, but something in me resisted. Something that lured me to the comfort of my routine here, to things that didn't change.

Mother would've been halfway there already. That thought sparked me into motion.

"Aye, the flats. Let's go. Dimwit, move!" I broke into a run with Petey on my heels and jabbed the transmitter I wore on my wrist. "Whirligig, you hear me?"

A faint electronic voice replied through the tiny speaker. "Affirmative, Essie."

"You and the others get out to the flats beyond the forest. A ship has crashed. Find it and report back."

Two beeps were all the response I got. 'Gig and the other five drones were well ahead of us at my shack and would cover ground more quickly than Petey and I could. So could Dimwit, but it lingered at my side.

"Don't suppose you want to pick up the pace and help the others?" I asked.

"Run Essie help Essie."

"Right, whatever."

We passed my shack and kept going into the forest that bordered that side of the settlement farthest from the mine. The moonlight didn't help much among the trees, shadows disguising the roots and stubborn undergrowth, but I didn't slow down. Petey fell a step or two back, but I knew he'd keep up well enough. Even with his age, the man was still fighting-fit.

Halfway to the flats, the receiver on my wrist pinged. I punched it as I ran. "Did you find it, 'Gig?"

"Affirmative, Essie."

"What do you see?"

Ticktock's voice cut in. "Garamite design, Class Three intra-system shuttle."

Garamite. Two orbits away from home and coming to the wrong part of Thanda. That made no sense.

"Condition?"

"Significant damage, specifics unknown," 'Gig said. "Infrared indicates possible fires in command and engine compartments. Instructions?"

"Try to get inside and pull out any people on board. Use medical protocols. And put out the fires!"

My muscles burned, but I ran harder, cursing the weight of my coat. If I dropped it, I'd have bigger problems. At least the snows hadn't come yet.

With the adrenaline pushing me, the eight links I could walk in an hour took under twenty minutes. But it felt like days. The drones could only do so much for the people on board; for all I knew, we were eighteen minutes too late.

I stopped at the edge of the woods to assess the scene. The flats spread before me, and the shuttle lay dead center. Not as bad a crash as I'd feared—it was still in one right-side-up piece. The sparks and smoke, however, didn't bode well.

Neither did the lack of people outside. A hatch gaped open at the rear of the shuttle, so the drones had made it in.

Petey caught up, along with Grayson and one of the miners. Just one. With Petey's stipulation of "sober enough to see straight," I wasn't surprised.

"Essie, I...I don't like the look of that smoke," Petey said.

I caught the look in his eyes. Worry, but also fear. He'd told me stories about a mine fire when he was younger, how he'd lost friends down there. Grayson was the kind of man who could only unpack jack-ale if Petey gave him bottle-by-bottle instructions, and the miner he'd brought wasn't one of the sharpest, either.

The people inside the shuttle didn't have time for this.

"The drones'll manage it," I said. "Come on!"

I forced more air into my lungs, ignoring the protest of my bruised ribs, and pushed on across the flats. The three men followed. "Got those fires out, 'Gig?" I said into my wrist transmitter.

"Affirmative, Essie. Secondary fire ignited in rear compartment...now extinguished."

True enough, the plume of smoke eased up as we approached. Still no sign of people. "Survivors?"

"One human male, command compartment."

Blazes, just one?

Petey cut in. "Well, why haven't you brought him out?"

"Medical protocol. Do not move humans with possible spinal or cranial trauma."

I clambered through the hatch into the engine compartment, coughing on the acrid smoke lingering in the air. It was the last thing I needed after a hard run, and I gripped my aching ribs with one arm. The drones didn't have the same problem. Clank and Clunk worked on locking down the electrical overloads sparking all over the ship, and Zippy put out a minor fire behind a control panel.

"Make sure the drones didn't miss other survivors," I told

Petey and the other two men, taking the medical kit from Grayson. "I'll get the pilot."

I left them to it, hurrying past two lateral rooms to the command compartment at the front, half expecting to find a dead body or two to climb over.

No bodies. The pilot slumped over the main console, his safety harness unfastened. All I could see injurywise was a nasty burn on the back of his right hand. Whirligig stood nearby as though unsure what to do, so I sent it to help the others. I pulled a scanner from the medical kit, and it gave me the details 'Gig couldn't.

Definite concussion, smoke inhalation, plenty of serious contusions, and several burns, but nothing to prevent him from being moved.

Before I could say as much, the console erupted in a new cascade of sparks, along with the panels to either side of me. I grabbed the pilot around the chest and pulled him back, hauling him out of the chair.

"Petey, a little help!"

The old man ducked in and took the pilot's legs, helping me carry him to the rear of the ship, electrical discharges showering every step. Grayson and the miner met us at the hatch and lent a hand getting us out.

"Cut the power—just cut it!" I shouted at the drones. "Anyone else alive?"

Petey had to cough three times before his voice could answer. "No, but no one dead, either. He was the only one on board."

We laid the pilot on the frozen ground, and I finally got a good look at him.

He was young, around my age.

"What in blazes is a kid from Garam doin' all the way out here?" Petey said.

I was thinking the same thing. Shuttle pilots were usually cantankerous and old, especially the types who traveled alone. And when they bothered coming to our planet at all, even black-market pilots went down to the Bands, not the mines.

The boy was also beautiful in a way that didn't make sense on a rock like Thanda. Golden skin that saw more sun in a day than we saw in a whole cycle, strong cheekbones and jaw like an artist had drawn him, and brown hair with just the slightest curl. The one less-than-beautiful feature was a bloody gash on his forehead.

I couldn't breathe. He was terrifying.

One of the drones swore, breaking my spell.

"You said it, Cusser. Come on, boys, let's rig something to get him back to town."

2

WHEN I'D SAID "back to town," I hadn't meant my own shack, yet that's where the men left the strange Garamite boy. Petey gave two reasons: it was closest to the wreck, and it kept our visitor farthest from the mine. Good reasons.

We'd sedated him to keep him out for the journey, but I'd seen plenty of worse injuries in Forty-Two. A smart-plaster on his forehead, regenerative wraps on his burns . . . The boy would be good as new soon enough.

And then what?

I would have been happy if he stayed asleep looking pretty for a few decades, but I doubted that would happen. Eventually, I'd have to deal with him.

A tap on the door signaled Petey's return from a quick stop at the Station. The no-good-news look on his face didn't improve my mood.

"Immigration officials on their way?" I asked.

"No, and that's the thing. There aren't any alerts about a

sanctioned shuttle crashin', but there aren't any about a *non*sanctioned shuttle crossin' the perimeter, either."

Hearing that Immigration wasn't on the way was a relief, but not enough to balance the new questions. "Scan-scrambler?"

He shrugged his slumped shoulders. "Must be. But it'd be a mighty powerful one to get through up here. What would a boy like this be doing with such a thing, and alone?"

That question piqued the part of my brain that craved new puzzles. "I'll find out. You're exhausted, Petey. Head on home." I cut off his attempt to protest. "You all have work to do in the morning, and if I can handle Jarom Thacker, I can handle one injured boy from Garam. I'll let you know if I find out anything."

He gave in and left again, slamming the door a bit hard on his way out—hard enough to rouse my mysterious guest, who began to stir. From the groan, I guessed I hadn't gone heavy enough with the painkillers. He wouldn't be feeling too spry, but I palmed a tack laser behind my back, just in case. As well as I could handle a fight, a makeshift weapon meant a lot less effort.

A second groan resolved into words. "Ow . . . What—where am I?"

"On Thanda. Mining Settlement Forty-Two."

His eyes wandered, unfocused, until they settled on me. Dark eyes with an unnerving depth to them. "Forty-Two . . . There was a malfunction, smoke everywhere."

"Aye, then you crashed about eight links from the settlement."

"Crashed?!"

He pushed himself up, too fast, nearly toppling over before I pushed him back with my free hand.

"Slow down. You're not going anywhere just yet."

"My shuttle. Is it—?" The boy gasped for breath, pain

contorting his face and raising sweat across his forehead. I thought about giving him a higher dose of painkillers, but decided I preferred him immobile.

"Still in one piece, but in a bit of a state. It's not going anywhere just yet, either."

"How bad is it? Can it be repaired? Is there someone who could do that?"

A snort of laughter slipped out. "The slugs around here are good enough at *using* machines, but haven't a baby's first gasp on how to make them work to begin with. Garamite brains like yours, you can manage yourself, right?"

"What? I...Not my area. Botany. I don't know anything about shuttles. But it has to be fixed. I can't stay here forever."

"True enough. Forty-Two's work crew is full up, and you don't seem the mining type. Mind telling me why you've gone to the trouble of scan-scrambling your way here in the first place?"

He paled enough to tell me it wasn't just about the pain. "What do you mean?"

"We may not be brilliant Garamites around here, but we know there's only one way to get to the surface undetected. There are *three* habitable planets in this solar system other than your Garam, and no one chooses Thanda for a vacation. So why are you here?"

"You'll laugh."

Unlikely. I told him so without a word.

"I'm treasure hunting."

"If you think you're going to steal one speck of merinium, those miners will make you wish we hadn't pulled you from that wreck."

My decided lack of laughter seemed to startle him. "No, not merinium! Not even close. Chasing stories, that's all. Doesn't much matter now, if my shuttle can't be repaired."

A sigh hefted my chest. He didn't have many options, and neither did we. Only two, really—report him to Immigration or not. No one in the settlement wanted government officials coming around if it could be avoided. We were happy to be far from the eyes and ears of the crown on Windsong. As long as this boy didn't interfere with our mine, no one would much care what kind of lawbreaker he was.

That left another two options to decide between: help him or leave him to fend for himself. His specially equipped shuttle was the only quiet way out. If he couldn't put it back together, he'd be stranded.

His problem, not mine. Not even sure I could help if I wanted to—a Garamite shuttle wouldn't be anything like a Thandan mining drone. I wouldn't know where to begin fixing it.

Do what needs doing.

I shivered. Memories of my mother's voice hadn't haunted me in years. It was right, though. Everything from my gut to my toes to the tips of my eyelashes told me someone had to help launch him back into orbit, save him from the trouble he'd fallen into by believing some ridiculous legend about treasure. He needed a favor on a planet where nothing came free.

Nothing except all the favors Petey had done for me when I first arrived in Forty-Two. I wouldn't have survived my first snows without him. Maybe it was my turn.

Tank it, then. If nothing else, the shuttle could be an interesting puzzle to solve.

"I might be able to help. No promises—depends on exactly what's damaged, but I can at least help you figure how bad it is. See where that takes us."

His brows furrowed. I wished he'd stop looking at me, but there wasn't much else to look at in the tiny bedroom. Something in those deep eyes made me want to move closer and run away at the same time, melding curiosity and fear into one confusing sensation.

"You? A doctor *and* a mechanic?"

I harrumphed. "Nothing close. I just know how to read the instructions on medical supplies. And as for machines, let's just say I'm better with their brains than their bodies most times, so like I said, no promises. But you don't have many options here, do you?" When he stared without answering, I rolled my eyes. "Look, do you have a name, Garamite?"

"What? Oh, Dane."

"Fine. Dane. It's the middle of the night, so I suggest you rest up while I do the same. In the morning we can see what there is to work with."

Dane settled back down, admitting his exhaustion. "Fair enough. What's *your* name, Thandan?"

"Essie."

"You saved my life, didn't you, Essie?"

"Looks like I did. Hope you don't give me reason to regret it."

Dane opened his mouth to say something else, but I didn't wait. I closed him in the bedroom, crossed the small kitchen and living area, and shut myself in my lab. Several half-finished programs called to me, but my muscles felt like they'd been injected with merinium. I checked the drones along the side wall—all seven of them in standby mode to recharge—and settled on the cot I kept at the back of the room.

I set the tack laser on the floor within easy reach...just in case.

A sleepless night never stopped me from getting up early, especially not with a stranger under my roof—not that any other stranger had ever *been* under my roof. While four of the drones set off for work in the mine and Dimwit reorganized my interface cables for the eighteenth time, I held Ticktock and Zippy back. I'd need Ticktock's help out at the shuttle, and Zippy needed some patching. During the rescue, it had overloaded several circuits by operating too fast...again. Maybe I could finally get its timing locked down.

Fixing Zippy came first—I couldn't keep both drones out of the mine all day—though my mind kept wandering to the shuttle.

"Ticktock, what files do you have on Class Three Garamite shuttles?"

"Production history, design options, safety records, artistic renderings—"

My mistake for asking a broad question. "Do you have any official schematics?"

"Negative, Essie."

"Okay, come here and plug in." I loaded up some crackcodes and scanned the off-planet networks I'd already broken into before, looking for an easy way to get something useful.

Garamites were clever with tech and had some blazing stubborn barriers on their computers, but I found a maintenance network that was less fiercely guarded. It had exactly what I needed. "Download those files and share them with the others."

I had hooked up Zippy to my diagnostic system and was tracing out the blown circuits. Then I replaced them, reworked the timing, and went back for more. My mind settled into the routine, stitching and testing, searching for the solution to yet another problem. A snip here, a patch of code there, a route I hadn't tried before.

Numbers. Logic. Puzzles. The clarity of the routine relaxed me.

"Essie, right?"

I jumped and nearly fried Zippy. Dane stood in the doorway to the lab, looking worn but a bit more alert, and he'd removed the smart-plaster from his forehead. His eye contact unnerved me as much as it had the night before, but then his gaze flicked to my hair. I had a small scarf tied over it to keep it out of my way, but hadn't tucked and wrapped it fully like I had for the fight.

"What, never seen a redhead before?"

He cleared his throat and averted his eyes, but I wondered if maybe he *hadn't* seen my hair's exact color before. The only dyes I could get were the ones the good-time girls used, and they weren't much for subtlety. Red mixed with a touch of purple had been the closest to a natural hair color I could manage. But it was better than risking recognition with the hair I'd been born with.

"Sorry," he said, hesitating. Then, "Nice computer."

My pride and joy had been cobbled together one component at a time when I won enough shares to buy them, stitched together from scratch when I didn't. I tapped the command to run another test on Zippy's timing algorithms. In the green—supposedly.

"The junk-tech here is scrap compared to what you have on Garam, isn't it?"

He shrugged. "Looks like it does its job, and that's what matters. Last night is a little fuzzy. Did you say something about *not* reporting me to the authorities?"

"Not yet," I said, keeping an edge of warning in my voice. I'd contacted Petey first thing to fill him in, and he'd agreed to my wait-and-see approach. "The miners would say the authorities are more trouble than *you're* worth, so just don't go making enough trouble to change that."

"I'm very interested in being trouble-free. You also said we could go check on my shuttle?"

"It's a long walk. Sure you're feeling up to it?" A glare was all the answer he'd give, and he did seem steady enough on his feet. "Right, fine. Just let me finish stitching up this circuit board."

"Stitching?"

"Working microcontacts is the closest I come to needlework. It's a bit of a joke for the men, so that's what we call all my fixing and coding and general fiddling." I made the last few connections to bring the drone back online and lugged it off the platform. "Right, then, Zippy. That should do you for now. Off to work you go."

Zippy whistled an acknowledgment and scuttled out past Dane. Still a little too fast to my eye. Maybe that one was a fight I'd have to forfeit.

"You should eat something. Here." I tossed Dane a nutri-bar, which he snapped out of the air. Good reflexes. "Your coat's by the door. Bundle up." *Blazes, now I'm saying it, too.* Of course, with Dane being from Garam, maybe it wasn't stating the obvious.

While he ate, I loaded a case with an assortment of gadgets and gear. Not that I had any real idea what I'd need. Working on the drones was one thing—I'd spent most of my time in Settlement Forty-Two fussing with their inner workings, teaching myself how they ran. Off-planet shuttles, not so much. But Ticktock had enough tools built in to handle most things... I hoped.

Dimwit held an interface cable I wanted, still determined to find the perfect order for the set. When I tried to take it, the drone latched on with a grip I'd never break. I gave two useless tugs, then reached toward its shut-off switch. It let go.

Dane was ready by then, so I shrugged into my own coat, slung the case over my shoulder, and shoved through the door. The pair of drones trailed after me, and Dane took the hint to follow. I let all of them pass so I could lock up. Despite his coat, Dane shivered.

"It's so dark," Dane said. "Storm coming in?"

"This?" I snorted. "No, cloudy through the day, clear at night... just another beautiful day on Thanda. Best way to keep warm is to keep moving."

The clouds may have meant no storm, but Dane quickly launched into a blizzard of questions. "What kind of robots are these?"

"Mining drones."

"So why aren't they in the mine?"

"Because Ticktock's loaded with a schematic of your shuttle, and because everyone agrees blowing up the mine is a *bad* thing. Not for nothing I call *this* one Dimwit."

"Dimwit Essie help Essie."

"And I can't seem to correct that 'loyal puppy' programming glitch."

We walked on, the faint hum and grind of machinery at the mine fading to nothing, leaving the quieter whirr and scuttle of the drones. Since Dane didn't know where he was going, I had a ready excuse for keeping in front. As nice as it was to avoid his unsettling glances, I didn't like having him behind me. My instincts said to keep an eye on him.

Side by side it is.

"Keep a sharp eye where you step," I advised as we got deeper into the woods. "And if you find yourself out here alone, mind you don't veer to the north. We've had a few sinkholes up that way."

"Lovely planet."

"If you wanted lovely, you should've crashed in the Bands."

"What are the Bands?"

Blazes, he doesn't know even that much?

"Equatorial zones," Ticktock provided, "comprising fifty-seven percent of Thandan population with native flora including—"

"That's enough, you," I cut in. "It's the one place on the planet that still manages a glimmer of warmth now and again."

"If it's better, why aren't you there?"

The incessant questions were getting me right rinked off, yet I answered just the same. "Busy enough here, aren't I?"

"Do you ever go down there?"

The men did. Every ten days—two weeks by Thandan reckoning—a different rotation of miners went down to the Bands for a five-day visit with their families, lovers, or bottles of something better than Petey's jack-ale. I could have, too, but I didn't. Ever.

"No, I don't."

"Why not?"

"No place nor need for me. The Bands is all women and children, and men too old or too crippled to work the mines anymore."

"You *are* a girl," he pointed out.

I braved his eyes long enough to shoot him a glare, and there was no doubt he felt the heat of it as his step stuttered. "I am, and I may be the only one living in Forty-Two. But I'm no one's wife and no one's good time, and I've no intention of letting that change anytime soon."

"I'm not saying you shouldn't be here. It's intriguing, that's all."

Intrigue ... not something I was looking for. A grunt was response enough, and he fell mercifully silent. The reprieve continued until we emerged onto the flats, where a sharp gasp signaled Dane's first sight of his damaged ship. His only sure way of ever going home no longer looked sure at all.

"Come on, now," I said, marching ahead toward the shuttle. When he gave no response, I turned back. Dane was leaning against the last tree, breathing heavily, his arm held tight against his ribs. "You all right?" I asked, heading back to him in case he collapsed. "I knew I shouldn't have brought you out here before you'd recovered."

He grabbed my arm. Fire shot through me at the point of

contact. My fingers curled into a fist, but he pulled himself upright and released me.

"I'm fine," he muttered. "Let's go."

To figure how seriously botched the ship was, I had to stitch up my own mess. When I'd told the drones to cut the power, they'd done a right thorough job of it.

"There," I said to Ticktock. "Splice that last connection. Try it now, Dane."

He threw a switch, and a flickering hum ran through the ship, but only a few indicator lights flashed to life. "We've got power. Looks like everything's offline, though."

"Good, that's how I want it. Last thing I need is another spark-shower."

He handed me a water-pack, and I pulled a thumb-size device from my pocket and waited for the readout to turn green before taking a drink. When Dane tilted his head curiously, I grunted.

"It's not personal," I said. "I always check the water. Right, time to see what we're facing." I retrieved a boxy contraption from my case and patched it into the ship's systems.

"What is that?"

"An Essie exclusive. Lets me have run of the place without asking its permission," I said, taking my slate from my coat pocket and initiating an interlink with both the panel and the schematics in Ticktock's memory banks. "This way I can run my own diagnostics. Given the state of this place, I don't trust its computer to tell me the truth."

"Makes sense. Anything I can do to help?"

I checked the results, and my heart plummeted to the mines. The first few lines on the diagnostic readout held nothing but headaches, and it only got worse. My instinct not to trust the computer had been dead-on. It was thrashed. Several subroutines had been wiped out by the overloads, and most of the others were a corrupted mess.

Then there was the physical damage. Most of it was superficial, but some key components had blown out, including what I suspected was the scan-scrambler. Ticktock cross-referenced what we saw with the schematic and maintenance files, detailing the repairs necessary. All that was straightforward enough.

Except the maintenance files assumed we had access to Garamite clean-tech. And the diagnostic wasn't even done yet.

Fixing everything would be more than a favor. More than twenty favors.

"You can tell me if you have anything valuable on board that we can trade for parts."

"Some merinium."

I couldn't help a laugh, but felt no humor. "That's the one thing we *don't* need in Forty-Two. We've got a mine full of it. Exactly what kind of treasure hunt are you on, Dane?"

When no answer came, I stared, daring him to remain silent. His eyes had changed, darkening, like they hid as much as mine.

"It's a story I heard." He spoke carefully, watched me as though my reaction would dictate each word that followed. "Something about a treasure big enough to change things."

"Change what kinds of things?"

"Things on Windsong, maybe."

Memories shuddered through me at the mention of that

planet—sunlight dancing on the mountains, rainbow orchids, birds singing every morning . . . shadows looming over me, pain and silence and must-keep-quiet—

"The rule on Thanda is to do what keeps you fed and warm and avoids interference from Windsong," I said gruffly. "From what I hear, your lot on Garam is spans better than ours, so what do you have to complain about?"

"We may not have to work in the mines, but we're not free. Not really. We create, and King Matthias and Queen Olivia take, giving just enough back to keep us complacent and working."

"And you think this mysterious 'treasure' of yours is enough to change that?"

He crossed his arms. "Wealth and power *do* go together, don't you think?"

"You're a blazing fool. No one stands against Windsong."

"Some people do."

"What, the Exiles? And you see all the good it's done *them*. Kicked out of their kingship on Windsong and relegated to the far side of the solar system for a few centuries, and now with their military battling in Windsong's outlands. *That* war's been going eight years, and no progress."

"The Exiles aren't the only ones who've stood against the crown. We've had rebellions on Garam, even uprisings on Windsong itself."

I scoffed. "Not in ages."

"Then maybe it's time for another." He exhaled sharply, then winced. "Not that any of this will happen if I can't get off the ground. What about the repairs? I'll find a way to get whatever parts we need—there has to be a way."

I looked at the readout again. Some things already in my lab might help, but trading for the rest would take more shares than I had at the moment, and blazes if I was going to go broke right before the snows for some strange boy.

My mind clicked through possibilities, trying to find another option. Petey might spot a loan if I asked, but I couldn't. He had family to support in the Bands. The easiest choice was to just tell Dane he was on his own and good luck to him. The next settlement was nearly fifty links away, though, and they certainly didn't have anyone who could handle tech like the shuttle's. Especially the new code that'd have to be written.

That's not my problem.

Mother wouldn't have thought so. She would've helped without worrying about what was in it for her.

I'm not Mother.

A chill seeped through my spine, telling me how true the thought was. But it didn't matter. All I wanted was to keep safe and keep to myself.

Then again . . . I could do this one thing my mother would've approved of. And as unhinged as Dane's idea sounded, maybe it could work. Maybe there really was a treasure, and he could find it, and it would be enough wealth for the Garamites to risk uniting against Windsong. And maybe with the Garamites' tech turned against the crown, Windsong would be defeated. The war would finally end, and the crown's lies would die with it. No more killing on either side.

That would be a good thing, even if it rested on some very shaky threads of "maybe." I sighed and prioritized the list of needed repairs.

"Give me and Ticktock an hour or so to finish stitching the

electrical so you won't freeze through the night in here. Then we'll go to the Station, see if Petey can rig a spur."

"What's a spur?"

"You know, spur of the moment."

"But a spur-of-the-moment *what*?"

I grunted and shouldered past him on my way to the forward compartment. "There are only two ways to earn extra shares in the settlements, and I already told you—I'm no one's good time."

3

BY THE TIME DANE AND I got to the Station, the midafter-
noon crowd had packed in. Most of the men were drinking, a few
over card games. Others picked up deliveries from MineNet...
then picked up a tankard and joined everyone else. If the stag-
gering drunks weren't enough to knock Dane over, the stench
was ready to do the job.

"What are we doing here?" he shouted over the din.

"I told you, getting enough shares to get you back in the
air. Now shut it." I shoved my way through the crowd, drawing plenty of glares that turned wary when they saw a strange
boy with me. Clearly word had spread about the crash and the
settlement's visitor.

Should've made him stay with his shuttle.

"Essie, there yeh are."

I turned at the voice, the gravel as recognizable as the
crooked nose. "Aye, here I am, Hawkins."

"I hear yeh're not willin' to fix up the botched transmission on the old pulverizer."

"Unwilling and unable. My hands are full with things the mech-bots *can't* handle." He opened his mouth, probably to repeat what Petey had said about the mech-bots only doing half a job, so I cut him off. "I'll get one of the drones on it when I have the time. Best I can do."

Hawkins protested, something about my having a finer touch than the drones, but I stopped listening and continued to push my way to the bar. The men didn't understand. There was no puzzle to solve when it came to mining equipment, just replacing worn-out parts and kicking it until it worked. No real challenge like Dane's shuttle offered.

"Petey!"

The old miner spotted me and waved for us to follow him into the storeroom, where the noise was more muted. "Our new friend's up and about, I see."

"In better shape than his shuttle, anyway," I replied.

"Still no alerts from Immigration Control," Petey said, shifting his gaze to Dane. "Listen, boy, yeh got in undetected, and no one here wants Windsong's watchdogs sniffin' around. But if yeh're here to make trouble—"

"I'm not," Dane said. "I just want to get where I'm going."

"And where might that be?"

A good question. Where *did* he think he'd find this treasure of his?

"The Umbergild Ascetics."

I stifled a laugh at the answer, and Petey did the same, letting a snort slip through. If Dane thought he could get information from the Ascetics, he didn't know nearly enough about them.

"They like to grow them delusional on Garam, and who are we to argue?" I said. "Repairs'll be steep, though. Think you can rig me a spur?"

Petey's mouth always had a bit of a frown, but at my question, the corners turned down even more. "Y'know I wish yeh wouldn't. Men from other settlements are one thing, but to fight spurs—"

"Fight?" Dane cut in. "What does he mean, fight?"

I spun on him. "What do you think that cage out there is for, storing jack-ale?" Turning back to Petey, I continued, "There are always men willing to fight me in a spur, so don't lecture me."

After a long scratch behind his ear, Petey sighed. "Lawrence Moray's been askin' for the next time yeh take one. I'll see to it."

Moray was far from my first choice, but I couldn't very well change my mind after all that. I gave Petey a nod and made my way to my usual washroom to prepare. Dane kept on my heels as doggedly as Dimwit usually did, shoving his way into the small room before I could slam the door.

Close quarters, no escape route, what weapons could I—? I snipped the thought and ignored him instead, taking off my coat and twisting my hair up to secure under a scarf.

Dane didn't feel like being ignored, it seemed. "You're going to fight one of the miners? In that cage? It's madness."

"Don't think a girl can handle herself? You wouldn't be the first to make that mistake."

"I'm sure you can, but it's still insane. How will this earn shares?"

"Those men out there are looking for some fun, and the

good-time girls don't come through near often enough for some. So the jack-ale starts said fun, and gambling on fights finishes it. Only sport we have on this planet."

"Fun...Why are so many of them here having 'fun' in the middle of the day? Shouldn't they be working in the mine? I heard Forty-Two had the highest merinium output of all the Thandan settlements. That's why I aimed to land my shuttle here when it malfunctioned; I didn't want to be stranded without help."

"Highest output is right, thanks to my great miscalculation. Tell you all about it later."

He puzzled over that, failed to understand, and shook his head. "Fine. I'll do it, then. I'll fight."

"What, so I can patch you up again?"

Dane raised an eyebrow. "Don't think a Garamite boy can handle himself?"

I looked him over. He was more than half a head taller than I was, broad-shouldered and fit. Something about taking in his build made my mind blank for a moment, but none of that changed my answer.

"You want your shuttle repaired? We need all the shares we can get, preferably in a single fight so we can get you on your way that much sooner. The men will bet more to see me take some hits, particularly after what I cost them in my last fight. Nothing like watching the legal beat-down of a girl."

His jaw tightened. "That's sick, Essie."

"Welcome to Thanda. Don't worry so much, Dane. I never said I'd give them what they want."

Lawrence Moray was the kind of man I typically kept well clear of—the kind whose gaze set off right nasty jitters under my skin. He'd tried sweet-talking me a couple of years ago, when I'd stopped looking like such a child. After I told him I preferred the look of him from half a link away, his attitude shifted from repulsive to spiteful. It was no surprise that he was looking for a spur with me.

It did surprise *him* that I landed the first hit.

He didn't move as well as Thacker had the night before, but he had more mass. When I went in for a second hit, he blocked it and grabbed my arm. I tried to slip him, but he socked a kidney-punch. Pain sparked through my torso, and he took advantage of the distraction, shoving me face-first against the cage wire and pinning me there.

The crowd cheered, banging their tankards on tables and shouting at Moray to let me have it. Through it all, I made out his voice snaking into my ear.

"Yeh shoulda been nicer to me, Essie."

His weight pressing on my back...

His ale-drenched breath spilling over me...

A shout ripped through my throat, and I thrust my head back, banging it into his eye. His grip loosened, and I slipped free. I embraced the rage and went at him with a knee to the groin. His elbow slammed into my gut, knocking the wind from me. The next swing clipped the side of my head when I didn't move quickly enough, and the world spun.

Moray's fist impacted my ribs, right on the bruise from the last fight. I gasped and staggered away, trying to stay clear. A whooping roar filled my ears. This was much better entertainment than the Thacker fight.

"Yeh've got her, Moray!"

"Yeah, show her what yeh're made of!"

"We'll get our shares back from her now!"

"Take that animal down, Essie!"

Dane's voice cut through the others. Calling attention to himself in that crowd was several sniffs from smart.

"Found yerself a pet, I see," Moray sneered. "Does he roll over when yeh tell him?"

I never wasted time with words midfight. When Moray opened his mouth to continue taunting me, I punched him in the trachea. Not hard enough—only a glancing blow. He tried to counterattack, but I twisted him around into an armlock. A little more pressure and something cracked or popped. I danced with him as he tried to maneuver his free arm to grab me and kicked the side of his knee. He went down, and I pinned him.

"Stay down, Moray," I said, "because this is the nicest you'll ever get from me."

Petey called the count and declared me the winner amidst the boos. I got out of the cage and crossed to the washroom quick as I could, but Dane still managed to trail after me.

"You're hurt."

"A little banged up is all."

"Bleeding is not 'banged up.'"

"What? Where am I bleeding this time?" I checked the mirror. A ribbon of blood trickled down my temple where Moray had clipped me. "That? I'm fine."

He stared at me, caught on something. "How often do you do these fights?"

"Once or twice a week, mostly."

"That's *beyond* madness. Look at you—you can't even stand straight."

The compounded bruise on my ribs ached every time I breathed, so he had a point. His concern put me on edge, though. He didn't know me. He had even less right than Petey to lecture me.

"Nothing I can't handle," I said, pushing him back out of the washroom.

He opened his mouth to continue his protests.

I slammed the door in his face.

By the time I patched myself up and calmed down, I realized leaving Dane among the miners hadn't been too sharp. The lack of noise hit me as I left the washroom. The men who weren't too drunk to stand had already stumbled home. Maybe I'd been in there longer than I realized.

"How's the take, Petey?" I asked, sliding onto a barstool.

"Solid. Most were confident Moray would finish yeh, knowin' how eager he was and that yeh had no rest from the last one. They're none too happy with yeh right now."

"They'll get over it."

"If yeh say so." He worked the MineNet terminal and nodded. "That's five-seventy-one over to yeh."

I ran the numbers in my head. That'd be enough to fix the shuttle without leaving me broke. "Good, I need to place an order."

He spun the terminal display to face me and watched as I

punched in a list of replacement parts. Not quite Garamite stock, but Ticktock seemed to think they'd get it done.

"Why're yeh helping that strange boy, Essie? We got him out of his ship still breathin', but we've got no obligation to him beyond that."

"And you had no obligation to me when I arrived."

"Is that how it is? A scrawny, half-starved child yeh were, but the sharpest mind I've seen. Helpin' yeh was a sound invest-ment. That boy looks like he can take care of himself, and what has he to offer for yer trouble?"

A small step toward making my mother proud, maybe, but I couldn't tell Petey that. Or that Dane's mad plan to unite Garam against Windsong made something jitter inside me, and the only way to quiet it was to help him. "Nothing, but he can't stay. You know that. The more I help, the sooner he'll be gone. Where is he, anyway?"

"Said he was returnin' to his ship, would see yeh in the mornin'."

I shook my head. "He doesn't know the way."

"Said he did. And it looked like Dimwit went with him."

"Great. They'll both get lost. Here, that's it."

Petey looked over my order and nodded. "Should be able to get that piped up from the Bands in a day or two. Yeh be careful out there. The men's frustration with yeh can only be pushed so far, y'know."

"Aye, I know."

"And bundle up. It's a cold one."

I resisted the urge to trudge out to the shuttle and check that Dane had made it there safely. If he'd gotten lost, it was his fault. Or mine for leaving him on his own, but I tried not to think that. Instead, I sat at my computer and cracked into networks I wasn't supposed to reach, searching for more information on the Garamite shuttle design.

It was a puzzle, no doubt, and different from any I'd encountered in the settlement. Sheer novelty was half the reason I'd agreed to help. But I couldn't deny that the mechanical systems were beyond me, so I downloaded what I found to the drones, adding to the knowledge base Ticktock had started. I couldn't keep the same drone back from the mine every day—the men would notice and make a fuss. Each drone had skills that'd be useful in repairing the shuttle, though. I'd make it work.

By morning, Dimwit was in its spot, recharging with the others, so Dane was probably fine. My assumption was confirmed an hour later when I arrived at the shuttle, Dimwit and Clank in tow. I banged on the hatch, and Dane opened it.

One problem I'd spotted in the schematics right away: Garamite shuttles weren't designed to be repaired by Thandan mining drones. Making the prettiest exterior meant the guts of the thing were awkward enough for *me* to get to, let alone the drones' bulky metal bodies.

"Where did Ticktock want us to start, Clank?" I asked.

"Repair coolant system to bring engine online," it said.

"Right, then. Pull up Ticktock's instructions and tell me what to do."

Dane's eyes stayed on me as I removed my coat and slid under a junction, watching how I moved, likely checking how hurt I was. Good thing I'd indulged in a rejuvenator patch for that nasty bruise. It still ached, especially when I stretched, but not so much that I couldn't keep Dane from noticing.

"You broadcast your punches," he said. "Anyone with eyes can see them coming."

"Well, I guess my opponents' eyes are occupied elsewhere most of the time, since I have a winning record. Thank you so much for the advice." The spark of a welder lit off to one side. "Dimwit, stop that."

"Tell me about the 'great miscalculation' you mentioned."

I sighed and forced myself not to wince. Clearly, Dane was set on making conversation rather than letting me work in peace.

"How much do you know about merinium?"

"Just that it's a versatile bio-mineral with lots of uses, which makes it valuable."

"And do you know where the 'bio' part comes in?"

"Something about a reaction with organic waste."

That was extremely understated, but most offworlders didn't know much more. "One of the few native animal species here is called the harri-harra. It's a giant worm that burrows in the bedrock and—Dimwit, I said stop! If you weld your feet together, I'm not fixing it. Anyway, the harri-harra leaves a trail of secretions and excrement in its wake that seeps into the stone, undergoes a chemical reaction and, after enough time, you have merinium."

I felt Dane's footsteps approach through the metal deck but couldn't see him from my position. "Okay, that's very educational. What's the miscalculation?"

"The harri-harra are still down there. They don't like humans, and that sludge they leave behind is deadly during the early stages. Flammable, too. Most settlements lose at least ten percent of their workforce every cycle. The drones were originally designed as remote-controlled tools to help with the heavy lifting, but I decided to try upgrading their programming to give them enough brainpower to do some of the dangerous work on their own."

"Remove damaged microduct," Clank instructed.

"I'm trying," I told the drone. It looked like the ship had seen better days even before the crash. "Dane, can you hand me that wrench? No, not that one—blue handle. So far, I've got six drones upgraded—seven if you count Dimwit, which I don't. Enough to manage belowground operations themselves, directing the dumb-drones."

Dane crouched nearby, having handed me the right item. "I still don't see the problem."

"Like you said, we have the highest output on the planet, thanks to the drones. Share value is based on output, so Forty-Two's shares are worth more than any other settlement's. As long as each man works an equal shift at the mine—or in my case, does work to support mining operations—they earn their shares. But with the drones, we only need a quarter-crew to monitor and direct from topside each shift. So I made it safer and more efficient, but I also made a settlement full of men with too much time and too many shares on their hands."

Dane was quiet for so long, Clank and I were actually able to replace the microduct plus a power conduit. I hoped he would keep it shut for the rest of the day so I could get more done, but no such luck.

"You saved their lives," he said. "But I heard them last night. A lot of them *liked* seeing you hurt."

I grunted, yanking on a bolt to loosen it. "Don't ask me to explain how their minds work. They're bigger malfunctions than Dimwit. All I know is they aren't always appreciative, and some wish I'd 'appreciate' *them* a little more."

Dane fell silent again for a few sparkling minutes. When he spoke, I got the feeling he was right worked up but trying to hide it. "Be careful, Essie. I also saw how they looked at you when you got out of that cage."

That was the second such warning I'd gotten in the last day. Hearing Dane say it felt different from when Petey did. But I'd been on Thanda eight years, most of those in Forty-Two. What made anyone think I couldn't take care of myself?

"Worry about yourself and eventually getting off this rock," I said. "Your problems are bigger than mine are bound to be."

Dimwit chose that moment to spot-weld one of its feet to the deck.

As usual, I didn't include that infuriating bucket of a malfunction in my tally of problems. After all, I could solve that one with a quick hour of dismantling work.

For some reason, though, I never did.

4

FOR THREE DAYS, I restored and reprogrammed bits of the shuttle's computer system, and I still had plenty left to do, especially in physical repairs. Petey got the parts and materials piped in from the Bands as promised, and it looked like they'd do the job. Maybe. As good as Clank was at microwelding and Clunk at fabricating, they weren't used to intricate tech that had to survive the vacuum of space. Half the time I could've spent programming went to keeping an eye on whatever drone I brought, making sure it didn't botch anything. Still, I could've been faster, but Dane never did figure how to shut it and let me work. I thought if I stayed quiet, he'd get the idea, but when he asked questions and I knew the answer, I couldn't shut my own mouth.

Part of me didn't mind. He made better conversation than Petey and Whirligig combined, and I didn't have anyone else to talk to. It couldn't hurt to enjoy it while it lasted, even if most of what I enjoyed was telling Dane how unhinged he was. But I kept the tack laser handy, just in case.

On the third day, the conversation he sparked was more serious. "After the crash, I told you more than I should've," he said, his footsteps approaching from behind me. "Maybe the head trauma, I don't know. But you haven't reported my plans to anyone. Not even Petey, really. Why?"

Stretching halfway into an exhaust manifold was an awkward way to work, so I wrenched the faulty regulator off the side and pulled myself out. I handed the part to Whirligig and sat cross-legged on the crate I'd been standing on, watching the drone fiddle with the regulator. So crude and clunky compared to the elegance of machine code.

"Like Petey said, we don't want the watchdogs sniffing around. And part of me hopes you'll see how impossible your odds are and just go home." I chose my words carefully. Part of me hoped he'd beat those long odds and succeed. It'd lift such a weight off me. But I didn't say that.

"And be happy with the status quo? I don't think you really believe that. Didn't you upgrade the drones because you thought it would make things better?"

No, I did it to make a place for myself, to create some standing that could protect me, with the side effect of helping the miners . . . selfish reasons.

I kept my answer simple. "You could say that."

"Right. And I have to keep trying to make things better for my people."

"With some 'treasure' that more than likely doesn't exist? If you want to make things better, just go ask the Exiles for help, offer a treaty, and see if they'll back your rebellion. Candara's coming close to us in its orbit right now. Put those sparkling Garamite brains together with the Exiles' military resources and you *might* end up less dead than you would otherwise."

He didn't answer, so I glanced up. His expression was tense and hesitant. I couldn't decide whether to smirk or smack him.

"Afraid the Exiles will 'possess' you, steal your secrets, and make you their puppet?"

That shook him out of . . . whatever he was lost in. "I've heard the rumors aren't true. I mean, I heard body-hopping isn't like that. The way I understand it, transitioning to another's aware-ness is more about empathy than control."

My breath caught. Transitioning. Empathy. Words my mother had used when talking about the Exiles. I took the regulator back from 'Gig, testing the contacts to ensure it'd been fixed. Focusing on work helped mask my reaction.

"Empathy sounds like just what you need, so why not go to them? Seems the more direct route to me."

"Garam won't unite against Windsong unless we can do it standing on our own."

I shrugged and pulled myself back into the manifold, set-ting the regulator in place. "Standing on your own will get you killed, Dane, and that'd be a blazing shame after all this work."

"I'm as capable of taking care of myself as you."

"Sure you are."

"Taking care taking care taking care—"

"Shut it, Dimwit."

When I emerged again, Dane offered his hand to help me off the crate. I ignored it and jumped down, but Dimwit scuttled past right in front of me, making me stumble into Dane. He helped me right myself, no big deal, but he didn't move away. Instead, he ran his thumb across my cheek.

I swatted his hand down and backed off, both fists up and ready in case he tried anything else.

"I—you—just a smudge of grease," he said.

Just some grease. You're twitching out over nothing, Essie.

Forcing myself to relax and lower my hands, I snorted. "A touch of grease is nothing new, is it?" Not with the perpetual dust and grime covering every inch of me. I liked it that way.

His head cocked to the side, confusion in his eyes. "No, I guess not."

I grabbed my slate and headed out of the engine compartment. "I'm going to work on coding the navigation system. Dimwit, stay!"

For once, the malfunction listened.

Leaving Dane with his shuttle at the end of the day brought a touch of relief. Solitude was familiar, comfortable. I needed that.

Back in my lab that night, I worked for hours, writing and testing subroutines, stitching together components that might or might not work. When I couldn't focus on the readout anymore, I gave it up and went to bed.

Working so late usually put me right to sleep, but not this time. I stared at the ceiling, wide awake, letting the imperfections in the metal above form patterns and pictures in the moonlight. A star. A logic circuit. A waterfall...but an ugly one. I'd seen better.

I sat up and opened the trunk at the foot of my bed. The

notebook was just where I'd left it. I flipped to the right page, and there it was. A high cliff, water cascading from the top, churning into foam at the bottom. Trees all around. Mother had captured it perfectly, down to the mist.

I thumbed through the sketches one by one until I came to my favorite—a dragonfly hovering over an orchid. I'd never been able to figure how she made a static image so alive with movement.

I'd never been able to figure how my mother did a lot of things. I'd managed to stop thinking about it until recently.

The past few days with Dane were botching my brain. Most of the last eight years had been filled with perpetual fear. Never able to trust anyone or let the truth slip free. I knew how to handle that, knew how to keep myself separate and safe. I confronted that fear in the cage, beating it down as I beat my opponents, showing them both I was in control.

Something about Dane made me feel very *out* of control.

I stood by my initial assessment. He was terrifying. I had to get him out of Forty-Two and get things back to normal. Soon.

I ran through my mental checklist of systems that still needed to be patched and found it wasn't as long as I'd feared. I'd send all the drones—other than Dimwit—to the mines the next day so I could focus on the computer subsystems. Another couple of days, maybe three, and Dane would be gone. I'd settle back into my routine. That assurance finally lulled me to sleep.

A scraping noise jerked me awake.

The door. I'd been in a hurry to get into the lab and lose myself in my work. I may not have engaged the lock.

Someone was in my shack. Someone big and lumbering, someone who'd never learned how to sneak around.

I barely had time to sit up before that someone entered my bedroom.

"Like I said, Essie, yeh shoulda been nicer to me."

One step into the room, then another. Panic flooded me along with the stench of jack-ale. He came closer, and I should've moved, my mind screamed to move, but my body wouldn't listen.

Tiny space, no room to maneuver, no escape route, no weapons. Big. He's too big—

It was too late. Moray grabbed my shoulder, his fingers digging in.

My surroundings went fuzzy, blurring with motion as something inside of me was yanked somewhere else.

To some*one* else.

A sniff of dizziness rolls through me, like I'm too close to the edge of the mine shaft. Like I'm too tall. But that's just because I'm standing over Essie.

Essie. I look down at her, slim but strong, small outside the safety of the cage. She doesn't even pull away from my grip. I squeeze tighter, digging my fingers into her shoulder, and she does nothing. She knows. She knows she was wrong.

I know no such thing! Blazes, he can't hear me. I'm stuck in here—my body there, my eyes are so blank, I'm helpless. But there's something here, something holding back. That voice, listen to the voice in the corner, Moray, what it says, listen listen listen . . .

My grip loosens. Hawkins and Petey. They might find out. Essie might take the drones and leave. We'd be like all the other mines, burying a man a week, like my uncle and my grandfather. She might, but I don't know. I don't know if she'd dare.

Yes, you know, Moray, you know I'll leave you with the harri-harra and their sludge and the dark, and you can die in its depths and I'll never look back.... Listen to that voice, you know it's right.

I release my hold on her shoulder.

My mind snapped back where it belonged, back to my own body. At least, I was pretty sure it was my body. It felt more like an old woman's, drained and worn. Moray stumbled out the bedroom door, but I still couldn't move.

I'd body-hopped him. It was a part of me I thought I'd shut down years ago, only using it with my mother and never since then. If Moray had any idea, if anyone else found out, I'd have more trouble than he'd already meant to bring. No one could discover I had any Exile blood. From there, it was a short dig to the whole truth.

It brought a new and very different panic, one that was cut off by a shout and a thud that shook the floor.

I pulled myself out of bed, bracing myself against the walls to stay up, and took a few steps toward the doorway and the cause of the noise. Moray was sprawled in a tangle with Dimwit and Zippy on the ground. It looked like he'd tripped over the drones.

"Get out," I said, pushing all shakiness from my voice.

When Dimwit sparked a microwelder in his face, Moray managed to get to his feet, only a little wobbly, and stagger out into the night. As soon as the door closed, cutting off the frosty wind, I turned to the drones.

"What are you two doing out here? You're supposed to be recharging."

"Essie was in danger and needed help," Zippy said. "Human male was in the wrong place, not the right place, not supposed to be here."

Huh. I hadn't programmed the drones to wake at signs of an emergency in the shack. Maybe I should have. Maybe the upgrades were taking them further than I'd realized. Then Dimwit offered its own answer.

"Dane Essie watch Essie help Essie."

Something flamed in my gut, churning with the panic and exhaustion. "Oh, he told you to keep an eye on me, did he? Well, *he's* the one who needs help, not me. Get back to recharging."

Both drones scurried back to the lab, and I triple-checked the locks on the door. By the time I got back to bed, I was gasping for breath, unsure whether it was more from the fear or the effort. Body-hopping was more work than running out to the flats. I didn't remember it being so hard when I did it with Mother.

I'd only gotten out of trouble because my control had slipped. That wasn't supposed to happen, ever. But if it hadn't, Moray might have overpowered me.

And maybe the drones would've come in and taken a cutting torch to his backside.

Maybe it was a good thing Dane had given Dimwit whatever instructions he had.

I vowed never to tell him what had happened.

The hike out to the flats felt twice as long the next day. I'd been both too tired and too worked up to do more than doze fitfully for an hour or so before giving up. Dimwit was chipper as ever, naturally.

It might have been the awkward moment the day before. Maybe something else. Either way, one look said Dane knew I'd had a rough night. Another look said he wasn't going to comment.

Whatever the reason, I accepted it and got straight to work.

Despite the exhaustion, I pushed hard, telling myself to take on one more system before I left . . . and then one more again. The more I finished, the sooner he'd be gone. And I was ready for him to be gone, for everything to be normal and dull and quiet. For the first time, he was silent most of the day, but he lingered nearby, handing me interfaces or reading off diagnostic results when Dimwit wandered away.

Finally, I'd done the last thing I could without more weaving and stitching in my lab, plus another round of cracking interplanetary networks. I closed out the coding matrix and tucked my gear in a corner. "I think I've convinced the stabilizers to coordinate with each other, but the thrust regulator still doesn't want to listen to the computer. Tomorrow I'll try some code with more teeth."

As I wrapped myself in my heavy coat and scarf, Dane stepped between me and the main hatch. "It's well past sunset and the temperature's plummeted. You should just stay here tonight."

Alone with him in the shuttle all night? I don't think so. "One of the moons is out—it's light enough."

"It's an hour to the settlement. You'll freeze out there."

I rolled my eyes. "We're not all from Garam, you know. Come on, Dimwit, we're leaving."

The drone whirred and beeped, skittering behind Dane to open the hatch. I pushed by and stepped out into the frigid night. The breeze bit the exposed skin of my face, but I strode across the flats without a word.

It took an unusually long time before the whine of the closing hatch reached my ears, so I glanced over my shoulder. The moon gave enough light to see the dark form of Dane trailing after us. Just what I needed after last night—a strange off-planet boy following me in the dark.

I walked a little faster.

Half an hour later, he was still behind us. Maybe he was just making sure we got back all right. I hadn't seen chivalry like that in years. It felt foreign. And it didn't make me like the feeling of being followed any better.

When we were far enough into the forest to cut off the breeze I'd felt earlier, I figured I could lose him in the trees and the dark.

"Wrong way wrong way," Dimwit said for the third time.

"Oh, shut it," I muttered. "You'd get lost in a one-room shack. I think I know my way home, thank you."

"Wrong wrong wrong—"

A cracking sound cut off the drone's electronic voice. I registered that it was a *bad* noise, but had no time for anything else.

I fell, swallowed by glacial water.

5

SINKHOLE. The only thing it could be, filled in and frozen over. Not frozen enough.

I fought off the reflexive gasp as my body reacted to the sudden change, but that was all I could do. Water soaked my heavy clothing, weighing me down. I clutched frantically at the fasteners on my coat, trying to shed my outer layers, but my fingers refused to work. Cold seeped instantly to my bones, sapping my strength. Gravity seemed to triple, fighting my efforts to swim back to the surface.

No hope. No chance. All I'd survived in seventeen years, only to be taken down by a frozen chasm on this ice-rock.

I kicked one more time. One last try.

Something clamped onto my shoulders, piercing all the way through to my skin. A corner of my mind that hadn't frozen yet directed my hands to reach up and grip the metal arms the best I could as they pulled me out of the pit.

When my face broke the surface of the water, I gulped icy air. A roar filled my ears, but Dane's voice sliced through it.

"Move, Dimwit, get her out of there! Essie? Essie, hold on."

If I'd thought the air cut into me before, I was wrong. As Dimwit and Dane both dragged me onto solid ground, my body shook like I was having a seizure. Then Dane began groping at my clothes, and instinct took over. I rolled away and pushed myself to my feet.

"D-don't touch m-me," I forced out.

"Unless you want to die of hypothermia, you need to get out of those wet clothes, *now*. Do it yourself or I'll do it for you."

Blazes if he wasn't right, and blazes if half of me didn't consider freezing to death over the alternative. Self-preservation won in the end. I turned my back on him and forced my rebelling limbs to start stripping off the layers of sodden fabric before they turned to ice.

"D-Dimwit, f-fire." Building fires was one thing the malfunction was good at—it had nearly burned down my shack three times. It raced around, gathering a respectable pile of wood before I'd gotten more off than my coat, scarf, and boots.

I heard movement and reflexively glanced back. Dane had moved closer, prompting me to choose between punching him and running. Both options dissolved when I saw he'd removed his outer coat. He held it between us, like a curtain, and a quick flicker of warmth clashed with the cold as I realized why. He was trying to let me keep a little dignity while staying close enough to help if the cold overpowered me.

That level of chivalry didn't exist in the mining settlements, ever.

Dimwit had the fire burning by the time I peeled off the last layers. Dane's sharp gasp elicited new panic, but another glance confirmed his coat was still between us. The most he could see was maybe my shoulders.

My shoulders... the mark.

"What, never s-seen a t-tattoo before?" I asked gruffly.

"I— No, you're bleeding."

"Grapples aren't m-made for grabbing p-people, are they? It's not b-bad."

Once I was naked, he wrapped his coat around me. It was much too large, but I was glad for that since it more than covered me. Then he sat me in front of the fire, working his fingers through my hair to encourage it to dry. If the drone hadn't built the fire so quickly, my hair probably would've frozen solid already. The convulsing shivers eased to a more normal level as I absorbed the heat. Half of what remained might have been more about Dane's closeness, the way he touched my hair. I shoved the thoughts away and focused on warming up.

Dimwit made itself surprisingly useful, rigging lines above the fire to hang my wrung-out clothes and dry them. It didn't botch anything.

"You aren't going into shock, are you?" Dane asked.

"Don't think so. Why?"

"You're just very quiet."

"Because I usually talk so much?"

His hand paused before continuing through my hair. "No. I guess not. It's... it's an interesting tattoo."

"Nothing special," I muttered. Last thing I needed was him digging into that. An elaborate S with filigree around it. Nothing more than a sentimental design, unless someone knew what it really meant.

He fell quiet, and I willed both time and heat to move faster. When my hair finished drying, he released it and scooted away from me a little. I appreciated the space. I'd have appreciated it even more if he'd scooted all the way back to the shuttle, but I didn't have the strength to demand it.

Sitting up took more strength than I had, so I shifted to lean back against the nearest tree. Only the crackling of the fire interrupted the silence of the woods. My eyes closed, just for a little rest, and the flickering flames lulled me into a doze.

I jolted awake, startled that I would let my guard down like that. Nothing had changed. Dane hadn't moved, still huddled in front of the fire, which Dimwit still tended.

"How long was I out?"

"A couple of hours, I think," he said. "You should go back to sleep. You're exhausted."

"No, I should get home."

I pulled myself to my feet and checked my hanging clothes, finding they were dry. My plan was to get out of the light of the fire and dress as much as I could without removing the coat entirely. Dane had different ideas.

"Stop. Here, stay where it's warm."

He stood and held the coat to shield me again until I was ready to put on my own. I wordlessly shoved my feet into my boots before looking over my shoulder and meeting his eyes, just briefly.

"Thanks."

"Don't thank me," he said. "Thank Dimwit. I was too far away."

"You didn't tell it to grab me?"

"No, he did that on his own."

I almost corrected him calling Dimwit a "he," but it didn't feel right at that moment. Instead, I watched the drone putter around to put out the fire.

"Maybe I should stop threatening to use it for spare parts."

"I think that would be fair."

"Come on, Dimwit, let's go home."

Three steps along, I felt Dane on my heels and stopped. "Your shuttle's *that* way."

He stopped, too, but didn't turn back. "You got halfway home and fell into a sinkhole. I'm making sure you get the rest of the way safely."

I knew I had a better chance of winning a cage fight blindfolded than talking him out of it, so I left it at a grunt and walked on.

We reached the settlement without further incident, but then I had another problem. I couldn't very well make Dane hike an hour back to his shuttle in the middle of the night. Or I could, but what if *he* fell in one of those sinkholes?

Oh, tank it.

"Go on, there's a cot in the lab. Get some sleep." I went into my bedroom and closed the door before he could respond. He probably wanted to point out that we could've avoided all this if I'd just agreed to stay in the shuttle.

But the shuttle was his. The shack was mine. It was different.

My mother's notebook lay open on my bed. I studied the sketches for twenty minutes, but not even the dragonfly could shut down my inexplicable anxiety. If anything, it made it worse. My brain knew Dane wouldn't try anything—he'd had plenty of opportunity out at the sinkhole. But knowing it wasn't enough.

The trunk at the foot of my bed was plenty heavy, full of old gadgets and nonsense. I dragged it over and blocked the door. Blocking Dane out, blocking me in.

Alone. Better.

I dreamed I was down in the mine as it flooded with water, yet the heavy machinery kept banging away. When I woke, I was relieved to find air instead of water in my lungs.

The banging, however, was real—someone pounding on the door of the shack.

Jumping out of bed brought a wave of lightheadedness, followed by pain as I stubbed my toe on the trunk. I'd forgotten it was there. I had to drag it away from the door to get out of the room. By the time I did, the pounding had stopped, and it was obvious why.

Dane had opened the front door, and Moray stood on the other side.

Bad, bad, bad.

I tried to shove Dane aside, but he stood firm, so the most I could do was stand next to him. Moray didn't like that, if his sneering glare was any indication.

"Oh, I see how it is, Essie. Not too good for the offworlder, are yeh?"

My face burned at what he was thinking while the rest of me froze, remembering what *he'd* aimed to do two nights before. I wasn't sure how much Moray remembered, what story he told himself to make sense of why he'd changed his mind . . . or if his microscopic brain had guessed what I was.

"Certainly too good for *you*," Dane said. "Don't you have a mine to work?"

Moray's eyes stayed on me. I held back a shudder. "Aye, I do, but another of yer blazin' drones mangled itself runnin' from a harri-harra."

He reached to the side and pulled Cusser into view. One of its four legs was dead as a rock, forcing it to stumble along.

I shook my head. "You blew out that actuator again, didn't you?"

It swore and tried to kick Moray with one of its operational legs.

"Come on, get into the lab. I'll have it fixed by tomorrow, Moray."

"Yeh'll fix it now," he insisted. "We need it down in the mine with the others."

"You do not. You can manage with the five of them running the dumb-drones below."

He glared, taking a half step forward. Dane took a half step of his own, blocking me. Moray shifted his glare to him. "Not with the massive gap they're leavin' in the northwest quarter, we can't."

Helpless blazing miners.

The transmitter I usually wore on my wrist had been botched in my unscheduled swim, but I had a spare in the lab. That meant turning my back on Moray, which I didn't like, so I retrieved it quickly.

"Whirligig, reconfigure for operations with team of five. Keep an eye out for more harri-harra." A pair of beeps told me the drone had gotten the message. "There you go, Moray. They'll be pulling merinium out of the northwest quarter by the time you get there. Have a sparkling day."

"I'm warnin' yeh, Essie—"

I slammed the door and locked it, uninterested in his warning. With the door solidly keeping him out, I exhaled the tension, surprised at how much my breath shuddered.

"Are you all right?" Dane asked.

He was definitely suspicious. Color rose in my cheeks at the thought of telling Dane what had happened the other night. I couldn't do it, so I shoved past him to get back in the lab.

Everything was in its place, and my computer lockouts were secure. At least Dane hadn't fiddled with any of it. Cusser waited patiently by the workstation, its botched leg in the air. I crouched down and got to work on the actuator.

"Essie, what aren't you saying?"

"If I told you, I wouldn't *not* be saying it, would I?"

He sighed and leaned against the workstation, too close for my liking. "How serious is the repair on Clank?"

"This is Cusser. It doesn't look a thing like Clank *or* Clunk."

"What? Maybe to you. Never mind. How long will it take?"

"Under an hour, I hope. Just as well. I wanted to take an extra drone to the shuttle today, anyway. But I still need to weave code for the thrust regulator, so maybe two hours before I can head back out. You can go ahead and I'll see you there."

"I'll wait," he grumbled.

Grumbling, that was new. Being woken up by Moray had me feeling pretty grumbly, too.

"Wait Essie shuttle Essie fly."

Dane spoke before I could. "Shut it, Dimwit."

6

CUSSER'S LEG PUT UP a fussy bit of drama, taking longer
than I'd hoped. Dimwit's constant stream of unhinged nonsense
slowed my programming work as well. By the time we set out
for the shuttle, I was right frustrated but still clung to the hope
that I'd have Dane off the planet by the end of the day, especially
with Cusser's help.

Then life in Forty-Two would be normal again, the way
I wanted it. Yet part of me felt as cold as the sinkhole at the
thought.

"Why did you veer so far north last night?" Dane asked as we
carefully made our way through the woods. "You said yourself
that it's dangerous up there."

"Maybe because I was distracted by *someone* following me."

He untangled one of Dimwit's feet from some undergrowth,
saving me from having to. "Or you were too tired to pay attention, and what would have happened if I hadn't followed you?"

"Oh, shut it. I did thank you last night, you know."

"I—Yes, you did. Sorry."

As we approached the shuttle, I ran through my checklist of things left to do. Try out the new code for the thrust regulator. Double-check the oxygen cyclers and scan-scrambler. Have Cusser rig a patch for the radiation shields from the materials in my case. Make sure the navigational subsystem hadn't fallen out of calibration again. Tighten up—

"Moray thinks something's going on," Dane said, knocking the checklist right out of my head. "I mean, with us. Not true, obviously, but why does it matter to him?"

Feeling a blush come on again, I picked up the pace to stay ahead of him across the flats, Cusser and Dimwit on my heels. "It doesn't. He's just rinked because I generally crack the kneecaps of anyone who tries to set foot in my shack."

"I've caused a lot of trouble for you, haven't I?"

"Aye, a bit, but it's nothing you meant to do."

He didn't say anything else, just opened the hatch, and I got to work.

The new thrust regulator code worked on the first try. The other repairs went pretty smoothly, too, probably because most of the systems were now patched enough not to botch any of the others in a cascade effect like I'd been dealing with the past few days. Or maybe the shuttle's systems were more afraid of Cusser's temper than mine. The radiation shields took some extra wrestling, and I nearly broke my hand on a bulkhead when navigation went out not once but twice before holding.

Not perfect, but compared to some projects—like trying to get Dimwit to function predictably—I couldn't complain.

Dane had kept quiet all day, staying out of my way until I was ready to test-fire the engines. He lit them up, and I ran checks on every system, especially the scan-scrambler. A few extra stitches in the computer and some last-minute tightening, and it was set.

"It's not good as new, but it's good enough to get you to the Ascetics if you're still set on that, then home again," I concluded, wiping my hands. "You'll want to look into more permanent repairs when you get back to your clean-tech."

He didn't look up from the command console. "Maybe you should come with me."

My stomach and heart collided in a race to my throat. "What? Still feeling that concussion, ridiculous delusions of romantic—"

"No! That's not what I mean."

Relief mixed with an unexpected sting when he said it so quickly. Of course he wasn't thinking that. "Well, what *do* you mean, then?"

"You don't need to stay here, with the way the miners treat you. People should appreciate your work. Your skills could be useful against Windsong."

No matter how much I wanted Dane to succeed, I couldn't help him. Not that way. My mother's voice whispered in my head again, trying to argue. I let my own words drown it out.

"Well, aren't you single-minded? My life here may not be some grand gesture, standing against a tyrant, but I like it the way it is."

"Do you really?"

"Aye, I do. Without you around, the miners leave me well enough alone, mostly."

"Being left alone . . . is that all you want?"

All I've wanted for eight years. I tucked my slate into my case. "I have my lab for experimenting, and the drones give me plenty of puzzles. That should be enough for anyone." When he didn't say anything else, I hesitated, then patted his shoulder. "Try not to get yourself killed, Dane. It really would be a shame. And a bit of advice: the Ascetics always lie to outsiders, so don't believe anything they say. Come on, Dimwit. Where'd Cusser get off to?"

The drone skittered ahead to the hatch at the far end of the shuttle. I heard Dane get up and follow me. Chivalrous to the end.

I spotted Cusser in the corner of the engine compartment, its lights dark. Shut down.

Every alarm in my body went off.

Something cold and metallic touched my neck. The shuttle skewed out of focus. My legs weren't under me anymore, but somehow I hadn't hit the floor. As my blurry world faded, I heard two things.

"Wait Essie shuttle Essie fly."

"I'm sorry, Essie."

Someone had injected steaming mine-slag into my brain. That was the only way to explain the searing spikes of pain in my head.

I tried opening my eyes. Bad idea. The light added two new skewers, one to each eyeball.

Take a breath, Essie. Get your wits.

I was lying down, curled on my side with my hands bound behind me. The floor felt like textured metal—exactly like the decking of the shuttle. It vibrated. My equilibrium felt a touch off. It could've been whatever had knocked me out, but it felt more familiar than that. Familiar in a haven't-felt-it-in-years kind of way.

Artificial gravity. We've launched.

More slowly, I tried opening my eyes again. Not so bad. My vision was still a little blurry, so I waited it out with a lot of blinking.

I was in one of the side compartments, which wasn't nearly as familiar to me as other parts of the ship. There wasn't a lot in the room. Just me, a couple of storage crates, and a powered-down drone. Dimwit, not Cusser. Dane hadn't left me a lot to work with.

Dane...The name lit a new fire, but in my gut instead of my head. I didn't know what he thought he'd get from taking me against my will, but I was going to show him the cost was higher than he could pay.

He may not have left me much, but he'd left me enough—the drones were never *completely* powered down.

"Dimwit, emergency protocol. Wake up."

Its little lights started blinking, and it rose up on its four legs. "Dimwit Essie help Essie."

"That's right, you're going to help me." I gathered my strength and rolled myself to sit up, fighting down the urge to vomit that came with it. "Come over here. I need you to cut off these restraints but *not* cut my hands. If you cut me, Dimwit, I swear, I really will dismantle you. Can you manage it?"

"Dimwit Essie help Essie."

That would have to do.

I stretched my arms as far from my body as I could while Dimwit scuttled around behind me. It had a few built-in tools that could do the job, and I hadn't told it which one to use. They were all too scary to think about coming near my skin.

A high-pitched whirr sounded, probably the little saw the drones used for cutting off mineral samples. Not a bad choice, as long as it didn't sever an artery.

Two seconds later, my hands were free.

Now what?

I didn't get much time to think. A new, rhythmic vibration rang through the decking. Footsteps.

Ignoring the lingering headache, I pulled myself to my feet and flattened my body against the wall by the door. Everything I knew from the cage about fighting someone bigger and stronger charged up in my head. That fire in my gut blazed into my limbs and made it hard to hold still, but I waited, unmoving.

The door slid open and Dane strode in. I launched my fist at his head before he could turn my way.

It hit empty air.

Before I could process how he'd dodged me like that, he got a grip on one arm, twisting it behind my back. I swung my free arm. Nothing. A thrust elbow, a kick, twisting and struggling... even more nothing.

He shoved me against the wall. One arm pressed against the back of my neck while the other pinned my hands, and he must have sprung extra limbs, because my legs were pinned as well.

A perfect hold. Can't slip it, completely helpless...

My panic attack fueled a renewed struggle, but Dane still held me in place. I felt his breath on my ear and shuddered.

"I'm not one of the half-drunk miners you're used to fighting...Princess."

He knew.

I couldn't breathe.

"I'm the 'treasure' you were looking for," I whispered.

"The treasure I *got*, the way I see it."

Get out now, *Essie.*

I dug for the old instincts that had let me body-hop to Moray before, focusing on the physical contact between us, willing myself to see through Dane's eyes, to see if I could find some way out of this.

I hit an invisible wall, bouncing back to myself. A new spike of pain drilled through my skull.

Dane's breath caught briefly, but his grip didn't loosen. When he spoke again, his voice was just as hard as before. "Not bad, but it won't work on me unless I let it."

That could only mean one thing. This trouble was even bigger than I'd thought.

Dane wasn't a Garamite at all.

He was an Exile.

7

EVEN IF DANE HADN'T been pinning me, I couldn't have moved. The part of my brain that ran my body had disengaged entirely. The part controlling my voice was a touch more stubborn.

"What in blazes do you want with me?"

"The truth, for starters."

"Truth? You're a lying mass of worm dung, and you want to talk about the truth?"

"You assumed I was a Garamite because my ship is," he said. "I gave you a story that fit with your assumption."

"What about your name? Dane isn't an Exile name, so who are you really?"

He pressed me harder against the wall. I was starting to lose feeling in my hands. "None of your business. You're going to tell me why you're able to Transition."

"You're dimmer than Dimwit, aren't you? Everyone has two parents, and I obviously didn't get it from my father."

"Matthias's first wife . . . Alaina?"

"My mother, yes. *She* was an Exile, only my father didn't know it."

Dane finally released me and stepped away. I rubbed and flexed my hands, getting the blood flowing back to them. I knew better than to try to go at him again. He was far too skilled a fighter. Maybe I still had a chance to talk my way out of the situation, though.

Maybe.

"I didn't know that," he admitted. "Why did she do it, breaking the law, hiding what she was? Just to become queen?"

No, I wasn't giving him that much. "Go to her grave and ask her yourself."

"Maybe I will. We're on our way there now."

Ice shot through the fire in my veins. Windsong. Home.

No. I couldn't go back.

"Why?" I forced out of my frozen lips.

His eyes ran over me from head to toe and back, forcing me to fold my arms tightly or risk trying to punch him again. "You're the king's only child. His efforts to find you have failed, so I think he'll find you a fair exchange for the Candaran prisoners."

A trade. He was going to trade me back to my father for the release of Exiles—Candarans, as they called themselves—like I traded mining shares for data processors and spare circuit boards. The fire surged back a little, but the buzzing vibration in the deck distracted me.

"I'd say I'd rather die, but you've already taken care of that."

"What are you talking about?"

"The shuttle! It might as well be patched together with slug spit. Enough to get to Garam, but Windsong is on the far side of the system right now. We'll never make it."

Dane moved toward the door. "A shame that I have more confidence in your repairs than you do. Dimwit, no more helping Essie. She needs to stay here, understood?"

"Dimwit Essie stay Essie."

I glared at the glorified scrap-heap. "You little traitor!"

"Dane Essie friend Essie."

"How do you even know that word?"

"You're very skilled, Essie," Dane said. "But you're not the only one who knows a thing or two about programming."

After everything—lying to me, knocking me out, kidnapping me—it was tampering with my drone that set my fury burning out of control.

"You rotten, festering smear of snail-scum!"

I launched myself at him—surely pure rage was enough to overcome his training—but I was too slow. He got through the door and closed it before I could reach him. My momentum carried me right into the solid metal, smacking my shoulder and knee.

I pounded my fists against the door. When that failed to satisfy me, I punched it until my knuckles bled, screaming every obscenity I knew. Pain was a problem for people who had something left to lose.

Dane had to hear me. My voice would carry through the ventilation system if nothing else.

Ventilation... the oxygen cyclers. The patch I'd stitched would last eight days, maybe a bit more, but nowhere near the time it would take to get to Windsong. If I'd had access to better materials I wouldn't have used a fuse that would burn out so quickly. But on Thanda, junk-tech was all I had to work with.

Saying I'd rather die than go back home was one thing. Actually dying of suffocation in the cold vacuum of space was another.

I stopped screaming. I stopped punching. I put one of the large crates between myself and the door, sank to the ground, and hugged my knees to my chest.

If Dane came back in, he wouldn't see me cry.

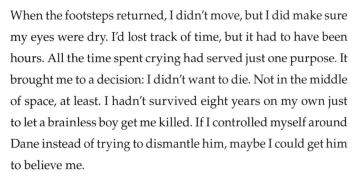

When the footsteps returned, I didn't move, but I did make sure my eyes were dry. I'd lost track of time, but it had to have been hours. All the time spent crying had served just one purpose. It brought me to a decision: I didn't want to die. Not in the middle of space, at least. I hadn't survived eight years on my own just to let a brainless boy get me killed. If I controlled myself around Dane instead of trying to dismantle him, maybe I could get him to believe me.

Maybe I could stall him, trick him . . . do *something* to buy myself a chance to get away.

"There you are," he said, coming around to the back of the crate and dropping meal- and water-packs into my lap. When I glared up at him, he took something from his pocket. My little water-scanner. It turned green when he ran it.

"See? Safe." He glanced at the dried blood on my knuckles but didn't comment. "Eat. You're not worth anything if you starve to death."

I agreed that starving wouldn't do me any good, so I silently opened the pack and started eating. If I looked at him too much, I feared my resolve to not kill him would fail.

He lingered a moment before walking back to the door. I waited until he was nearly out of the compartment before speaking.

"I mean it. The ship won't last."

"It will. I'm getting you to Windsong, and I'm getting the prisoners back."

His voice had no give, no room for doubt. People so driven and committed wouldn't listen to reason. I'd have to get creative.

Good thing creative was my specialty.

I spent hours at a time in my head. The compartment that made up my prison had a small lavatory attached, and Dane brought food twice a day. A stack of my clothes lay in a corner, and Dimwit oh-so-helpfully informed me that it had retrieved them from my shack under Dane's orders. I didn't need anything else, just time to think. Sometimes I sat on the crates, sometimes I paced, but always I thought and calculated and planned.

This was just another puzzle for me to solve.

My gear and supplies weren't anywhere in the compartment. Even the small multitool I kept in a hidden pocket of my jacket was missing.

Dane must have searched me while I was unconscious. It took twenty minutes to calm the revived homicidal rage when I realized that.

Focus, Essie.

Dimwit had been told not to help me, and I didn't have the

equipment to access its programming matrix to override that order, but it was useful in other ways. I asked it for the date and time, and it told me. Assuming we'd left Thanda shortly after I'd been knocked out, assuming we were on a direct course to Windsong at the shuttle's maximum speed... That was a lot of assuming, but it gave me an idea of our position.

We had to get onto a planet. Once we had an atmosphere around us instead of a vacuum, I'd have more options. Any logical course to Windsong would take us right by Garam before skimming past the sun....

The sun. I definitely had *not* patched the radiation shields well enough to handle the onslaught that came with a solar near-pass.

I had a single plan with any chance of working, and it wasn't a great chance. If my calculations were right, though, I only had a small window to try, and no time to come up with anything better.

In rummaging through the storage crates, I'd found a sturdy metal brace with a thin edge... thin enough to pry the cover plate off an electrical junction on one side of the room.

"Dimwit Dane help Dane."

"Shh!" The drone had all but ignored me for ages, but it must have recognized I was up to something. "Dimwit, your new directive is to help Dane. I get it. If I don't do this, Dane and I will *both* be killed. The ship won't hold together all the way to Windsong. Do you understand?"

"Essie right way Essie."

A vote of confidence if I'd ever heard one. Dane had underestimated Dimwit's tricky logic algorithms.

Behind the cover plate, I found far too many conduits, and

I didn't have anything I needed. I needed Ticktock to tell me exactly which conduit went to what. Even Cusser would've been helpful, but at best it was still powered down in the engine compartment. I hadn't bothered downloading the full schematics to Dimwit. All I wanted to do was send an overload to the oxygen cyclers and force the fuse to burn out a little early.

A precision job with imprecise gear.

Better than sitting here doing nothing.

I wrapped my hand with a thin piece of rubber sheeting, took my best guess at which conduits would do the job, and used the metal brace to cross-connect them.

Sparks exploded out of the junction, and the shuttle lurched, throwing me against one of the crates before righting itself. An alarm blared and lights flashed as the deck continued to heave and shudder under my feet.

I'd definitely damaged more than the fuse in the oxygen cycler.

The door to the compartment was open. Either an emergency measure or I'd shorted it out, too. I didn't really care which. I dove through the opening, out into the corridor, and staggered up to the command compartment.

Dane sat at the main console, madly working to get the shuttle back under control. Through the viewer, I saw my timing couldn't have been more perfect. The tan globe of Garam hovered just off to one side. My aim, however, was several sniffs shy. Flashing lights on the console told me the oxygen cyclers were fine. The stabilizers and thrusters *weren't* so fine, and right when Garam's gravity well had a hold on us.

"You did this, didn't you?" Dane shouted over the alarm.

"Of course I did! Set it down on Garam or we'll both die."

"With the thrusters misfiring like this? We'll never make it."

I glanced at the readout on his panel. He was right. I'd sabotaged myself right into a corner and had about five minutes to get both of us out of it.

"Where's my gear?"

He shot a glare over his shoulder. "How bent do you think I am?"

"Dane, I did this because I don't want to die! *Where is my gear?*"

One more pause, one more violent lurch of the misfiring thrusters, and he gave in.

"Engine compartment, storage cabinet."

I was already halfway there. "And tell Dimwit to help me! Cusser, emergency protocol. Wake up."

My gear was in its case, right where he'd said, but working on systems midflight was not something I had a baby's first gasp about. Unlike when I'd done the other repairs, the entire ship had power running and parts moving. Every attempt could get me burned, electrocuted, or worse. Doing nothing, however, had more certain consequences.

Cusser powered up and swore. "Shuttle trajectory inconsistent. Danger to human occupants. Correction necessary, and blazing soon."

"No kidding," I muttered. Midflight repairs were an even worse idea for the drones. Metal-on-metal contact in a live electrical system was a bad combination. I'd have to do it myself, but Cusser could help. "Pull up the shuttle schematics, tie into the monitoring systems, and tell me what to do."

I stitched faster than ever, rerouting power and cross-connecting hardlines, ignoring the burns when sparks flew at my fingertips and the cuts when the ship bucked just as I reached my hand between components. Cusser rattled off a steady stream of instructions, and Dimwit handed me gear before the words were halfway from my mouth. It didn't wander off once.

The stitches weren't elegant and neat. They were fast and sloppy...and temporary. They only had to hold long enough.

I jammed the last connector in place. The shuttle settled to a rumbling vibration. Not perfect, but better. Steady enough that I could get back to the command compartment. Garam loomed before me, much larger already.

"Will it hold?" Dane asked.

"We'll find out soon enough."

He glanced back at me and started. I followed his eyes. My hands and forearms were a bloody, burnt mess. They shook, and I couldn't stop them. My cheek stung. Another burn.

"Dimwit, get her strapped in," he said, nodding to the other command seat.

I willingly collapsed into the chair, and the drone fastened the safety straps around me. Once I was in, I told Dimwit and Cusser to go back to the corridor and mag-lock themselves to the wall.

As we entered the atmosphere of Garam, the vibrations grew, but the shuttle held a steady line.

Then we hit turbulence.

I really hoped Dane was as good a pilot as he was a liar. We both had to survive the landing.

It was the only way I'd get a chance to kill him.

8

DANE MANAGED A SOLID LANDING near a Garamite colony. Hardly a scratch on the exterior, I would guess. By the time we were on the ground, though, I didn't really care. My adrenaline had faded, and all I knew was pain. My hands felt like they'd been held under a tack laser, like they had no skin left to protect them from anything. They throbbed with every heartbeat, pulsing with pain from the inside out. Every breath was an effort not to scream or cry.

"Here, let me see," Dane said. He had a medical kit out on his lap, ready to go.

I didn't want him touching me.

I wanted the pain to stop.

I couldn't do it myself.

Tank it. I held my hands toward him, still shaking madly.

His medical supplies were different from what I was used to, more like what I remembered from Windsong when I was little. He cleaned off the blood and sprayed something onto the worst cuts to seal them, better and faster than a smart-plaster. Then he smoothed a cooling gel over the burns, including the one on my cheek. I fought not to flinch, keeping my eyes locked on the desert landscape on the viewer.

"If you just hadn't started any trouble—"

"You *kidnapped* me, Dane. Kidnapped me and stole two of my drones. If you hadn't done that, you could've gone home to Candara. It's only a little farther than Garam. My patches could've managed that much, but there's no way we were getting to Windsong."

"It's not like I'm the first."

My gaze turned sharply to him. "What?"

"The people who kidnapped you eight years ago. Who were they? How did you escape from them? That's why you were hiding in Forty-Two, right? Or was Petey one of them, got you on his side so he didn't have to lock you up?"

That was enough, and I looked away again, my breath hitching in my chest. But it had nothing to do with my injuries. "Oh, you know *so* much. You don't need me to tell you anything."

He grabbed my chin and turned my face back toward him. I couldn't use my hands yet, and I was at the wrong angle to kick him.

"I know that when you were taken, my people were blamed, and your father arrested all the Candarans on Windsong, people living legally in the embassy. People like...People who hadn't done anything wrong."

I froze. *If* he was telling the truth—and it seemed likely he was—I hadn't known. I knew the war with the Exiles had started just after I left Windsong, but I didn't know about the embassy. Still, he didn't understand the situation, why I couldn't go back, and I had no desire to explain it to him.

"I hope you didn't steal this shuttle," I said softly.

"Of course I didn't." He finally released me and moved away. "Why?"

"Because the locals have sent someone to greet us."

Dane turned to the viewer to confirm my claim. A sand-skimmer large enough to carry several Garamites was making a straight line for us. With the vehicle's speed, they'd arrive within minutes.

"I aimed for *this* colony because I have contacts here," he said. "It'll be fine."

Fine for him, maybe. "Are you going to tell them who I am?"

His pause told me he hadn't thought about it yet, but he found an answer quick enough. "I think it's better if they don't know."

I wasn't sure whether I agreed or not. Between the royal tutors and listening to the miners, I knew a few things about Garam. First of all, Garam had no central government. Each colony on the planet ran itself, and as long as they gave my father what he wanted, the on-site presence from Windsong was kept to a few officials at the spaceports.

My tutors had said Garamites were mercenary as a rule and politically fickle, leaning toward whichever side seemed most likely to let them do as they pleased. And "what they pleased" usually meant anything they could call an advantage.

A lot like Thandans, really. Except Thanda only had one advantage—the merinium mines. Garam, on the other hand, had some of the best tech in the system, know-how that no one else could figure, and more solar energy than even they could use, thanks to their proximity to the sun.

Garamites had backed the crown during some attempted uprisings and gone against it in others, depending on which seemed most profitable. That was why I'd swallowed Dane's story about looking for enough independent wealth to persuade the planet to unify. I had no idea how the Garamites would react if they discovered the missing royal heir was in their grasp. Maybe they'd send me along to Windsong faster than Dane could. Maybe they'd keep me away to spite my father.

Maybe they'd kill me just to simplify their lives.

If I could figure their inclinations, maybe they could help me escape.

Dane must've been thinking on a similar track. "Question is, will *you* keep quiet while I get the shuttle fixed the *right* way?"

I supposed screaming that I'd been kidnapped was an option. Didn't feel like a good one, though. Not until I had a better idea of the people I was dealing with. Dane was one; they were many.

"Me?" I said. "Don't exactly like people knowing my business, do I?"

Besides, with the shuttle fixed, I could use it to get back to Thanda . . . once I rigged a way to dispose of my captor.

Dane told Dimwit and Cusser to stay hidden inside the shuttle until he gave them further instructions, and to attack anyone who found them before those instructions came. So even with his "contacts," he accounted for the possibility of trouble. Good to know.

He also thought it would look better if we stood outside waiting to meet the Garamites, leading me to discover I did *not* like Garam's climate. As soon as the hatch opened, the air seared my skin, particularly the halfway-healed burns. The colony lay to the shaded side of the shuttle, and the sun was already low in the sky, so it could've been worse, but not by much.

Three men and two women emerged from the sand-skimmer. They all wore loose-fitting clothes in bright colors, and a swath of thin fabric covered their noses and mouths to keep blowing sand out. Each of them also had an electronic pack on their belts with narrow tubes running to the seams of their clothes. A cooling system, maybe.

One of the men—older than the others—stepped forward and shook Dane's hand. "Good to see you, lad."

"You know them, Brand?" asked one of the women.

"Dane, yes. He's from a good family, never ones to take advantage. His friend, however...I don't know her."

"This is Essie," Dane jumped in. "I went to Thanda to see if I could arrange a better merinium trade. Instead, I found her. She's a decent mechanic and was looking to get out of the settlements."

I could've sworn he smirked when he referred to me as a "decent mechanic," but I kept my mouth shut.

"Emigration from Thanda is strictly controlled." The woman again. Her eyes were more suspicious than the others'.

One of the younger men laughed and nudged her. "Come on, now, you know those restrictions amount to 'If you can pay, you can come and go anytime.' Besides, can you blame him for skirting the rules? Look at her!"

If my face hadn't already been red from the heat, it certainly would have colored at his remark. I might have tried knocking the attitude out of him, but Dane shouldered in front of me.

"I brought her for her skills." He carried off the lie so well, I might have believed him if I didn't already know he was rock-scum. "Unfortunately, the tech on Thanda wasn't up to the repairs I needed to get home."

"We don't have a repair bay large enough for it here, but we can certainly manage," the second woman said. "And we'll determine a fair price. But first, Essie, you're injured?"

I glanced down at my hands. Dane's patches did a pretty good job but were still little more than a head start. "In-flight repairs. Not my sharpest move."

"Let's get you out of the sun and into the colony, then. We have doctors who can take a look."

Doctors... I hadn't seen one since leaving Windsong. As long as they kept their "looking" to my obvious injuries and nowhere else—say, the back of my left shoulder—I'd go along with it.

Anything to get out of that blazing heat.

⁕⁕⁕

Thandans thought "grand architecture" meant a shack with the slightest feature beyond utilitarian, like a decorative texture on the paneling. I still had my memories of the palace on Windsong, the sweeping towers and arches, the terraces with their intricate balustrades overlooking gardens. But I'd gotten used to the shacks, the grime, the world existing in shades of gray and black.

The Garam colony was a new experience altogether.

The original settlers had taken a massive impact crater and built the colony within it. Perhaps at first they'd sought the shade the crater walls provided during all but the midday hours, but they didn't have to worry about the sun anymore. They had a solar screen, an energetic field forming a dome over the colony, allowing the right amount of sunlight through and converting the rest to usable energy. That was in addition to the solar collectors dispersed planetwide.

The sand-skimmer had large openings on the sides and roof, letting hot air blow through. Our vulnerability as we passed through the energy field made me anxious, but the man piloting the skimmer didn't seem worried as he tapped the controls. I spotted the word *polarization* on the readout as he did, and the skimmer's vibrations changed just a sniff. We got through easily. The polarization must have formed a safe buffer around us.

As soon as we were on the other side of the screen, I felt the difference. Still far warmer than Thanda could ever hope to be, but refreshingly cool compared to the bare desert. The Garamites lowered their masks and deactivated their belt packs. I didn't have to squint nearly as much, either, so I could take in more of my surroundings.

Green.

Trees and shrubs and flowers and grass. Not like Thanda, where stubborn, hardy plants barely clung to life. These flourished, lush and unfettered.

And in the midst of the foliage was a city—large by Thandan standards, small by Windsong's. Buildings with more shapes, sizes, and colors than I could take in at once. Bold colors, too, like vibrant tropical flowers. Nothing hinted at the harsh landscape beyond the perimeter.

Yet with all that, I found myself looking up at the sky. The field made it strange... fuzzy-looking somehow. I was stuck next to Dane, so in an attempt to resist hitting him, I focused on my curiosity.

"How does it work?" I asked.

"How does what work?" said the man who'd teased me earlier.

"The solar screen. I've heard of them, but didn't realize they could create such a wildly different climate."

The man smiled in a way I didn't like. A way that said he thought he was better than any lowly Thandan mechanic. "Ah, that's one of the great secrets of Garam. And we don't tell our secrets to strangers."

Secrets all around, then.

We slowed as we got farther into the colony and consequently drew stares from passersby. Most of the stares were directed at me. Dane didn't look any different from the Garamites—so at least I hadn't been right dimwitted to swallow his lie on that front. But no one on this planet had skin as pale as mine.

"Here we are," said the second woman—Liza, I'd heard the others call her. The skimmer came to a stop in front of a sleek blue building. "Essie, we can get those injuries treated inside."

"Meanwhile, Dane," Brand picked up, "perhaps we should discuss arrangements for your repairs."

Dane tensed so much, I felt it. "If it's all right, I'd rather stick with Essie. Besides, she knows what the shuttle needs better than I do."

"Very well."

Brand and Liza both got out with us, and the others continued on.

The blue building felt more like a clinic than a full hospital. Certainly it was nothing like the bustling hospitals of Windsong, but it served far fewer people. A doctor saw to me right away . . . and couldn't stop staring, narrowing his shrewd eyes at my grubby clothes and the grime under my fingernails. On Thanda, a perpetual state of dinginess meant blending in. Here, they looked at me like some kind of botched science experiment.

"Got something to say, Doc?" I prompted when I couldn't take it anymore.

He cleared his throat and finished healing my hands. No scars. No new ones, anyway. I still had the jagged scar on my wrist, courtesy of Cusser when I first upgraded it. It was no mystery where the drone had picked up the habit that spawned its name.

"I think you'll find accommodations here more sanitary than you're used to," the doctor said.

"I'll try not to leave a trail of stains in my wake," I retorted.

Dane glared. I ignored him. I was there against my will. Just because I was keeping quiet about it didn't mean I had to be polite.

Liza cleared her throat. "What's the extent of the shuttle damage?"

I rattled off some things I knew were botched, some I thought were botched, and some that might very well be botched but I'd been too busy trying to stitch things together to notice.

Brand gave me a look like he couldn't believe we'd landed in one piece. "Repairs like this won't be cheap," he said. "How do you intend to pay for them?"

"I have enough merinium for some," Dane said. "For the rest, I'll work it off in the support lab, same as usual. Essie, too."

"Indeed. Let's get you something to eat and settled for the night. We'll get things started in the morning."

Dane, continuing his trend of being a worm-ridden fleck of stone-scum, didn't argue when the Garamites offered a single room on the ground floor of a short-term residential building. That added credence to their earlier assumption of why he'd brought me along, but I knew better than to believe that was his motivation. He probably just wanted to make sure I didn't try to sneak off.

He shouldn't have worried. I didn't have enough information to run away ... yet. I needed the shuttle repaired. Failing that, I needed to figure where I could run to, how I could get there, and how to twist the situation to get myself back to Thanda. Either way, I had to wait.

The residential buildings were all consolidated in one corner of the colony. The short-term facility had smaller units rather than full apartments. Those catered to people coming from other colonies to collaborate on projects, or occasional visitors from Windsong coming to learn maintenance on some form of tech. Brand and Liza took us to a vacant unit and tapped a code on a control pad before letting us in. A panel above the door lit up with a blue-and-green pattern and Dane's name underneath.

I glanced up and down the hallway. Many doors had darkened panels, but all the other lit ones had a solid blue band. We were being singled out.

I waited until Brand and Liza left us before positioning myself very carefully on the far side of the room from Dane.

"That panel above the door—it's that important for everyone to know where the offworlders are staying?"

He collapsed on the bed and kicked off his shoes. "That's for me, not you. So everyone knows not to engage me one-on-one. We won't be allowed to go anywhere alone, either."

As much as I wanted to leave it at that and ignore him the rest of the night, my curiosity wouldn't let up. Gathering information was important, and I remembered what Brand had said—*never ones to take advantage.* "They know you're an Exile, don't they?"

"They know I'm *Candaran.*"

"You told Brand 'same as usual.' You've been here a lot?"

"A few times. Just because Garam won't help us against Windsong doesn't mean they'll turn away a fair trade from either side."

"Then why don't they trust you 'one-on-one' if they know you that well?"

Something in Dane's expression shifted, as though the question bothered him. "They also know Transitioning only works on one person at a time, and they know the signs to watch for if I try it on someone. Of course, they don't know about *you,* so if there are only two of them, we could get around that."

"Not likely," I grunted. Not with the blankness I saw in my own eyes when I body-hopped Moray. I couldn't leave myself defenseless like that.

You have to coordinate two parts of yourself, the part that Transitions and the part that stays behind. Like bouncing a ball with one hand and drawing a circle with the other.

Mother had tried to teach me about Transitioning, but she'd died before I could learn much. Mostly I'd learned that I shouldn't use it at all because no one could discover what I was. Years of not practicing made hiding the ability easy—until I panicked—but left me with no real skill. Just vulnerability.

"I wouldn't do it anyway," Dane said, unaware of the memories pummeling me. "The people here don't automatically assume the worst of Candarans. I wouldn't jeopardize that."

"Clearly they don't know you as well as I do."

His jaw set as he glared again. "Get some sleep, Essie."

I grabbed a blanket and pillow from the foot of the bed and curled up on the floor.

"Don't try to run off," he added as he dimmed the lights.

"I won't. Don't you come near me, or I'll bite your hand off."

"I'd expect nothing less."

9

THE SUPPORT LAB WHERE we were to work to pay for the shuttle repairs was an insult. "Drudge-work lab" would've been more accurate. Just a place for people to do minor technical tasks that needed doing but were beneath the brilliance of most Garamites.

It was exactly what I needed.

I had my own workstation with a computer terminal and a full set of gear. The computer displayed the work order, and components showed up behind a sliding grate. Everything was sleek clean-tech, but the repairs were beyond boring. Replace three fuses. Fix a faulty regulator. Reconfigure a conduit for reversed polarity. Each work order came complete with step-by-step, even-Dimwit-couldn't-botch-it instructions on the monitor.

To keep me from dawdling too much, each task had a time limit I had to meet, or we wouldn't get credit toward the shuttle repairs. A ridiculously long time limit. The Garamites seemed to have a pretty low opinion of a Thandan's capabilities.

Dane worked at the station next to mine, debugging code and writing simple routines. Work I'd rather do, even if it still amounted to puzzles any child could solve. We could hear each other, but a divider meant he couldn't see anything I did. Couldn't see me finish each repair in a fraction of the allotted time and spend the rest exploring the computer network—on-planet networks I hadn't been able to access from Thanda.

I figured the Garamites could access a log of my aboveboard activities, and I didn't dare push my cracking efforts too far. Their code was the most sophisticated I'd seen by links and spans. Didn't matter. Some gentle nosing around told me they were like everyone else in the solar system. They expected computer fiddling through software, but upgrading the drones had taught me plenty about finding hardware work-arounds. They'd given me all the necessary gear to pull the identification chip from the terminal and recalibrate it with a tag for a location on the other side of the colony. If they traced my activities, they wouldn't know it was *me*.

"How's it going over there, Essie?" Dane said.

I snapped the modified chip back into place. "Positively sparkling. You?"

"The same."

Once the computer forgot it was in the support lab, I dove in. I had more important things to do, but I couldn't help satisfying my curiosity about the solar screen first. Some of it got too technical to unravel between mindless stitching assignments. One particular component caught my attention—the control for modulating and stabilizing the field. It used a core of crystallized merinium. I'd never heard of anyone using the mineral that way.

Interesting as it was, it didn't help me.

I needed a way off the planet and back to Thanda. I probably couldn't stay in Forty-Two, but I could take the drones to another settlement, do a better job of staying hidden. Make it harder for Dane or anyone else to find me again. Petey would help me find someplace safe.

Petey, who had no idea why I'd disappeared or what was happening. I was halfway to sending a message to him before I stopped. I couldn't risk the communication systems. Getting word to Petey would have to wait, and I refocused myself.

The Garam colony had plenty of short-range vehicles such as the sand-skimmers, but the nearest spaceport was a hundred links away. I filtered through piles of network data until I came across an intercolony trade schedule. Transports regularly went from one colony to another with goods and passengers.

The next one heading for the spaceport would arrive in four days, but the price was steep. Not as steep as the repairs for the shuttle, but steep enough. And then I'd have to negotiate for off-planet passage . . . if I could convince anyone I wasn't illegally off Thanda in the first place.

Or I could stick with the shuttle and its scan-scrambler, but that meant getting aboard without Dane. As much as I still really liked the idea of killing him, I just didn't see any way it could work. His insistence on one room left plenty of murderous opportunities every night as he slept, but then what? I had to get from the colony to the shuttle without anyone catching me, and once they found the corpse, I'd be done. Maybe I could rig a way to get to the shuttle quickly enough for it to work. I ran through scenarios, looking for a solution, but kept stopping cold at the "murder Dane in his sleep" part.

Face it, Essie, you're no killer.

The computer beeped, warning me that I only had a few seconds left to finish calibrating a thermal sensor. I slid the part back behind the grate and waited for the next one to arrive.

"Keep up with that timer, Essie. You won't get credit if you finish late."

Killing, no. Maiming, on the other hand . . .

"Worry about your own blazing work, Dane."

I made sure the terminal didn't beep again.

Around midday, the door to the lab slid open and several sets of footsteps entered.

"Dane? Essie?" Liza's voice called. "A moment, please."

My timer paused, so I stepped out of my workstation's cubicle. The Garamite woman stood waiting with two boys, thirteen years old at most.

"The technicians have completed their initial survey," she said, turning to the boys. One handed a slate to Dane.

"Here are our findings and the cost for repairs," the boy said. "Minus the merinium you already provided."

"*These* are the technicians?" I blurted.

"Essie."

I ignored the warning in Dane's voice. "I'm stuck here doing the most mind-numbing work of my life while *children* are repairing the shuttle?" After a glance at the tally on the slate, I was doubly outraged. "It'll take twenty days to work it off at this rate! I could do it myself. All I need are a few parts and some help from—"

"Essie!" The danger that time stopped me.

"We've seen your so-called repairs," the boy said. "Not very elegant."

Hitting a kid wasn't my style, but his sneer made it tempting. I'd done what I could with what I had.

"I'm sure it's different on Thanda," Liza said kindly. "But education here relies on students being given real tasks. With Tobias as their instructor, they're more than capable of making the repairs."

At that price, I certainly hoped so, but I kept my mouth shut.

"We accept the terms," Dane said.

Liza made a note in the slate, and the three of them left. I turned to go back to my workstation, but Dane grabbed my arm.

"Do not mention the drones. I signaled them to stay where the technicians won't look, but if anyone finds them . . . Well, let's just say that when Garamites want something, they make it difficult to say no, and trying makes them a lot less friendly."

"Why would they care about my Thandan junk-tech?"

His gaze riveted my feet to the floor. "Those drones aren't 'junk-tech,' and you know it. Keep quiet about them."

I yanked out of his grasp and went back to work without a word. My head, however, was a riot of nonstop noise.

Twenty days. That was plenty of time for them to find Dimwit and Cusser. Plenty of time for Dane to form plans of his own to keep me from escaping. Plenty of time for the Garamites to find out who I was, with or without Dane telling them.

Worst of all, twenty days in that lab, performing stitch after lifeless stitch, wasting away.

Like you were wasting away on Thanda.

I shook my head, dislodging the sudden thought. Thanda was safe, hidden, out of reach.

Do what needs doing, Essie.

I'd do what needed doing, all right. There had to be a more efficient way of earning a little extra on this planet. I just had to find it.

We got more visitors in the lab the next day, but the footsteps passed my workstation, stopping at Dane's. I kept my eyes on the fuses I was replacing, my ears on the voices floating over the divider.

"How's your work coming along?" Brand asked.

"Slowly," Dane said. "But we'll get it done."

"Good." He lowered his voice, but not so much that I couldn't hear. "We haven't had a chance to talk. Still no word on your father?"

"No, nothing."

A sigh. "Shame. Eight standard years is a long time, especially if the tales of Matthias's prisons are true."

I dropped my micro-spanner, and both attempts to pick it up failed. My fingers felt numb.

Dane's father . . . The arrested Exiles who'd been living legally in the embassy when I'd disappeared . . .

That hadn't been part of the equation.

I shivered and willed myself not to throw up, focusing intently on the replacement fuses instead.

Dane mumbled something I couldn't hear. Then a voice came from directly behind me, drowning out Brand's response.

"And how is our clever little Thandan doing today?"

I glanced over my shoulder enough to confirm it was the man I hadn't liked from the beginning, the one with the superior smirk frozen on his face. "Well enough," I told him. "Better if you leave me to my work."

"If this is too advanced, perhaps we can find something more basic for you."

I bristled but resisted the urge to turn. "This'll do fine, thanks."

He started to say something else, but Brand interrupted. "Leave her alone, Tobias. Let's go." So the smirking man was Tobias, instructor to the technician brats. Figured.

The footsteps retreated, each beat echoing in my head. Dane's father was one of the prisoners. It changed things, broke my defenses, and set my mother's voice screaming in my ears.

Windsong needs you.

I needed to get off of Garam and back to Thanda, fast.

There had to be a way, and I redoubled my efforts to find something useful on the network. Every planet had routes to speedy wealth—one of the few consistencies in the system. Those routes were always risky, but so was sticking around a day longer than I had to.

I found plenty of games of chance that seemed popular, but I didn't know enough about them to work the odds in a gamble. The same went for some skill-based competitions I came across. Maybe I could succeed at one, but I didn't have time to learn the rules and get that good.

I needed something quick, something I could pull off.

Something obvious.

By the time Brand and Tobias returned to escort us to our

room, I'd figured the answer. One other thing was common to all the planets: everyone loved watching two people try to beat each other senseless.

"What would it take to set me up for a fight?"

Dane whipped around to stare at me. "A what?"

"I'm not talking to you," I retorted.

Brand stepped in. "I hardly think that's the kind of thing—"

"I have a winning record in the Thandan fight circuit. Go on and check their networks, you'll see. Fight winnings will pay off the repairs a lot faster than patching broken components."

"Then I'll do the fighting," Dane said.

"My idea, my fight." Besides, getting the winnings in my name would make escaping that much easier.

Even with Dane arguing, Tobias didn't take his eyes off me. He was looking at me like the men on Thanda did when they were certain a risky bet would pay off big. I wondered how he'd feel if I took him out for a warm-up spur right then.

"With all due respect, Dane, watching a trained Candaran fight won't bring in the credits she will. A girl who bested Thanda's mining brutes will be an incredible draw."

"She's never used VT."

"You keep telling us how smart she is. I'm sure she'll catch on."

Dane opened his mouth to argue more, but I cut him off. I'd seen VT mentioned on the network, but no definition. "What's VT?"

"Virtual-tech," Tobias explained. "Fighters engage through our computer network, the audience watches, and no one has to leave their colony."

It didn't sound any worse than the cage fights I was used to. Possibly better.

That didn't explain why Dane looked so unhappy about it.

Brand and Tobias took us by a VT facility to let me try out the technology. It was complicated, involving neural transmitters and kinetic sensors, redirecting the signals from my brain to the computer. I couldn't begin to guess how it all worked. They got me hooked up and ran a demonstration.

It felt real.

The rational part of my brain knew I was in a small room full of equipment, unmoving in a reclined chair, but every other part was convinced I was walking along a cliff overlooking an ocean. Salt wafted on the breeze tickling my skin, and the sun made me squint just a little. As I explored, I stubbed my toe on a large rock. That felt real, too.

It was amazing. My brain responded to the signals the computer sent, and the simulation responded to my brain's own signals. I could fight like this.

Tobias turned off the simulation and disconnected the equipment. "So, are you in?"

I answered before Dane could. "Definitely."

"All right, we'll arrange a fight for sometime tomorrow and see how many credits you rack up. If you're as good as you say, I might consider sponsoring you into the professional circuit. There are a lot more credits to be won that way."

And be your pet fighting Thandan? Not likely.

I kept my mouth shut as I followed the others out. My toe still hurt. Odd.

Maybe that had to do with why Dane didn't like it.

His bad mood lingered as we returned to our room. I waited until we were alone before saying anything.

"What's your problem? You want to use me to get your people back. Why not use me to get on with it faster?"

"It's different."

"Using is using, from where I stand."

"I didn't like you fighting Moray, either, remember?"

"Aye, but that *was* different. We were friends then."

Dane flinched. Once I said it, I realized it was true. He'd felt as much like a friend as any I'd ever had, up until he knocked me out. My anger morphed to a wrenching pang.

You should've known better than to trust him, Essie.

His face hardened as he stuck to his original track. "Why are you doing it? You're the one who acts like you don't want to go home."

I couldn't tell him I had every intention of using my winnings to leave Garam *without* him and head in the opposite direction of Windsong. To my *real* home, the one he'd stolen me from. There were plenty of reasons to be in a hurry, though.

"You've seen how Tobias looks at me. And you said yourself that when Garamites want something, they make it hard to say no."

"I would *not* let that happen!"

All I'd meant was how Tobias viewed me as a commodity, something that could bring more credits his way. Dane was talking about something else . . . something more personal. His dark eyes flickered, punctuating his sincerity. A twisted knot formed somewhere behind my ribs.

I turned away. "Well, much as I don't want to go to Windsong, I don't want to stay *here*, either. I can find new ways to botch your plans once we're off this fireball." I curled up in my blanket, intending to think through possible plans, but the urge to speak up refused to fade. I needed confirmation before I could even think about what I'd do after the fight. "What Brand said... Your father is one of the prisoners you want to trade me for, isn't he?"

"Good night, Essie."

That was a yes.

I turned away from him, but I felt off, and it wasn't just the lingering twinge in my toe. The knot in my chest wouldn't loosen. I was annoyed with Dane and still wouldn't mind breaking his nose along with a few other things before I left, but the fire of rage I held toward him went so weak I could barely find it.

Kidnapping me to trade for political prisoners made him a despicable smear of buzzard dung. Trading a girl he'd just met for the father he'd lost eight years ago... that made him something else.

⊶▪▦▌▌▌▦▪⊷
⊶▪▦▌▌▦▪⊷

As fight-time drew nearer, Dane couldn't shut it with the advice.

"Remember what I said before. Don't let your body show what you're going to do until you do it. Each action lives in its own moment."

"Aye, I heard you."

Liza finished connecting me to the VT unit. "Here's the current data on the wagers," she said, pointing to a monitor. "And your percentages for either a win or loss, depending on the length of the fight."

I took in the data. If I won, I'd be set. Enough to get to the spaceport, maybe even enough to get passage to Thanda. I could work out the other logistics. If I lost, it would take a few more fights to earn enough, depending on how long I lasted each time.

Or I could pay off the repairs and slip away. In either case, I'd be gone.

Tobias moved as though to clap a hand on my shoulder, but my glare stopped him. "Make it a good one, Essie."

"Always do. Let's get it going."

The tech initiated, redirecting my brain's physical and sensory signals away from my body and into the virtual world. Nothing as serene as the cliff-lined shore greeted me this time.

I stood on the floor of a large arena, the stands filling quickly. So quickly, I had to blink twice to assure myself I wasn't imagining it. People weren't walking in and taking their seats; they just popped into existence, already in their places.

I stood in one corner of a large red square. Clearly a fighting ring, though with no cage surrounding it like I was used to. Not even a rope or railing to reinforce its boundary. My opponent appeared in the far corner.

I'd never fought a woman before. This would be different.

I ignored the noise of the gathering crowd to get the measure of her. Tall, nearly Dane's height. The kind of muscular build that was achieved for its own sake, not from lugging heavy equipment around a merinium mine.

She had strength, weight, and reach on me. And from the cool look in her eyes, I knew it wasn't her first fight.

A voice came from everywhere and nowhere. "Wagers are now locked in. Fight to commence in three...two...one...begin."

I never got the lady's name or anything, not that I cared. Especially when she ran straight at me.

Instinct took over. I dodged, landing a kidney punch as I did. All it elicited was a grunt.

She twisted, grabbing me—I didn't move fast enough to escape her hold—and threw me across the ring.

I'd thought there was no cage. I was wrong. Thousands of tiny hooks jerked my muscles from the inside out.

A shock-field lining the ring. Charming.

The woman came at me again while I was still down, swinging her leg back for a kick. Dim move, and one I anticipated. I pivoted and brought my own leg up, thrusting my heel into the kneecap of her anchor leg. She went down, giving me enough time to roll to my feet and move away from the ring's perimeter. I did not want another dose of that shock-field.

My opponent was warier when she got up. She circled me, calculating her next move...smiling.

I hated it when they smiled.

Three attempts to knock it from her face failed, and I took three slamming blows to the gut in return.

She swung at my head, and I moved my left forearm to block. My arm didn't slow hers down at all. Her fist crashed through my defense and collided with the side of my head.

From there, the fight came unhinged.

I staggered away but kept to my feet, weathering a small shock from the cage. She stayed right with me. Another swing, and another. My blocks did nothing—I felt them more than she did. A bone in my left forearm snapped, and I cried out.

It's not real it's not real it's not real.

It felt real enough.

I let myself get angry, let the rage fly. It bought me a little space and a few bruises for her, but she kept coming.

I'd lost fights before, plenty of them. Most times, I knew it would happen long before it was decided. This was no different, and I always shifted to the same strategy.

Hang in as long as you can, Essie. And hope you don't get yourself killed.

10

FOUR ROUNDS. Somehow I pushed through four rounds before my body and brain both refused to cooperate any longer, and I passed out.

Passing out while hooked up to the VT unit was not a pleasant experience.

As soon as the fighting ring faded, a jolt ripped through me, waking me in the real world. My body still wanted the oblivion of unconsciousness and rebelled. I didn't have a single injury, but the lower functions of my mind wouldn't accept it, convinced I was a bleeding pile of broken bones. My eyes blurred as I shook, sending even more phantom pain shooting through my body. I wanted to throw up, but my brain couldn't get the signals worked out right.

"What's wrong with her?" Dane's voice.

"She pushed too long." Liza. "The beating she took, she should have blacked out much sooner. She overloaded on neural stimuli."

"What does that mean?"

"It means her brain is very confused. She'll be fine once she sleeps it off."

"Knock her out, then."

"We can't interfere with her neurochemistry further. That'll make it worse. Let's get her back to your room."

Hands on me, touching me, but I was in too much agony to stop them. Then I was moving, but my feet didn't touch the ground. Someone might have been carrying me. Too hard to tell.

A standard year must have passed before I stopped moving. Something soft cradled me. Probably a bed.

"You're too blazing stubborn, Essie."

I remembered how to make my mouth form words. "Another fight or two should do it."

"No. You're not doing that again."

I had to. I had to get away. Before I could rig an argument, my brain got what it wanted, and I passed out for real.

<hr>

I spent a full day in and out of consciousness. Sometimes I saw Dane, and sometimes I saw my mother, so I figured it was better to assume everything was a dream.

When I awoke the following morning, the pain had faded, and my surroundings felt real. I pushed myself to sit up—still a right mess of aching—and spotted Dane occupying my usual corner of the floor. He was awake, staring at the ceiling.

"We should get back to work."

He turned to look at me with a strange stillness in his face, but didn't get up. "No, I should. You should rest."

I found my boots on the floor and pulled them on. "Done enough of that already, haven't I?"

"Maybe. How are you feeling?"

"Like I went through the pulverizer back at the mine. But it's not real."

"Your brain decides what's real. That makes it real enough."

I groaned, stretching my arms over my head. Maybe if I gave my muscles some legitimate signals to send, my brain would unconfuse itself. "Very philosophical of you."

If he had a retort, I didn't get to hear it. A chime sounded to announce someone at the door. When Dane opened it, Tobias entered with a man I didn't recognize.

"Oh, good, she's up," Tobias said.

"I am. What do you want?" I asked.

"For you to finish paying off your debt. Come on, time to go."

Tobias took one step toward me, but Dane moved to block him. "She's not doing another fight."

"You're right. She isn't. Harper, tell them what you found when you checked the Thandan networks."

The other man smirked, making me wonder if he and Tobias were related. "A lot more than a fighting record. The safest, most productive mine on the planet, and it's all down to Essie."

"What does that have to do with anyone's debt?" I challenged.

"The payment is simple," Tobias said. "You'll tell us everything you know about merinium mining on Thanda and hand over complete schematics and codes on the drones you upgraded."

I got my aching body up off the bed to stand next to Dane. "You're all so sharp, design your own drones."

Harper raised an eyebrow. "You don't realize what you've

done, do you? Drones with the ability to make decisions, with complete autonomy. We've tried for years, but no one's managed it."

"Now that you know it can be done, I'm sure you'll figure it," I retorted. "Why is that worth so much to you anyway?"

"Because if you've made mining operations on Thanda less of a death sentence, we know quite a few Garamites who'd be willing to take over."

"Why would you do that?" Dane asked.

The pieces of the puzzle clicked into place, and I had the answer before either Garamite could give it. "You need more merinium for the solar screens, more than Matthias gives you. That's how he keeps you in line, how he keeps you supplying him with tech, how he keeps your colonies small and limited. The tiny amounts of merinium that black-market traders manage isn't enough to make a difference."

"Very good, Essie." More condescension from Tobias. "If we control the merinium, we can transform the rest of this planet. No more answering to Windsong."

"What about the Thandans?" I demanded.

"They're nothing but grunts King Matthias keeps alive to work the mines, and you've made them expendable. No great loss."

I couldn't breathe, and it had nothing to do with the false aches lingering in my body. Tobias was talking about war between Garam and Thanda—a war Garam would easily win even without uniting the colonies.

Another war.

Did it matter? Certainly if they wanted to blast Moray to pieces, I'd hand them the ammunition. But Petey, and the men who'd left me alone like I wanted, and the families in the Bands…I didn't want any part of hurting them.

"I won't do it," I said.

"Trust me, you will."

Harper's hand locked onto my arm. A jolt of panic triggered the push-and-pull on my consciousness—just like when I'd body-hopped Moray—but I fought it down. Before I could break Harper's grip, Dane did it for me, knocking the Garamite's hand away. When he did, I saw something on Harper's belt. Something that looked like a gun.

This could turn into a disaster right quick.

"Those aren't the terms we agreed to," Dane said.

Tobias snorted. "You know the rules, Dane. If you Candarans want to trade with us behind Windsong's back, *we* dictate the terms. And we reserve the right to change our minds."

For five seconds, Dane said nothing. No one did. Everyone just glared. When he finally spoke, his mouth barely moved.

"Go with them, Essie."

My shock at Dane's words rendered me immobile. Harper took the opportunity to grab my arm again, and Tobias latched on to the other. They guided me out into the hallway, despite my efforts to break free. I couldn't decide who to be angrier at, the Garamites or Dane. For all the things Dane was, I couldn't believe he'd let anyone destroy the lives of all those Thandans. I twisted to look over my shoulder, to yell at him or spit at him or *something*.

He looked right at me and held up two fingers.

I got the message. *Two of them. Two of us.*

If I did it, if I body-hopped, the rest of me would be helpless.

But Dane was a full Exile. He had to know what he was doing.

I tilted my head toward Harper, and Dane nodded. I focused on the contact between Harper's hand and my arm, remembered the feeling the night Moray broke into my shack. The push-and-pull returned, and I rode it into Harper's mind.

A moment of dizziness makes me tighten my grip on the Thandan girl's arm, even though she's stopped struggling. It's strange—I was feeling fine before. I get my focus back and pull her along. We can't afford any mistakes. Her knowledge is too valuable.

Where are his doubts? There! In the corner, push them forward, Essie. Make him hear. Harper, what if you can't get enough Garamites to unite behind you? What if Windsong intervenes and defends the Thandans? What if the Exiles do? Can you—

Dane punched Harper in the back, and the pain shoved me back to myself, stumbling as my legs turned to lead. The body-hop had been brief, but I was already worn out. Adrenaline would have to make up the difference.

Tobias, who'd taken a hit of his own from Dane, was retaliating. While Dane handled him, I didn't hesitate, slamming my fist right into Harper's face. Without any protective hand-wraps, my knuckles stung sharply, but I embraced the pain—it was *real*.

In moments, both men were on the ground, unconscious.

Dane caught his breath and went back into the room. After several taps on the computer terminal, he snatched up the few items we had with us, tossed them in a bag, and came out. He grabbed my arm, more gently than Tobias had, but I still pulled away.

"Don't touch me!"

"Fine, but we've got to go."

"Where? The shuttle repairs—"

"Are finished."

Unbelievable. "Those little brats finished it already?"

"Essie, come on."

Too many thoughts, too many changes, too much for my weary head. It didn't fit my plan. I'd never get to the spaceport, but Dane seemed to have a plan of his own for getting to the shuttle. No one was in the hall, but that could change at any moment. If they found out we'd body-hopped . . . Not good. Better the Exile I knew than the Garamites I didn't.

When Dane went for the exit, I stayed right with him.

Outside, some early-rising Garamites walked along the causeway. They gave me more funny looks than Dane, so they probably didn't know who—or what—he was. Still, the obvious offworldliness of my clothes meant they knew I should be escorted. I thought about the size of the colony. Was it possible they would think Dane was one of their own, assigned to accompany me?

It seemed so for the first link or two, as we walked quietly through the residential sector without incident. Then a voice called out behind us.

"You there!"

I turned and recognized the woman as the suspicious one from the greeting party when we first landed. She definitely knew who Dane was and knew we shouldn't be out on our own.

"Time to run," Dane said.

It was exactly what my instincts had longed to do for days, so I did. The woman shouted at a man up ahead to stop us, but his face blanked. I had no proof, but I suspected Dane had body-hopped him. A total stranger, without touching him, without missing a step—a full Exile's abilities, just like my mother's. The man turned away as we passed him.

I glanced back at the woman again. She was older and not very fit. She wouldn't catch us on foot, but I figured she wouldn't have to.

"We can't run our way out of this crater," I said, pushing to keep up with Dane's long-legged stride. My body tried to tell me it wasn't up to a workout like this just yet. I ignored the burning in my muscles. "She'll have someone in a sand-skimmer on top of us in two minutes."

Dane dodged a startled couple walking a dog. "Taken care of."

"What do you mean, taken care of?"

"Didn't you see how they have *everything* connected to their network? I launched a virus at all their ground transports. They'll have to do a full reboot."

I blinked, remembering the brief set of commands he'd tapped in before we took off. Too brief to be code for a virus.

"You had it ready?"

He didn't answer. Clearly I wasn't the only one who'd found some extra time in the support lab.

Blazes, why didn't I think of that?

We left the residential area, which meant fewer people at that time of morning. Any we came across either chose not to get in our way or got body-hopped by Dane. I couldn't be sure which most of the time, except once when he slowed down. This much

was an effort, even for him. Fewer people also let me think about where we were going.

"Dane, the solar screen! We can't go through that."

"On it." He took something from his pocket—my wrist transmitter. Rage flared up again, seeing it in his hand. "Dimwit, get to the solar screen and disrupt a sector, just like we discussed. Cusser, get the shuttle ready to go."

"Dimwit Dane help Dane."

"That's right, and hurry."

He had this all planned out so well, I didn't bother asking how we'd get to the top of the crater. As we approached the wall, I saw the answer for myself.

"A ladder?"

"They have lots of old evacuation routes. Go on, you first."

I didn't argue, just started climbing. And climbing some more. Less than a quarter of the way up, my arms and legs screamed. Most of the false pain had disappeared, but my body was still worn and didn't appreciate the strain. I paused near the halfway point to catch my breath and glanced back.

A glint of light below me caught my eye. The shiny surface of a sand-skimmer. The Garamites had gotten through that reboot.

I climbed faster.

At the top, I dropped to my knees for a second of rest. The edge of the solar screen was less than a link away. A faint gray blur on the other side might have been Dimwit.

I remembered the shock-field in the VT fight. Walking into the solar screen would be much worse.

"We can't go through there," I said as Dane came up over the edge. "That useless malfunction will botch it. You should've sent Cusser."

He took my arm and got me up and moving again. "Haven't you noticed? Dimwit never botches anything that's really important."

I'd have argued that the time the drone narrowly missed shooting a rivet through my arm was plenty important, but I didn't have time. The fuzzy distortion of the field loomed closer every second.

Nearer...nearer...then a patch wasn't fuzzy anymore. I could see Dimwit clearly at the edge of it.

"Go! I don't know how long he can hold it."

I ran harder, instinctively ducking as I went through the gap.

Fire blazed over my skin, convincing me I'd been caught in the field. But no, I was on the other side, yet it still burned. I fell forward onto the sand, my lungs flaming with the searing air I sucked in.

Dane hauled me up yet again. "No stopping, Essie. They'll be up here any minute. Dimwit, let's go."

He kept hold of my arm and dragged me along. I couldn't keep going. It was so hot, I couldn't understand how anyone wouldn't burn to ash in moments.

If I fell down dead, the Garamites couldn't use me, and Dane couldn't make me go home. Problem solved.

Tempting as it was, I still had a few self-preservation instincts left. I'd find another way.

Somehow I kept my feet under me, letting Dane's momentum carry me forward. He glanced over his shoulder and ran faster, saying nothing. He didn't have to—I knew he'd seen the sand-skimmer behind us, too.

"Dimwit, go on ahead," he said. "Help Cusser fire up the engines."

The drone scuttled past, kicking sand in my face. Grit stung my eyes and caught in my teeth, but it was the least of my problems. My head throbbed, sweat soaked my clothes, and every breath came in a heaving gasp.

Moments after Dimwit disappeared through the hatch, the engines roared to life. That little drone had become frighteningly reliable.

I heard something else, too. A higher-pitched sort of whine, very much like the sound of a sand-skimmer. I didn't dare look back to confirm it.

We scrambled through the hatch and bumped shoulders as we both ran up to the command compartment. I fell into the second chair, giving myself a moment to breathe in the climate-controlled interior.

"Close it up, Cusser," Dane called, skipping all the usual preflight checks. He jabbed at the controls, and my stomach dropped to my feet as the shuttle launched into the air.

I checked the viewer. The sand-skimmer was right where we'd been a moment before, its occupants firing energy weapons at us. They were too weak to do worse than singe the shuttle's exterior, though, and quickly fell out of range. We were safe.

Safe from the Garamites. I wasn't safe from Dane.

As we cleared the atmosphere, I stood and shoved him out of the way, entering a few quick commands on the control panel.

"What are you doing?"

"Setting a course for Candara."

His mouth snapped shut. I was pretty surprised, too. Not like I'd actually thought it out before doing it, but it was the only option I had left. He'd never take me back to Thanda, and I refused to go to Windsong like he wanted.

"Why?" he asked.

"I'm your prisoner—fine. But it occurs to me that if this were an official Exile move, they wouldn't have sent a kid to pull it off. I want to see whoever's in charge. *They* can decide what to do with me."

He stared at me for several moments, both our hands hovering over the controls, daring the other to make a battle of it. His eyes hardened, and a finger twitched.

"It won't change anything."

"Then the detour won't matter, will it?"

At last, his hands relaxed. "Fine. We go to Candara."

I sat back down, too worn to do anything else. Dimwit came into the compartment, probably looking for new instructions. I turned toward it to thank it for doing a good job.

Then it stepped on my foot, nearly crushing my toes, and I changed my mind.

11

THE SHUTTLE QUICKLY BECAME a very awkward place.

Dane didn't try to confine me in the side room again, but I went there myself to drink some water and rest. It was easier to be alone, particularly when I wasn't feeling well. Before I went, he gave me a tube from his bag. Dye stripper. He'd either traded for or stolen it from the Garamites. In his words, if we were going to Candara, then I was going to be recognizable.

A few minutes in the lavatory took care of that. No more not-quite-natural red. Instead, my hair was the barely natural white I hadn't seen in years. When I came out and returned to the command compartment, Dane raised an eyebrow but didn't say anything.

He wasn't subtle about keeping an eye on me, either. I put up with it for about two hours before I couldn't anymore.

"I'm not going to crash us again," I finally told him.

"And I'm supposed to take your word for that?" he retorted.

"You're not taking me to Windsong just yet, and I already decided I don't want to die in space if I can help it."

He fussed with the controls. Running a general system check, it looked like. "Why are you so set against going home?" he asked. "It doesn't make sense."

Something clicked. The look I'd seen in Dane's eyes ever since he took me. He'd expected me to be glad to go, that he'd be doing me a favor and getting his father back in the process. My resistance had botched his brain.

The truth botched my stomach, and I pushed it down. "People often *don't* make sense, I've found. You, for instance. Why'd you want to body-hop Tobias and Harper? You're a trained fighter—you could've stopped them without it."

"Transitioning, not body-hopping. Didn't you see the weapons on their belts?"

"I did, but you've proven yourself quick enough to manage that, I'd think."

He shrugged. "Didn't want to chance it. Transitioning always causes a moment of disorientation. I hoped it'd be enough for us to take them down before they could pull their guns."

"Aye, they were disoriented, and *I* may as well have been sleepwalking for all the brains I had left. Sparkling plan you had."

"You—what?"

"If I'm in someone else's head, I'm not exactly in my own, am I?"

"That's how it is when we Transition to non-Candarans as children, before we learn to split our attention. You never learned?"

I bristled and didn't bother hiding it. "My mother didn't have a chance to teach me everything about it before she was killed, did she? And she kept the focus on making sure no one discovered I could do it at all. The most we figured is I can't do it without touching the person, and I'm not very good at it."

Dane looked at the controls again, perhaps considering an apology, but it didn't come. "Either way, we were lucky. Tobias was too committed to using you. I couldn't Tip him."

My brows knit. "Tip?"

"No matter what they say, we can't just turn people into puppets. Not really. But you were right about us stealing secrets. Not that we do—but that we can. When we Transition, they can't hide anything from us. It's like we *are* them. People make decisions all the time, and sometimes they could go either way. If they're uncertain about a decision, we'll know it when we Transition, and we can sometimes nudge them in one direction or the other."

"Make them listen to the voice in the corner."

"Exactly. We call it Tipping. Doesn't always work. I—we try not to do it if we can avoid it."

I remembered Moray looming over my bed and restricted my shudder to just a slight clenching of my toes. "Sometimes a nudge can save your life, can't it?"

Dane's jaw muscles twitched, like he wanted to say something else, maybe ask what I meant. I was glad he resisted. Cusser came into the command compartment, checking the system status display, and seeing the drone sparked another question.

"We were lucky to stop Tobias and Harper, then. But having

the virus ready, prepping the drones to breach the solar screen and get the shuttle running? More luck?"

"Let's just say I don't trust easily, and I plan ahead."

His plan had been better than mine. I had to give him credit for that. And I had a pretty good idea where those trust issues stemmed from.

"Some of your other plans are making more sense. Tell me about your father." When he stayed silent, I pushed harder. "Tell me why you're doing this, or I'll decide *you* aren't included in my promise not to botch anything."

He held back a moment longer before the words burst out. "I was born on Windsong, all right? At the embassy—only it was hardly an embassy at all, just a place they could keep a few 'Exiles' contained. We were activists Matthias barely put up with, trying to show that we wouldn't Transition uninvited, that we wouldn't 'possess' or control anyone. Trying to bring this system back together. All of us came from Windsong once. We used to be one people."

We were, hundreds of years ago. Before merinium was discovered on Thanda, before the technology was developed to tame Garam. And before people became so afraid of a subgroup that had a peculiar genetic quirk for body-hopping, before my ancestors led the Liberation that ousted the body-hoppers from the throne.

Dane wasn't finished. "My mother died when I was born, so I grew up in the embassy with my father. He sent me away to live on Candara when I was eight because he thought Windsong was becoming too dangerous. He promised he'd follow soon, but then you were taken and they were all arrested."

My throat cinched shut. I wanted to say I was sorry, but I couldn't. An apology was nothing in the face of something like that.

"There, I answered your questions, Essie," he continued. "Now tell me the truth. Why didn't you jump at the chance to get off Thanda? Was I right about Petey?"

"No, absolutely not. It's because I didn't want to go home," I said simply. "I still don't."

"What do you mean? Who were the people who took you, then? How did you get away from them and end up alone in a mining settlement?"

I didn't want to answer. The answer made everything even worse. It admitted my failure. It made all the bad things that had happened my fault.

"Why didn't you go to the Bands, tell the officials who you were?" he pressed.

The instinct to run pushed me to my feet. I only got as far as the compartment threshold before the truth spilled out.

"Because no one kidnapped me, Dane. I ran away."

I kept busy in the engine compartment whenever I could, making Cusser double-check the Garamite brats' work and ensuring everything held together. When those tasks were done, I pulled out my slate and fell back on my old routines. Being busy meant filling my head with simple, logical thoughts rather than memories I'd struggled to keep buried for years. Better to solve a trifold number matrix puzzle than consider the ramifications of choices made by my nine-year-old self.

Dane let me be sometimes, but when I refused to answer his questions, he came up with his own theories. That I'd run away because I was angry with my parents, or I didn't like the pressure to be queen someday, or I feared they would realize I was part Candaran. Perfectly good theories, so I let him think he was right.

Surely, he figured, I'd stayed on Thanda so long afterward because I was afraid of the trouble I'd caused and how angry my father would be.

Sounds good, Dane. Let's go with that. I wouldn't say the words aloud. Nor would I tell him the truth. All I said was, "You might just as well kill me as take me back there."

Two days after our escape from Garam, Cusser reported that a relay for the radiation shield was being a bit twitchy, adding a few choice adjectives of its own. So much for the repairs being simple enough for schoolchildren to do. I checked the diagnostic while hoping the kids got failing marks. Software problem—the relay wasn't communicating properly with the rest of the system—so I activated a console and set about stitching up the code. Dane leaned against the adjacent wall and watched me work.

"There's something I can't figure out," he said. "How did you do it? Just nine years old ... How did you get all the way from Windsong to Thanda and survive there on your own?"

His questions scraped against my nerves, but this was something I supposed I *could* tell him. "Had a bit of help early on. Someone who got me away from the palace." A member of the Midnight Blade—the queen's guard—but that bit was none of Dane's business. "I cut my hair, kept my head covered. I was clever enough to get to a spaceport and stowed away on a transport that got me to a merinium barge bound for Thanda. Only off-planet passage I could find."

"And once you got to Thanda?"

"I pretended to be a boy at first, made things a sniff easier. Got down to the Bands and scraped by. Learned to fight because there were always bullies about. Once people knew I was handy with tech, being a girl didn't matter. Like I told you, though, they only have a few uses for girls in the Bands, and I decided I'd be better off in one of the mining settlements. You know the story from there."

He remained quiet until I got the relay to play nicely. "My uncle told me what the palace on Windsong was like," he said when I was done. "All lazy luxury. Servants making sure you don't have to lift a finger, cleaning drones so efficient you never actually see them at work. Hard to believe a girl who grew up with that could handle life on Thanda."

"Well, you adapt quickly when you have to. Can't be that surprised. You came to Thanda knowing I was there, didn't you?"

"Sort of. Eight years with no sign of you, so I picked the least likely rumor to try first."

"Rumors?"

He looked at me like I'd suggested going back to Garam. "Yeah, the rumors of Windsong's missing princess. You haven't heard them?"

"We were lucky to get much *real* information from outside Thanda, let alone rumors, and most of that only when I cracked a network or two. I thought everyone believed Exiles took me."

"Well, we Candarans knew better, and a few others questioned the official story."

I almost didn't want to know. "What were they saying?"

"You were uniting the Garamites against Windsong, you'd died in an accident and the kidnapping story was a cover-up, you'd never left Windsong but were being kept in a secure location. Lots of others. No one really seemed to think you were on Thanda, though."

An itch started in the back of my brain. "And you happened to crash-land near the mining settlement where I happened to be?"

"It's not where I expected to find you. I really *did* think you'd be in Umbergild. Isolated, comfortable, seemed like a reasonable place to keep a princess prisoner. Like I said, I figured landing near the most prosperous settlement on the planet would mean some chance of getting help."

Yet another result I could blame on my great miscalculation, doing *too* good a job improving the mine. And Dane hadn't been far off, thinking to look for me with the Ascetics. Just several years too late. "I was right, wasn't I? About this being a scheme of your own, not your government's?"

Dane's turn not to answer.

I sighed. "The mark on my shoulder tipped you off?"

He nodded, and I fought not to blush at the memory. "I expected either kidnappers or royal agents keeping guard, not a girl tinkering with drones in the settlements. The red hair was a nice touch, too. Otherwise I'd have known who you were from the beginning. You don't exactly blend in."

I grunted and sat on a coolant tank. "The day I was born, my father was more interested in unusual weather for the season. He chose my name and had some genetic resequencing done."

Dane flinched slightly. "That's supposed to be painful."

I just shrugged. It wasn't like I remembered the experience.

"He wanted what he wanted. So I was made Princess Snow, eyes like the sky and hair as white as my name. You remember Windsong, though. My appearance wasn't as uncommon there as on Thanda."

"I suppose not."

After a few minutes of silently watching me double-check a power junction, he left me alone in the engine compartment. I began to wonder: how different would it have been if he'd known right away who I was?

Only one answer came to me. He'd have given himself away . . . and I wouldn't have been fool enough to think he was my friend. No one could act *that* well.

After Candara neared, my anxiety grew more pronounced. Diverting Dane to his home planet was a good stalling tactic, and I was proud of myself for coming up with it. If the Exile leaders were anything like every other governing body I'd known, it would take them ages to make a decision about what to do with me.

That didn't change the fact I had no idea what they might do with me meanwhile.

Although busying myself with the engines had its appeal, I stayed in the command compartment the day we reached Candara. The globe we approached looked very different from Garam's mottled tan. Much of the surface was covered in the blue of oceans swirled with white clouds, and varying shades of green made up most of the land masses.

It looked a lot like Windsong. Fitting, I supposed, since they were called mirror planets. Nearly identical orbits, but separated by half a cycle, one always on the opposite side of the sun from the other.

We entered the atmosphere, and Dane communicated with some kind of flight authority who gave him permission to land in Gakoa, their capital city.

I hadn't seen a real city since leaving Windsong, and I wasn't sure what to expect. I'd been told Exiles were militaristic people who drilled in formation three times a day. With Dane's fighting skills, I could believe it, but as we flew over Gakoa, I didn't see anything like that.

Instead, the city was full of sweeping buildings made of stone, striking in their simplicity. Almost grand, in a way I'd never seen before. Trees lined the causeways, and open green spaces dotted the city. Parks. No military drills seemed to be taking place anywhere. As we flew lower, I thought I spotted children playing—something I hadn't seen since *I* was a child in the Bands.

We approached a large cluster of buildings at one end of the city, butting up against a rising mountain range. The governing complex, Dane told me. It had its own small spaceport, and he carefully guided the shuttle into the hangar.

No more time to back out. No chance for an easy escape back to Thanda. I was officially in enemy hands.

Except my mother had been one of them.

"Let's go," Dane said, gesturing for me to go ahead of him. "Dimwit, Cusser, stay here."

The spaceport attendant seemed to know who Dane was, merely nodding as we passed. As we worked our way into the complex, we came across other workers, guards, and low-level officials. All of them seemed to know Dane. No one questioned him or tried to stop him. Or seemed surprised to see him, for that matter, though they gave *me* a few curious looks. Guards opened doors without a word.

I got the feeling I was missing something.

We took a lift up several levels—maybe *all* the levels—and came out in a foyer with a pair of large doors attended by a matching pair of large guards. Again, they said nothing, just pushed the doors open. We entered, and I quickly took it in.

The vast room had a high ceiling and a wall-size window overlooking the city. In the center was a table surrounded by at least a dozen chairs. More stark simplicity, as there was no other furniture, no computer terminals, nothing. The floor, walls, and table all appeared to be made of marble, though the room was light and the table dark. Most of the chairs were occupied, and the occupants—all of them at least as old as Petey—turned from their slates to look at us.

This room radiated importance, and so did the people in it.

"Dane!" a man said as they all stood. "Where have you been? We've been trying to reach you for half a season, and nothing! No word on where you'd gone! It's irresponsible."

That was all the confirmation I needed—my kidnapping had been a solo operation. Dane took the rebuke, his shoulders squared, before responding.

"I've been to Thanda. And I've brought back Princess Snow."

These people were old, and I never expected them to move so quickly. They surrounded me, hands grabbing my shoulders and arms, too many to shake off.

"Let me go!"

"What are you doing?" Dane demanded.

Ignoring him, they dragged me forward and shoved me hard against the table, holding me down.

Someone pulled my sleeve off my left shoulder. Their fingernails scratched me. I struggled harder.

"The mark!"

"But is it authentic?"

"Get the windows."

The room darkened, and I twisted my head around to glare at them. A bluish glow approached from the side. It was a black light. I knew what they'd see—the fluorescing nano-ink forming my tattoo, designed to keep it intact as I grew up. Only the royal family had access to it.

Strong footsteps sounded on the other side of the room.

"It's real."

"It *is* her."

The hands released me as the room lightened again. I shoved them away and backed up, pulling my sleeve into place.

"What have you done?!"

The new voice resounded off the marble walls. My eyes followed it to a tall man with dark hair, younger than the others, who grabbed Dane by the shirtfront and slammed him against the wall.

The man glanced my way, quickly turning back to Dane when I met his eyes. I knew his face.

It was Kip.

It was the guard who'd helped me escape Windsong.

12

I COLLAPSED INTO ONE OF THE vacated chairs. No one noticed; all attention was focused on the confrontation across the room. One of the men who hadn't been involved in examining the royal mark tapped on his slate as if he had better things to do. Dane glared at Kip but made no move to escape his grasp.

"I did what no one else managed in the past eight years. I finally got us the leverage we need to make Matthias release the prisoners."

"She was safe where she was!"

Safe ... We have to get you safe, Princess. ... You have to run.

Dane's glare faded, replaced by confused horror. "You knew? You knew she was there? All these years my father and everyone have been held and *you knew?*"

Some of the others gave Kip looks of their own, some confused, others accusing. A few turned to me.

"Tell us what *you* know, Princess," said the man who'd first greeted Dane. He had silver hair, harsh eyes, and jowls that quivered when he spoke. "Who took you from Windsong, allowing us to be blamed?"

You must keep it a secret. Never tell anyone the truth.

I couldn't answer. If Kip hadn't betrayed me in all these years, I wouldn't betray him now.

"No one took her," Dane said. "She told me she ran away, but she wouldn't say why."

Kip gave the answer before anyone asked me. "She ran because Queen Olivia tried to have her killed."

"What? How do you know that?" Dane pressed.

Kip gave me the same look he'd given me that day eight years ago. A look full of horror, regret, and self-disgust. A look I'd wished erased a thousand times since, but none of it had faded.

"Because I was ordered to kill her."

"You were the one," Dane whispered. "The one who helped her escape."

A knife in Kip's hand, both of us staring at it, staring at each other . . . The indecision in his eyes fading only when he hands it to me.

Kip released his hold on Dane, but then pulled him into his arms like . . . like a father would. Dane neither fought nor returned the embrace. Now that I looked, there was a resemblance between the two of them. Something in the lines of the jaw and nose. They had to be related.

"I'm sorry, Dane. It was my fault. I didn't realize Matthias would move on our people so quickly, and there was no time."

His words twisted in my gut. I knew how much it *wasn't* his fault. How much it was mine.

Dane pushed away but didn't say anything, just looked between me and Kip. I avoided his eyes.

"The fact remains, we have her now," said Quivery Jowls.

"Dane is correct—Matthias would likely trade the prisoners to get her back. We're certainly not making progress on any other front."

"Didn't you hear what I said?" Kip protested. "The queen wants her dead."

"That was eight years ago, Kip. Many things have changed since then."

"Perhaps there's a better use for her," said another, a woman with unusually straight posture. "She *is* the heir to the throne."

"For all we know, she's as bad as her father or worse," Quivery Jowls cut in.

"But if ever there was a time for a coup—"

That jolted me free of the memories. "Do I *look* like anyone's blazing queen?"

Everyone stared at me, their faces saying the same thing—I absolutely did *not* look like any kind of queen.

"Glad we're all clear on that," I continued. "Now ship me off for a trade, lock me in a dungeon, or send me back to Thanda to mind my own business, but don't be thinking I'll be part of some unhinged revolution."

The thin man who'd been tapping on his slate looked thoughtful as he spoke for the first time. "This is not a decision to be made lightly. We should gather more information and discuss this carefully and thoroughly. Meanwhile, Your Highness, I've asked that a room be prepared. Someone will escort you."

"I'll take her," Kip said.

Anything that got me out of that room sounded good to me, and I knew from experience Kip wouldn't stab me in the back. I got up and followed him, glancing at Dane one last time. His expression was difficult to read. Anger and confusion, perhaps, but something more, something deeper.

I had big enough problems. He could deal with his own.

Kip led the way back into the lift. We rode down several levels before he touched a control, bringing us to a stop, yet he didn't say a word. Just stared at the panel.

"Who were those people?" I asked.

"The governing council. Members of the First Families of Candara."

"And how do you know Dane?"

"He's my nephew. His mother was my sister."

His sister, Dane's mother. The woman who'd died before Dane could even know her. I angled myself to see Kip's eyes. They held the same hesitance they had years ago. The same indecision.

"You're thinking about helping me escape again."

"I can't let them send you back there." His gaze moved from the control panel to me. "It would be easy enough."

He could do it. He could get me on the shuttle, convince someone to clear it for departure, and have me on my way before Dane and the others knew a thing. The solution to my problem.

Or was it?

"How much trouble would you be in?" I asked.

"You don't need to worry about that."

"I think I do. The last time you helped me, Dane's father landed in prison."

Kip shook his head. "I promised your mother—"

His words stabbed into my gut. He was willing to help me run away.

But I couldn't do it.

Not again.

"Aye, well, I made her plenty of promises I've long since broken. A dead woman can't very well punish either of us for that." He stiffened, but I turned away. "Take me to my room, Kip. I'll manage this myself."

After another pause, he set us moving again. We got off the lift and wound through serpentine corridors before stopping at a particular room, where Kip pressed his thumb to a panel. The door slid open. Inside was a suite the size of my whole shack, with flowers on the dresser and a window with a sidelong view of the mountains. My clothes from the shuttle were in a neat stack at the foot of the bed.

"Did I ever thank you?" I asked.

"I don't remember. And it doesn't matter." He looked around the room. "You'll be confined here for now. I'll check in on you later."

I nodded, unable to find any other response.

When I remained silent, Kip opened his mouth but stopped himself, refusing to meet my gaze. After a few more seconds' hesitation, he shook his head and left. I couldn't blame him. The situation redefined awkward for me, too.

Once I was alone, I set about inventorying my temporary home. The arrangements made by the thin, thoughtful man had been both quick and thorough.

A spacious private bath was attached, lined with marble and tile. I could practically swim in the tub. The huge bed was softer than anything I was used to. The closet was full of clothes in my size, the kinds of silky, pretty things I'd worn on Windsong. Completely useless things. Likewise with the vanity, lined with perfumes and makeup and jeweled combs I had no idea what to do with.

The mirror above the vanity caught my eye. I'd never paid much attention to mirrors. Something about me looking back at myself twitched me out. Nothing I saw there surprised me, but I still found myself staring. A ragged scarf tied over my head, keeping my hair trailing down my back instead of getting in my face. Then there was my face—weather-beaten and pale. My eyes looked as weary and worn as my clothes.

Definitely no one's queen. Better off that way, too.

Confinement in a luxurious suite in Gakoa was the worst punishment ever devised.

Being alone wasn't a problem. I liked it that way. But on Thanda, I had things to do in my lab. When Dane crashed, I had the shuttle to work on. When he kidnapped me, I had sabotage to figure. When we landed on Garam, I had trinkets to repair and plans for escape.

My room here had nothing except a simple communication console by the bed. I'd already taken it apart and put it back together for lack of any more interesting puzzles to solve. No one had bothered to take away the small tools in my pockets.

I'd never been so bored in my life. I wondered if Dimwit and Cusser were as bored, stuck in the parked shuttle. If the hangar exploded, I'd have my answer.

Kip had checked in once after leaving me. He said the council was deep in discussions, and they were gathering reports of current conditions on Windsong. There was no knowing how long that would take. He also said he'd try to find better things for me to do than tear my room apart—he'd arrived just as I got the console broken down to individual pieces.

After sleeping on the gigantic bed and waking to find myself huddled on the very edge of it, I couldn't imagine how I'd get through a full day without coming unhinged. Fortunately, the door signal sounded, and answering it gave me something to do other than brainstorming extreme measures.

Dane stood on the other side.

"You should have told me, Essie."

That was some greeting. "Told you what?"

He looked at me like I'd declared harri-harra sludge a rare delicacy. "That you ran because the queen tried to have you killed."

"Would it have changed anything?" I countered. "Your father is still in prison, regardless of my past. *Because* of my past."

"It might have changed *something*." He glared at me another moment, then shook it off. "They left clothes for you, didn't they?"

"Aye, but I like my own better."

He shrugged. "Fine. Kip said you needed something to keep you busy. Here," he said abruptly, handing over my slate.

Better puzzles. Less boredom. "Thanks."

"The council also said you can leave the room if you're escorted. Come on, you should see the city while you're here."

Even getting stared at by strangers sounded better than staying in that room, number puzzles or no. I twisted my hair up under my headscarf before following Dane out.

We were quiet all the way down to the main level. I didn't know what to say to him anymore. The hatred had died when I found out about his father. The anger still came and went. Sometimes I thought it made more sense to be mad at myself, but I hadn't sorted it out yet. I couldn't figure where his head was, either. I'd expected him to avoid me, but obviously he wasn't. Then again, as we made our way out of the building, he kept his hands in his pockets and didn't walk too close.

Just as well. Maybe he didn't have a choice about babysitting me. Punishment for acting behind the council's back.

Somehow during our flyover, I'd missed one key fact about the governing complex. It was directly across from the largest park in the city. The expansive space contained trees and flower gardens, footpaths and benches, even play areas for children.

And there were children there.

Regular children, not like the bratty technicians on Garam, and much younger, too. They ran around the play areas, climbing brightly colored structures, sliding and spinning. Laughing. They looked my way, cocked their heads curiously, and waved at Dane, who waved back. Then they went back to playing and laughing.

Is that what childhood is supposed to be like?

I needed distraction.

"How are things sounding with the council?" I asked.

"Hard to tell. Conditions on Windsong haven't been great. Your father's hold on the population is tight, and we haven't been able to get word about the prisoners in years. Kip is arguing for letting you stay here as a citizen, forgetting your connection to Matthias. Stindu wants to go with my plan to trade you for the prisoners, maybe more if we can strong-arm Matthias into a few things."

With the chance to get his father back, I couldn't imagine

Dane cared much about "maybe more." I just hoped strong-arming didn't mean the war moving from the outlands into more populated provinces. "How soon will they decide?"

"A few days, maybe. More reports should be coming soon. They're nowhere near ready for a vote."

I nodded. "Okay."

Watching the kids was too uncomfortable, and the conversation with Dane wasn't as helpful a distraction as I wanted, so I focused on everything else. The breeze tickled the back of my neck, and the sun warmed my skin. Not the searing heat of Garam. Not the freezing death of Thanda. A beautiful, perfect day. I tried to remember the seasons on Windsong. This felt like late spring, maybe.

The pond out beyond the orchid gardens, chasing dragonflies, Mother laughing.

The memory shuddered through me. I shook it off just in time to notice a woman step directly in our path. She was about the same age as Kip, a few strands of gray weaving through her auburn hair.

"You're her, aren't you?" she said, glancing hesitantly at Dane before turning back to me.

"Depends what 'her' you mean." The retort came automatically, without much thought, but I hadn't missed how rattled she was. Her demeanor set me off-balance.

"Ametsa's daughter. Kip said I'd find you here."

That name. My mother's real name. The hidden name woven into the drawings in her notebook. The name I only discovered when I deciphered her secrets years after her death.

My throat closed up, and I just stared, so Dane cut in.

"And why did my uncle send you here?"

"He knows Ametsa was my friend when we were children. Oh, you look so much like her—if you had dark hair, of course."

Did I look like her, beneath the ragged clothes and callused skin? Not according to the memories I had. Not even close. Maybe Ametsa of Candara hadn't looked the same as Alaina of Windsong. Didn't matter. I still couldn't speak, and my heart seemed intent on breaking free from my ribs. The woman assumed my silence meant I needed more.

"You know, she left our city when we were about your age, said she was going to do something important. Something that might make things better for everyone. It's the main reason I work for the council now. I wanted to be like her. To help people."

This woman knew my mother. She was her friend. But she didn't know why she left, and I did.

To become a queen on a planet that hated her people. To have me. To be killed.

Windsong needs you. . . .

My mother's voice again. After the memory of the pond and the dragonflies, it was too much. I turned and ran back to the complex, ignoring Dane's shouts.

One thing hadn't changed since he took me from Thanda—I still would not let him see me cry.

13

THE GUARDS TRIED TO STOP ME when I barreled into the complex without Dane. I didn't want to argue. I wanted to hit them until they got out of my way. Before I committed to that ill-advised strategy, one of them touched a device in his ear. He didn't say a word, just opened the door for me.

Every guard after that did the same, opening doors until I got to the lift. Dane must have called ahead.

I got to my room and found that my thumbprint opened the door, even though I'd already discovered it didn't work from inside. Dane could open the door as well if he wanted to, so I grabbed my slate and cracked the interface, then cut off its communication with the rest of the network. Not too complicated. Now it wouldn't recognize anyone's thumbprint.

For good measure, I shut myself in the bathroom. Finally, I let the tears go.

Stop being such a child. Crying won't bring her back.

Olivia's voice this time. My stepmother. Crying never got me anything but a slap across the cheek from her. She haunted the edges of my earliest childhood memories. Then a season after my mother's death, she'd been everywhere, berating me, judging me, telling me I was unfit for the kingdom, unworthy of my father. She was inescapable... until I escaped.

If Dane and the council—or men like Stindu, at least—got their way, I'd be back under her shadow.

Many things have changed since then, one of the men had said. I wondered what he meant, or if he really knew. Maybe when I disappeared, Olivia realized her hatred of me had been misplaced. Maybe she'd missed me.

Right. That was likely.

We'd all be better off if Kip won the vote, letting me stay quietly on Candara, disappearing into a lab somewhere. Except for Dane's father and the other prisoners. They wouldn't be better off.

My mother's voice burrowed into my mind again, and this time I didn't shut it out. *Windsong needs you to give them better than they have.* It was something she'd told me every night as she put me to bed.

I cried harder. I wasn't the girl she'd hoped I'd be.

Eventually, the tears ceased, and I left the bathroom to curl up on the bed. Much later, the door signal sounded, and I ignored it. Then Dane's voice interrupted my focused effort to do nothing.

"Essie, I know you can fix the door faster than I can get a repair crew here, so will you please just let me in?"

I should have thought of the blazing intercom. If I refused to let him in, he'd just get that repair crew anyway. I got up and restored the panel. The door slid open. When I saw the slimmest hint of sympathy in his eyes, I looked away. I didn't want that, least of all from him.

"Kip suggested I get you out to the park, but I didn't know he'd arranged for that woman—Laisa—to meet you. And she didn't mean to upset you."

"I know, it's just...I didn't want to talk about my mother, that's all."

"I get it. I let her know your mother died several years ago. If you're up to it, she'd like to meet with you sometime, tell you some of her memories."

That should've sounded nice, but I wasn't sure I'd ever be up to it. Besides..."I probably won't be here that much longer, right? And I couldn't tell her anything *I* knew about my mother. No one here knows what she did, going off to Windsong, lying about what she was."

"No, all that was definitely a surprise." His voice held a hint of darkness when he said that, but I didn't ask. He pulled himself away from that darkness, and I kept studying random bits of code on my slate. "The council wants to talk to you, see if you have anything to add."

"I don't have anything better to do, right? Let's go."

Anything not to stand there another second.

Back in the council chamber, I got a lot of down-the-nose looks. They must've expected me not to show up in my old rags. Too bad.

Kip guided me to a chair at the table. After the stunt with Laisa, I wasn't sure how I felt, but I didn't protest as he sat next to me, quietly telling me the names of everyone I didn't know. Dane stood behind him. The other council members filled in the remaining chairs, eyeing me suspiciously or glancing at each other.

A crawly feeling in my stomach said maybe I should've stayed in my room.

Quivery Jowls—Stindu—spoke first. "Princess, we realize you're likely to have knowledge that may aid us in our efforts against King Matthias. We would appreciate your cooperation."

"It's been eight years since I left Windsong, and I was a child. What makes you think I know anything useful?"

"You're a clever girl. I'm sure you learned a few things growing up in the palace."

My mouth stayed shut. Aside from Kip, I didn't know yet whether these Exiles were my enemies or my people. Based on the way Stindu and several of the others looked at me, enemies sounded more likely all the time.

Stindu sighed. "Very well. A trade it is. Matthias is more likely to be generous if we keep the humiliation to a minimum, so it will have to be done quietly."

"Wait!" Dane cut in. "Essie, please."

My neck twinged as I turned too quickly to gape at him. Trading me had been *his* idea. It was what would reunite him with his father.

Kip spoke to me before I could figure what his nephew was getting at. "You don't have to betray any confidences. Just ... is there anything you can tell us that would help us understand the situation better?"

"I don't have any confidences to betray. But I'm not going to help you kill more of the soldiers there."

"We haven't killed anyone on Windsong."

Now they thought I was ignorant just because I'd been living in a frozen wasteland for eight years. I rolled my eyes. "I've read the newsfeeds about near-constant battles in the outland territories."

"We know. But it's not us."

"It's your father," said Lunak—the thin, thoughtful man I'd noticed before. "The battles are staged quite theatrically, with his best soldiers posing as Exile insurgents. A theater that's all too deadly for the Windsong militia, however."

The blood rushed away from my face. It may have left my body entirely. I'd seen images on the networks I'd cracked, bodies strewn across the outland fields, bloodied and broken. Always the corpses of Windsong infantry . . . the Exile casualties carted away quickly by their own army before images could be captured.

It made sense, though. I should have noticed it. Let the Exiles gain just enough ground to frighten the public and make them remember they need a strong leader to protect them. Push back just enough that the people think their leader is doing what he promised. Neither side really made any progress, but only if you saw the long scheme. In each moment, the war was dynamic and hard fought, looking like their dutiful king was keeping them safe.

That kind of strategy was just like him.

And if the war was fake, was it still my fault? People were still dying, fake enemy or not.

I shook my head. "It's unhinged. You'd think the blazing poisons would be enough."

"The what?" Kip asked.

I looked at him. "You don't know? You were a Midnight Blade, one of Olivia's guards."

"She was selective about what she trusted me with because I was your mother's guard first. The order to kill you was a test."

A test he failed. "Do you know about Olivia's job as royal theurgist, her 'magical' healing abilities?"

Lunak steepled his fingers. "We do, and we have wondered. Of course, as people with an...*unusual* gift ourselves, we try not to rule anything out. You know something about those abilities?"

"Aye, I think so." I thought back to memories I didn't want, things I'd seen and heard in the palace, along with what I'd deciphered from my mother's notebook. "There are poisons, different kinds, that create symptoms to look like diseases. My father and Olivia slip targeted doses into the water supply. A house here, a shop there. Doctors can't make anything of it, but Queen Olivia can save them. But there's no magic. It's just the antidote. She's done it for my father since before I came along."

"That's why you always check the water," Dane muttered.

Stindu sniffed, apparently not hearing him. "Seems you *do* know a few things of use."

I glared. "Oh, I do indeed. How to rig every gadget you touch to short out your heart, for one."

The members of the council shifted restlessly, some even looking to the doors with the very large guards on the other side.

Go ahead, Essie, threaten planetary leaders. Sharp.

Kip held up his hand before anything became of the murmurs. "That's not necessary. We didn't know about the poisoning. Thank you."

"I didn't know about the battle staging. Thanks for that, I

suppose. I still don't understand, though. You aren't the ones battling in the outlands, yet you *are* enemies of Windsong. You're talking about things like coups. They exiled you to this planet, they fear what you can do—why not just leave them to their fate? Or use your Transitioning to take the upper hand?"

"We *were* working toward peaceful coexistence," Dane said. The sudden heat in his tone startled me. "We had the embassy, we kept the law, but your mother broke it. She kept her identity secret, she risked all of us, she even risked you. If it weren't for her—"

"Dane!" Kip cut in sharply. Good thing, too. My fists balled so tightly, my nails cut into my palms. "You don't have the whole story."

Dane's posture went rigid, and his mouth barely moved. "Maybe now is a good time to fill me in, Uncle."

The straight-backed woman I'd noticed the first day—Mura, Kip had called her—answered. "Queen Alaina didn't risk us. We risked *her*. We created her false identity, altered her appearance, orchestrated her marriage to Matthias. She did it all at our request."

My body stayed frozen, but a fire sparked within. It hadn't been her own ridiculous idea. Mother had been a spy. All of it a plan—one that had gone horribly wrong.

All of it?

Dane processed it more quickly than I did. "But . . . my father, he says we always have to be honest about what we are, keep the law, *always*. It's the only way we can get others to trust us again."

"You were young, Dane," Stindu said. "That was the role you were to play at the time."

Those words broke me out of my silence. "His *role*, was it?

You had it all engineered like a bit of Garamite clean-tech. So neatly planned, every piece in its place. So what about me? Was I planned? What role did this council rig for me before I was born?"

The old leaders looked at each other. No one answered.

"Tell her," Kip pressed.

"We hoped Alaina would be able to gather information to help us bring down Matthias from the inside," one of them said. "Barring that, she was to ensure Matthias's heir would be a very different type of leader. But she died when you were young, leaving no assurance of the kind of person you'd be, and then you were gone as well."

A simple plan. One my mother had believed in. She'd left me many of her secrets but kept the most important one—that she'd put her trust in people who couldn't protect her. People who maneuvered lives like strategically placed pawns.

Leaving only me, the last pawn to play, but I'd been knocked off the board years ago.

"All the planning in the world, but you couldn't account for Olivia, could you? My mother dead, and one of your own men ordered to kill me. Sparkling job. Congratulations to the First Families of Candara."

I didn't want to hear anything else they had to say, so I did the only sensible thing and left, forcing one of the guards to follow and make sure I went to my room. It didn't matter what the Exiles did with me. They didn't have what it took to outwit my father.

If my mother couldn't, no one could.

14

BOREDOM MEANT TOO MUCH TIME to think, and thinking only led to confusion. Facts and emotions got all tangled and knotted, and I didn't want to unravel any of them, too afraid of what I might find underneath. Avoiding that meant I had two choices. I could lose myself in puzzles on my slate, or I could demand that the drones be allowed to come keep me company.

Neither option would keep my problems at bay for long. Fussing with Dimwit and Cusser would keep me more than busy, though. Especially if Dimwit set something on fire. It'd be better than staring at the ceiling.

I rolled over to activate the communication console, but my hand missed as the bed shifted beneath me. My momentum carried me over too far and I fell, smacking my head against the console's hard edge.

At first I thought I had a concussion—and maybe I did—but two failures to get up off the floor told me the room really was moving.

Not moving…shaking. A lot.

Only a few things could make a room shake like that. Too prolonged for an explosion. Too intense for weather.

An earthquake.

Father's stories of the dark kingdom, where the ground swallowed whole any who dared speak against the king—

Silly stories, Essie.

It was easy enough to tell myself that, but harder to believe. I focused on the scientific explanation of why quakes happened, massive continental plates butting against each other, building pressure until something gave way. The governing complex hadn't collapsed on top of me yet, so it probably wouldn't.

Of course if it did, I'd be buried by so much stone and marble, they'd be lucky to find a smear of me.

It won't, though. Right?

The trembling stopped after a minute or two…in the building, anyway. My body, curled on the floor, kept shaking for long minutes after.

"Essie?"

Dane's voice finally pushed me to my feet. The room moved unnaturally again, but this time I knew it was my woozy head. One deep breath and I managed to cross the room to the door.

"If you're here to continue blaming my mother for every bad thing—"

I stopped. Dane wasn't alone. His uncle stood next to him. Kip's eyes went straight to my forehead, and I realized the wet trickle wasn't a bead of sweat.

Running through a palace corridor, turning too quickly and crashing into a pair of legs…the black-and-gray uniform of the Midnight

Blade...worrying the guard would yell at me...Kip helping me up, making sure I'm not hurt.

Years later, both of us staring at the knife...

The memories collided, making the pain in my head more pronounced.

"Let's get that taken care of," Kip said, gently taking my arm. It sounded like a good idea.

"We usually have more warning when a quake is about to hit," Dane said from behind.

"This kind of thing happens a lot?" I asked.

"All the time. The tectonics on this planet aren't too stable. We built Gakoa here because the quakes are less severe than everywhere else."

"Right lovely place, then, isn't it?"

He harrumphed. "It's not bad. And it's not like we have any-where else to go. This is the place no one else wanted."

I turned to Kip. "Was there damage? Was anyone hurt?"

"There are bound to be some minor injuries like yours, but nothing serious," he said. "And no major damage. Come on, right through here."

The only real difference between the doctor who patched up my head and the one who'd healed my hands on Garam was that the Exile was female. Her expression of disdain matched the Garamite's down to the little furrow between her eyebrows. Apparently Thanda was the only planet in the system where people weren't afraid of a few scars and well-worn clothes.

"I want both of you to come with me," Kip said once the doctor finished.

I hadn't changed my mind about letting him help me escape, but I doubted he wanted to discuss that. Dane and I followed him to a lift, up several levels, and down a long corridor to another lift. As we went into the second, I saw Dane's tension increase, like he was bracing for a fight. I edged a little closer to the corner.

The higher we went, the heavier the silence became. I wasn't about to break it, not between those two. They may have been family, but they occupied very different parts of my history. I hadn't figured how to reconcile their connection just yet.

Finally we arrived at a short hallway with a door at the end. Nothing seemed especially remarkable, except the very sophisticated lockpad with fingerprint scanners in the numbered keys.

Kip took five steps from the lift to the door and turned to Dane, waiting.

"We shouldn't be here," Dane said.

"It's the one place you *should* be."

Dane glared, exhaled sharply, and jabbed a code into the lockpad, using a different finger for each number. The door slid open, and I peered between the two of them to see what the big deal was.

The big deal was a big room, with a bigger view.

We walked in, and I discovered the room had a hexagonal shape. Three of the walls were floor-to-ceiling windows, and the whole city of Gakoa spread before us, and beyond. A river snaked along the edge of the city, sunlight glinting off its surface, then farther to green fields and forested hills. We were high enough to see everything, higher than any building in the governing complex. I thought back to the flight over the city—a glare of reflected sunlight off a particular point on the mountain. I'd thought it was some kind of sentry or lookout post. In a sense it was, I supposed, but no guard was stationed inside.

For the briefest moment, I wondered what sunset would look like from there.

When I finally tore my eyes away from the view, I noticed the rest of the room. Soft benches lined the perimeter, some facing out, others in. All blanketed with a layer of dust. No one had been in this room for a while.

I turned back toward the door. Maps covered the walls on either side. One looked familiar, so I took a few steps closer. Windsong. Every part of it, from the outlands to the capital to the whistling canyons that gave the planet its name. The other wall mapped Candara. I recognized nothing, but I found Gakoa. All of the other labeled cities were in the same province.

"All right, Kip, why are we here?" Dane asked.

"To remind you that you have a decision to make soon, and I want you to stop avoiding it."

I had no idea what they were talking about, but it felt distinctly like a family conversation, something I shouldn't be part of. I continued examining the map. The areas without cities had other things labeled. Volcanoes. Major fault lines. Lots of them.

"My father will be back before I have to decide, so it doesn't matter."

"It doesn't matter? Even if getting him back means sacrificing *her* life? Is that really what you want?"

So much for not being involved. I felt their eyes on me but refused to look, instead studying a chain of Candaran islands just off an area marked with the words TYPHOON ZONE.

Silence hung around us like the cold on Thanda. Unbreakable.

"Princess," Kip said finally, "I'm sorry."

No more excuses, so I turned. "Sorry for what?"

"For ignoring you far too long. Are you all right?"

"Aye, the doc did a fine job patching me up."

"That's not what I mean. Eight years on your own, and Thanda is not a gentle planet. How have you been all this time?"

Oh, so he didn't mean ignoring me since we walked in the room, or even just since I arrived on Candara. I glanced at Dane, who knew exactly what my life there had been like. He stared out the window, unfaltering. "All right enough. Or I was, anyway, until a certain impulsive Exile crashed near my settlement."

Kip ran a hand through his hair and paced a stretch of the marble floor, but said nothing further. Dane continued to pretend I wasn't there.

Another uncomfortable silence loomed. I had to break it. "How does all this marble hold up with the quakes?"

That got Dane's attention. "With everything going on, you want to know about architecture?"

"Dane," Kip cut in, holding up a hand to silence him. "Our first permanent settlements two hundred years ago didn't hold up so well, but we learned. The marble's been modified, and all our buildings here in Gakoa have been carefully engineered to cope with the stress."

"Ah, stress," I said. "Good to know *something* around here copes with that."

Dane shot me a look, proving he felt the dig. "Any other questions?"

"Aye, for Kip. When did you leave Windsong?"

"Same time you did," Kip answered. "Or nearly."

"Not enough time to get Dane's father and the others out with you?"

Kip sank onto one of the dusty benches, his manic, pacing energy drained. "No. I thought...I thought if I went to the embassy, if I even sent word to warn them, it would be taken as a sign of collusion. If I just left, I thought the queen would believe I acted alone, wouldn't make the connection that I'm Candaran. I didn't know an entire half of her plan was to blame the embassy for your death. Even when I didn't return, she framed them for an attack."

"You didn't even *warn* them?" Dane burst out. "You just left them? Why didn't you ever tell me?"

"How could I? You know your father is a brother to me. How could I tell you I made a choice that landed him and so many of our people—so many of my friends—in Matthias's prison while I walked free? The choices I made, Dane, so many...I'm not proud of them."

Kip and me staring at the knife, staring at each other.

"It's not only the choice you made that haunts you," I said quietly. "It's how close you came to choosing the other way."

"What?" Dane pressed. "What do you mean?"

"Like he said, he was the one ordered to kill me." I turned to Kip. "I saw it when you held the knife. I saw you consider it."

"Princess, no! That's not what you saw," he said. "I wasn't thinking about *using* the knife! I was thinking about whether to keep it and bring you with me."

My memories of it seemed so clear, though. Kip looking at the knife, trying to decide if I had enough of my mother in me to be worth saving.

Maybe I'd been the one wondering that, not him.

"Why *didn't* you take me with you?" I asked.

"I thought—I don't know. I thought you should have a chance

at a life away from all this, including us. That you were safer away from me and the wrath I was bringing down on myself. So I sent a nine-year-old to fend for herself on the next best thing to a prison colony." Disgust sharpened the edge of each word.

"I fended well enough, didn't I?"

He shook his head. "You shouldn't have had to. Forgive me, Princess."

Now I understood why he let me convince him not to sneak me away a second time. He couldn't repeat his mistake. Except it didn't feel like a mistake. Not the part where I ended up on Thanda, anyway.

"Nothing to forgive. I told you, I'm all right," I said. "But Dane's father and the others certainly aren't."

Dane spoke up. "My father would've done the same thing. He would have saved you even if it meant prison for them. How could anyone let a child die to save themselves?"

Those shouldn't have been the only choices, with others paying the price to keep me alive. It made my fingers twitch with the same helpless energy I'd had ever since my escape. Energy that told me to do something, when there was nothing I *could* do.

Or would do.

Kip straightened his shoulders. "That's why I'll do everything I can to convince the council not to trade you. We can't give Olivia another victim."

Another. "Did she kill my mother, then?"

Something flashed across his eyes. Pain. "I don't know whether she did it herself or had it done, but yes, I'm confident it was her."

Oh, I knew Olivia well enough. She'd likely have done it herself. Only . . . why had she left the job of killing me to someone else? Maybe to make sure Father never connected it to her. Or maybe the idea of killing a child was too distasteful, even for her.

I wasn't a child anymore.

While I thought on that, Kip continued. "You may have doubted me, but I never had to question. I always saw Queen Alaina in you, Princess. I still do. She was very brave. And, Dane," he added tersely, "I'll not have you speaking against a woman who did nothing but sacrifice for our people."

"If I'd had all the information I *should* have, I wouldn't have said it," Dane said, giving Kip a meaningful look. "I'm sorry, Essie."

They were both being too nice, too sympathetic. I hated it. Kind words didn't change anything. They didn't bring my mother back, remake my childhood, or return me to Thanda. They didn't return Dane's father or end the killing on Windsong, either.

The twitchiness in my hands sharpened. Too much standing around talking. Too long without doing anything. My mind swam with codes and algorithms, trying to push away the memories of my mother. She pushed back.

Always do what needs doing, even when it's hard.

She always knew what needed doing, or so it seemed. Then she got herself killed.

Windsong needs you.

I hadn't just failed her. I'd failed an entire planet. Maybe two.

I couldn't stay in that room, couldn't take the view, couldn't face the two Exiles. I turned and strode back to the door. It wouldn't open.

"Dane, let me out of here."

If he heard the tremor in my voice, he didn't show it, just keyed in the code for me.

"Tell the guards I'm going down to visit the drones, and I'll break anyone who tries to stop me."

15

IT TOOK ME TWICE AS LONG as it should have to find the spaceport hangar on my own, but Dane had clearly called ahead as requested. No one gave me any trouble. The attendant even opened the shuttle's hatch for me.

"Will there be anything else, miss?" he asked.

My glare was enough to send him scurrying back to his station.

I went aboard, knowing I'd be left alone. With the shuttle's landing struts held by the hangar's docking clamps, I couldn't have stolen the thing if I'd wanted to. Some of the tension leeched from my body as I walked into the engine compartment and caught a slight whiff of coolant. The shuttle was the one truly familiar place on Candara. Best of all, there were things to do. I found the drones on standby.

"Wake up, you two."

Their little lights sparked to life, but I noticed a slight high-pitched whine as Dimwit's systems came online. "Dimwit Essie."

That was all it took for tears to press at the corners of my eyes. *This blazing emotional nonsense is getting right embarrassing.*

"I missed you, too, you walking disaster. Sounds like that business with the solar screen might've done a number on you. Cusser, how are your systems doing?"

"All systems nominal, Essie. Assistance required?"

"You want to help stitch up Dimwit? Grab the gear."

Cusser got the requested items, but its arm fell dead before it got back to me, causing it to swear even more colorfully than usual.

"Truly, what do you do with your actuators when I'm not looking?"

"Cusser blowout Cusser."

"Shut it, Dimwit." Cusser's retort was unexpected but unsurprising. It had certainly heard me say the same thing enough times.

"Settle down, I'll get both of you stitched," I said.

Without my own computer and tailored diagnostics, it wasn't quite the same, but I settled in and started tinkering. The usual patch worked on Cusser's arm. Dimwit had a few connectors loose—whether from the stunt with the solar screen or ordinary wear and tear, it was hard to say. I tightened those up and tested out the contacts on its primary circuit boards.

The work soothed me, drawing the itching-and-twitching out of my hands. Circuits and actuators, puzzles and programs...that was the world I belonged in. The one that made sense.

A pair of voices approached outside the shuttle. I tensed and paused in my work until I could make out what they said.

"—told her not to bother." Male voice, sounded young.

"As you should. I keep telling you, Pondu, looks aren't everything." Also male, but more gravelly, possibly older.

"I know, I know. So what have we got today?"

"General systems check on number eight, and a complete power boost on number eleven. Come on, now, you need to keep up."

Their footsteps faded as they walked on. Just a couple of maintenance engineers. I got back to working a stitch on Dimwit's rear pair of legs. They'd sounded a touch grindy.

"Come on outside," I said after a moment. "Let's see if you can run, Dimwit."

We exited through the hatch but only got two more steps before both of Dimwit's back legs locked up. Cusser swore on Dimwit's behalf, probably out of sympathy. I sighed and crouched down to find the problem. The legs were losing the signal somewhere along the way. Probably more loose connectors than I'd expected.

I spotted the two engineers across the hangar, doing that systems check on a small hover-vehicle. They spotted me, too, but looked more curious about the drones than me. They eyed Dimwit for a minute before turning back to their work. With my scarf covering my hair, I wasn't that interesting. Their voices carried easily, but beyond their checklist, all I gathered was that the younger one—Pondu—had a girlfriend the other, Mikat, thought he shouldn't be with.

"There, can you at least move the left one now, Dimwit?"

It could, but only through the first joint. I went back to tracing out connections.

"Whatcha doing?"

I jumped at the voice behind me, but quickly relaxed. It

belonged to a little girl, maybe seven or eight years old. She looked like she wanted to come closer but wasn't sure she dared.

"Just repairing this drone. What are *you* doing?"

"I'm here with my dad." She pointed to Mikat but kept her eyes on the drones. "What are their names?"

"This here's Dimwit, and that's Cusser."

She frowned. "Those aren't very nice names."

"Aye, you're probably right, but they're fitting."

"Why do you talk funny?"

"Tatsa!" Mikat called out before I had a chance to answer. "What're you doing over there?"

"Systems checks are *boring*, Dad."

He gave her a definite Look but spoke to me. "Sorry, miss, is she bothering you? She has a particular fascination with robots."

"Please can I help?" Tatsa asked. "I'm a really good helper."

I supposed I didn't mind, though her father might if Cusser decided to demonstrate how it earned its name.

"It's fine," said another voice behind me. This one was familiar and got Mikat to smile and turn back to his own work. "I'm sure Essie could use a hand."

Tatsa's eyes lit with similar recognition. "Hi, Dane!"

"Hi, there," he replied, sitting on the floor next to me. "I bet Essie needs the rest of her gear. Still in the shuttle?"

I nodded, and Tatsa scurried up the ramp to retrieve the case.

"What's wrong with Dimwit?" Dane continued, but more quietly. "I didn't botch something when I adjusted his programming, did I?"

The urge to say yes tempted me, but I didn't have any reason to believe that was true. The tone in his voice made it hard to concentrate, so I kept my eyes on the drone. "I don't think so.

Just need to tighten up the signal transfers, and its gait calibration might be out of sync."

Tatsa jumped off the side of the ramp with my gear bouncing against her leg. "Here you go! What do you need?"

"A narrower signal tracer, for starters."

She handed me the right tool before I could explain what it looked like. Not a bad assistant, even if she was awfully small. Then again, I was that small once.

"Do you come here often with your dad?" I asked.

"Kind of. Why?"

"Just seems like it could be dangerous with all the shuttles and equipment."

She shrugged. "Nah, I'm careful. It's just as dangerous for you."

"Dimwit Essie protect Essie."

The little girl giggled at the pronouncement, but I rolled my eyes. "You think you're going to protect me, do you? Did you get a defense subroutine I don't know about?"

"Essie writes all drone subroutines," Cusser answered.

Tatsa bounced on her toes. "You *should* program them to fight! I bet they'd be great at it."

"Not a bad idea," Dane murmured. I dared a glance at him but couldn't read his expression. Like he was thinking about something else, but then he shook it off. "Does Cusser need anything?"

"No, I—Don't say it, Cusser!" Its arm chose that moment to lock up again. "I *just* fixed that."

"Come here, I'll take a look," Dane said. "Maybe Tatsa will have some ideas."

He set to work while I kept at it with Dimwit. Tatsa handed me whatever tools I needed. When Dane already had one, I got it from him directly.

There was something very different about the way Dane's fingers brushed mine as he handed me a tool. Tatsa's touch was light, fleeting, while Dane's lingered. It prompted me to glance at what he was using a few times and find an excuse for needing the same thing. There was something else, too, in the way Dane talked to the little girl, listening to her prattle and letting her make a few adjustments herself.

It made me think of the person we pulled from the shuttle on Thanda rather than the one who knocked me out and took me away.

We tinkered and stitched until all drone limbs were functional. Just as we were finishing up, Mikat and Pondu walked back across the hangar.

"Come along, Tatsa, time to go," Mikat said. He offered another smile to Dane before turning back to his companion. "All I'm saying is, with that much aggravation, is she worth it? Is one girl worth it?"

Tatsa thanked us and ran after her father, but I wasn't listening. Dane and I gathered the gear and got the drones back in the shuttle, but I wasn't paying attention to any of that, either.

"Essie, are you all right?" Dane asked as he walked me back to my room.

"Aye, I'm fine."

The answer was automatic, but it was also a lie. Mikat's words about Pondu's demanding girlfriend shouldn't have meant anything to me, but that didn't stop them. They rattled and cycled and festered inside me, refusing to leave me alone.

I couldn't figure why the words bothered me so much. But they did.

For three days, I kept busy with the drones down in the hangar, stitching solutions to new problems, brainstorming for a basic defense subroutine, and pretending a second quake didn't faze me. Dane kept me company most of the time. Our conversations centered around actuators and coding options. Nothing about the council, Windsong, my father, or the so-called war. It made our days working together strangely relaxed, but it couldn't change the truth.

The council began deliberations leading to a vote. In response, I spent a good part of each night staring at the ceiling of my room, Mikat's words pounding in my ears.

Is she worth it? Is one girl worth it?

What am I worth?

Do what needs doing, Essie.

Only one answer made sense.

"Essie, get up!"

I had enough time to register Dane's panicked voice and open my eyes just before he grabbed my arm and hauled me to my feet.

"What—what's going on? Quake—attack—?"

"No, not that," he said. His eyes darted to the door and back to me. "It—I just—oh, tank it!"

One hand still had my arm, and the other went to my cheek. He pulled me close—too close—and pressed his lips to mine. By the time I processed that he was *kissing* me and started considering what to do about it, he'd moved on to dragging me out of the room.

"Come on. We have to go."

None of this made sense. My brain couldn't keep up, not when I'd been sound asleep moments earlier. We were out in the hall before I came up with words again. His panic hadn't faded, and the unfamiliarity of it made me anxious.

"Dane, what in blazes—where are we going?"

"I've got the shuttle prepped. I'm taking you back to Thanda."

Back to Whirligig and the others. Away from the uncertainty and fear. Back to hiding. Away from responsibility. Too many emotions vied for my attention. I couldn't figure where to start, and my indecision gave Dane time to drag me around a corner and into a lift. Finally I went with the easiest response.

"Now? *Now* you're taking me back? Why?"

Dane's eyes were anxious, his whole body tense. "Kip's getting outvoted. They're going to trade you for the prisoners."

"So? It was *your* idea."

"I can't do it! I didn't know about the queen, and I can't trade your life for theirs. It's not right—it's not what my father would want."

His father. A man who'd been captured because of my escape years ago. Because Kip refused to kill me. And he wasn't alone.

Thanda, my lab, and the drones felt farther away than ever.

"Dane, it's the only way to get him back."

"I'll have to find another."

He dragged me along another hall before I dug in my heels. I had to do what needed doing. "No. I'm not going. My life is worth saving a dozen or more."

He looked at me the same way I looked at Dimwit when it tried to repair a blown gasket with a block of wood. "That's absolutely not true."

Dane took my arm again, but I wrenched it away and shoved him back, the words bursting from behind an eight-year-old dam. "What good am I to anyone, then? Help a few miners so they can be lazy drunks? Hide on a frozen rock? What good is that? What blazing good have I ever done anyone?"

"You can do anything you want, because you'll be *free* and *alive!*"

The fire left my voice. "I've been both of those for years, but it was borrowed time. I was never meant to be either."

"What's wrong with you, Essie? Why are you talking like this?"

I tried to evade the question by heading back to the lift, but Dane was too quick, blocking me. "The cost of my freedom was too high, all right? I didn't ... I didn't know that until I came here. Blazes, that's a lie. I knew about the war, knew it was my fault, but I didn't do anything about it. And I didn't *want* to know what happened to Kip and anyone else on Windsong when I left. Didn't want to think that people lost their families because of me. But now I can try to make it right."

His eyes widened. "It's my fault. If I hadn't taken you from Thanda, you wouldn't be thinking this way."

"Willful blindness is no way to live."

He crossed his arms and stood his ground. "I'm not letting them trade you like a case of merinium. I'd rather not knock you out again to get you on the shuttle. So what do you want me to do?"

I thought about it. "I want you to tell me why you kissed me *before* you explained what's happening."

Dane didn't expect that, and it got him to shift a little. "Figured once I told you about the council, you'd break my nose and make your move to steal the shuttle yourself. So my last chance was before I told you. Kind of thought you'd break my nose *because* I kissed you, but I took the risk."

"Why?"

"You're not what I expected to find on Thanda. Not a spoiled princess, and not a tyrant's daughter."

"I *am* a tyrant's daughter."

"No, it's like Kip said. I didn't know your mother, but there's more of her than Matthias in you. You're not like him. You're nothing like I expected, and with everything you *are*..." He trailed off, shaking his head. When he spoke again, his voice held no arguments, no explanations. Just an ache I'd never heard before. "How could I *not* kiss you?"

I'd thought my mind was as settled as the frozen poles of Thanda, that I would let myself be traded to repay the debt I'd incurred years ago. But that was before I had to endure Dane looking at me like he was, with new determination flickering in his eyes.

"Please, Essie," he said. "Let me take you home. Let me make it right."

If I went through with the trade, Dane would blame himself, and I didn't like that. He may have taken me from Thanda, but it was just one step on a path I'd begun with my escape from Windsong. If I let him take me back to hide behind mine-drones and cage fights . . . it would never be the same. I couldn't forget the price of my freedom.

There had to be another choice.

I had to create one.

Do what needs doing, even if it terrifies you.

Only one option remained. The one I'd never been willing to acknowledge, but now I had to.

"Right, then, I'll go home." Dane relaxed and smiled at my words, but I wasn't done. "Home," I went on, "is Windsong."

His smile vanished. "Essie—"

"I have an idea. Tell the council I'll see them in two hours."

Emotions battled in Dane's eyes. At last, he let me by, but not without calling after me. "Why *didn't* you break my nose?"

I only had one answer to give, and it troubled me most of all. "I don't know yet."

Back in my room, getting more sleep was out of the question. I had too much to do.

First, I spent a heap of time figuring the frivolous items the council had stocked my room with. Exfoliants and moisturizers, buffers and balms, and things that had names I couldn't make sense of. Whatever they were called, they succeeded in getting my skin soft and smooth, my nails shining rather than chipped.

I gave up my headscarf, leaving my hair down, straight and sleek and white as my name. I considered the jeweled combs but didn't know what to do with them. My own clothes weren't good enough, so I rifled through the contents of the closet. It held row upon row of satin and silk, too much to choose from. I finally selected a red silk tunic with delicate silver trim and paired it with black pants. The fabrics felt like a warm memory, yet at the same time made me squirm. The last step was the trickiest. I didn't have any experience with makeup, but I remembered watching my mother apply hers. A steady hand for eyeliner and mascara, just a touch of blush and red lips, and I was finished.

My mirror-self stared back at me with one piece that still echoed my mother—my eyes. But hers had never shown such uncertainty. I couldn't let mine show it, either. A few deep breaths steadied everything, from my hands to my nerves. I didn't look like myself. No problem—I had to be someone else for what I was about to do.

Two hours after leaving Dane in that random corridor, I arrived at the council chamber. The guards couldn't hide their surprise at my appearance, but they threw open the doors without a word.

Shoulders straight, Essie. Chin level. Just like Mother.

The council sat around the large table, caught in the midst of an argument. Dane was the first to spot me, his lips parting in mute surprise. The older council members followed his gaze, and the room went silent.

"You wanted a queen," I said solidly, pushing my Thandan accent aside. "You've got one."

16

DANE MANAGED TO FORM words amidst the gaping, sort of. "Ess—what?"

I turned from him to Mura. "You said it yourself the day we arrived: I'm heir to the throne and your chance at a coup. My mother tried to destroy my father's rule from the inside. I can finish what she started."

"Princess, no!" Kip protested. "I told you, I will not let you be traded back into Olivia's hands."

Dane's eyes were still on me—I felt it—but I continued to avoid them. The new depth in them confused me, and I couldn't look at him and say what I had to at the same time. "There won't be any trade."

"What precisely are you suggesting, then?" Stindu asked.

"You were right before when you said my father would insist on a trade being carried out quietly, sparing his ego. That kind of secret trade would give Olivia time to get rid of me before my return could be announced. If I'm not traded—if I return freely, in a way my father can acknowledge officially—we'll have public fanfare and celebration. All eyes will be on the palace, and Olivia will have to be more careful."

The members of the council exchanged glances, thinking it over. Kip still looked conflicted. "We won't be able to hurry news of your return," he began. "The crown controls all broadcast frequencies. We have a handful of spies left, and none positioned in the Royal City. Olivia might still get to you before the public knows you're back."

"Let me worry about that. And I'll get the prisoners out."

Stindu wasn't finished with his doubts. "As you said, you were a child when you left. You don't have the wealth of inside information it would take to thwart your father from so close."

"Though you knew about the poison," Mura pointed out. "I can't believe Matthias willingly told you about that."

"Of course he didn't," I said. Time to give up another secret I'd kept for years. "My mother told me. Well, sort of. Her notebook did."

"Her artwork," Kip murmured. "You had it?"

I nodded. "I kept it in that bag I took everywhere, so I had it when I escaped. Took me a while to decipher the information in some of the drawings, things she was gathering for you and hadn't passed on yet, I guess."

Stindu's eyes lit up in a very disturbing way, like I'd just offered him all the merinium in Forty-Two's mine. "Do you have it with you now?"

"No. *Someone* took me from Thanda without giving me a chance to pack first. It doesn't matter, though. I memorized everything and destroyed all but the more innocent sketches a few years ago. If you want this done, you need *me* to do it."

Some of the council members nodded, gesturing for me to take one of the empty seats at the table. They believed me, believed I could do it. It would work as long as I kept those shadows of uncertainty from my eyes.

"You'll need a story," Dane said, forcing me to look at him. I couldn't read the stillness of his expression. "They believe we took you. If you return on your own, they'll suspect you're on our side."

"That's the beauty of the plan. I'm very good at telling convincing stories."

His jaw set. "Better find a place in that story for one more person. I'm going with you."

"Fine. Because the story I'm thinking of using is yours."

The council didn't like the idea of Dane going with me to Windsong, but he held firm. They couldn't stop him. I didn't know if I could. Worse, I couldn't decide whether I wanted to or not.

Yet I didn't understand *why* the council couldn't put its collective foot down to keep Dane on Candara. The dynamics didn't make sense. The observation room up in the mountain that Dane could access, the way the council looked at both him and Kip, something about a decision for Dane to make . . . His family was clearly important even among the all-important First Families. But the council could still outvote Kip on matters like what to do with a runaway princess.

The easy solution was to ask, but that wasn't easy at all. Kip kept too busy to catch, and I wasn't about to ask anyone on the council. That left talking to Dane alone—something I carefully

avoided. He'd kissed me. I hadn't broken his nose. And that concerned me far more than the intricacies of Candaran politics. Whatever made him special wouldn't make any difference.

Day after day of planning sessions kept me busy enough. Plotting to take over the government of a planet that was perpetually on the opposite side of the solar system from all your resources was no small thing. The people of Windsong thought a war already raged in their outlands. They didn't realize the distance plus the iron grip my father had on the planet made such a brute-force approach impossible.

We knew Dane and I could get to Windsong. We also knew the two of us couldn't defeat my father's entire regime alone. The biggest question remaining was how to work Candara's military forces into the plan.

So we hashed out details and argued about strategies. Stindu kept his mouth shut more often now, while Mura often suggested bolder, riskier courses. Lunak put Mura in check, advising caution and further consideration.

It didn't take long for me to wonder how they ever got anything decided.

"Unless you're suggesting we leave both Dane and Princess Snow completely on their own, I don't see how sending *no* troops could possibly be an option," Mura said.

Lunak tilted his head slightly. "I'm not suggesting that at all. I'm merely reminding you—again—that once detected by Matthias's defenses, we endanger both of them."

This argument had sprung up several times already and never reached a conclusion. I rubbed my temples as it got rolling yet again.

As expected, Lunak wasn't finished. "Matthias will not react well if he finds Candaran ships in the vicinity soon after the miraculous return of his daughter. We mustn't reveal ourselves until the proper moment."

"Of course, but we can't simply wait here for them to call for help. You *do* understand the distance involved, don't you?"

I raised my head. "You *should* wait here. Or wait somewhere, anyway. The problem is that you can't get within seven spans of Windsong without your ships' signatures showing up, right? So launch your ships, send them to a safe point along Windsong's orbit, and wait for the planet to come to you. Cut everything but life support. Then we just have to rig a way to shield any heat readings. You'll be invisible until Dane and I can clear a path."

Mura and Lunak both remained silent.

"That's very clever, Princess," Kip said. "It could work. The timing would be narrow."

He had a point. Once Windsong moved into range of the powered-down fleet, we'd only have so many days before we moved *out* of range. "It's likely to be narrow no matter what. I'll also need to rig a way to contact you from the planet's surface. Cusser's good with communication systems. It might be able to help us find a way."

Dane spoke up. "Essie, it means we'll be there on our own for a long time at first."

Back in the palace with Olivia and my father, staying alive long enough for the plan to work... I was trying not to think about it. "I'll have to be very convincing. And there'll be plenty for us to do before we're ready to make our attack, right? Laying the groundwork and all that, building my father's trust."

Everyone agreed that my plan was the best course—or at least the one with a better-than-zero-percent chance of working.

We moved on to debating what Dane and I should do and when we should try to do it, how many days to allow for each task, trying to calculate where the Candaran fleet should position itself to wait.

When Lunak and Mura geared up for another useless spur, I got to my feet. "If you'll excuse me, I'm going to get some air in the park." Now that I was on their side, I was allowed to come and go as I pleased, and I'd decided to take advantage of that.

I didn't make it past the foyer outside the council chamber.

"Essie, wait a second."

Dane had followed me, and he inclined his head, silently asking me to follow him down a side corridor rather than going directly to the lift. I followed even though it put us alone, away from the eyes of the guards.

I was terrified Dane would kiss me again. I was also terrified he wouldn't. Mostly that he would and I'd have to hit him. Maybe.

How does that make any kind of sense?

"Is everything all right?" he asked.

"Yes, it's fine. Like I said, just going out to the park."

"Want some company?"

"No. Thank you," I added quickly. "I just need a bit of quiet to settle my wits after all the talking in circles in there."

The small smile he offered was one I hadn't seen on him before, making me wonder when I'd started cataloguing his smiles. "Yes, they're good at that, aren't they? Enjoy your walk."

Before heading back to the council chamber, he brushed his fingers along my arm. So lightly, so gently, my usual instincts to lash out didn't surface. I focused on the tingle his touch left behind, wishing it wouldn't fade so quickly, and nearly changed my mind about letting him join me. Nearly. But better to do this alone.

Or so I thought. When I got to ground level and exited the complex, Cusser stood waiting for me.

"Cusser will accompany Essie," it announced.

"Oh, will you? These new instructions from Dane?"

"Affirmative."

At least the drone was honest. "And if I told you to go shine your circuits because I'm fine on my own?"

Cusser told me to do something much ruder than shining my circuits.

"I figured. Come on, then."

The park soothed me and made me uneasy at the same time, particularly with the playing children. Cusser kept me anchored, though, one familiar thing in such a foreign place. Maybe Dane had guessed at that when he gave the drone its instructions. The Candarans undoubtedly found the scene surrounding me commonplace. Groundskeepers tended to some damage from the latest quake—tears in the turf, small cracks in the decorative curb around a flower bed—while others trimmed the grass and added new flowers.

What was it like to live on a world where the ground couldn't stay put more than two or three days at a time? Where instability was so normal that only a fraction of the land was habitable?

What had it been like to grow up here?

I walked along a footpath, ignoring curious glances split evenly between the drone and me, until I reached a particular bench and sat down. Cusser settled next to me, inspecting its input/output ports, while I picked at the blue satin of the clothes

I'd chosen that morning. A few minutes later, a woman with gray-streaked auburn hair approached and sat with us.

"Thanks for meeting me, Laisa."

"No, thank you. I'm so sorry I upset you the other day."

I steadied myself, acknowledging that only part of me *wanted* to do this. The bigger part knew I needed it before we moved forward with the plan. I couldn't talk to my mother; I *could* talk to her friend.

"You startled me, that's all. I wasn't expecting to run into someone who knew my mother. I wasn't quite seven when she died. What do you remember about her?"

"I'm not sure words are adequate. Would you like to Transition?"

My hands jerked in my lap. "I'm not very good at it. And I can't do it without touching."

"That's fine. Please."

The last two people I'd body-hopped—Transitioned—had been Harper and Moray. Other than my mother, I'd never been in any head I really wanted to be in. Laisa had been Mother's friend, though. It wouldn't be like it was with Moray.

I reached over, lightly touching her hand. The next step was to search for the push-and-pull, but I didn't have to. I didn't hit an invisible wall like I had with Dane on the shuttle. So easy, hardly a thought, and I was there. Like Laisa's own mind drew me in.

I sit quietly on the bench as the breeze wraps itself around my hair. The memory of Ametsa warms in my heart, where her daughter can feel it—where she can understand all of it.

I do, Laisa! I feel how daring she was in the face of the highest trees and walls, how brave she was when others made fun of you. This kind of friend, I've never felt this. I never had a sister. Your daughters—you see your friendship with my mother when they play. You see my mother everywhere, just like I hear her.

But Kip and Dane are wrong. There's little of me there.

I pulled my hand away, pulled back to myself to catch my breath, and wiped away a threatening tear. It wasn't the same as it had been with Moray, pushing myself, struggling to Tip him. My left-behind face hadn't looked as blank, either. But it still took effort, leaving me with a heavy feeling in my limbs. It wasn't natural like it had been with Mother, and that thought deepened the ache. Silence filled the emptiness inside me until I dared break it.

"And she never said anything about why she was leaving?"

A smile played on her lips at some memory. "No. Like I said, just that it was to make things better. I'd thought perhaps she was coming here to Gakoa to work in the governing complex. When I followed and couldn't find her, I imagined she'd joined the embassy on Windsong. Was she one of those prisoners taken years ago?"

"She died before that."

The smile faded, replaced by warm sympathy in her eyes. "I'm very sorry. I'm sure you miss her. I have, too."

I'd felt that when I Transitioned to her. The ache in Laisa's gut resonated with my own. Before I could admit it, her gaze shifted to something behind me, and I turned. A commotion at the far end of the footpath sent people stumbling. Someone ran full speed, heedless of anyone else. Nearly half a link away, but I recognized the jacket. Dane.

"Essie!"

I could barely hear his shout, but the tone pierced me—a tone holding all the dread of Dimwit telling me "wrong way." I looked around and muttered some of Cusser's favorite words; I'd been too distracted by stories and memories to notice several of the groundskeepers working their way closer to us. Six of them. One a very familiar Garamite.

Tobias had the look of someone wanting to collect a debt with interest.

I grabbed Laisa's arm and stood, ready to run toward Dane and the safety of the governing complex.

"Not this time, Essie."

Too late.

The "groundskeepers" dropped their gardening tools, and I spotted guns on their belts, ineffectively hidden by jackets. I knew they didn't want me dead, so when all six came at me, I didn't hesitate to lash out. Neither did Laisa, as she struck one of Tobias's friends in the neck.

Maybe there was some truth to those rumors about Exiles all being fighters after all.

Six on two was still steep. Cusser tried to even the odds, engaging its new defense subroutine. It set two of its saws buzzing, keeping anyone from getting too close, and pulled a tack welder. As I gut-checked a man who swung for Laisa, I couldn't help thinking I'd done a pretty good job with that little program.

Possibly too good. Cusser caught one of the men with the tack welder, burning a band of flesh along his thigh. The man screamed and swore—Cusser swore back. Then the man pulled his gun, twisted a setting, and fired.

I spun to dodge a right hook, so I heard before I saw. A terrible scratching squeal. The stench of melted alloys. Finally, my eyes found the source. Cusser was on the ground, a hole blasted straight through it.

All its lights were off. Dead.

I couldn't breathe, couldn't swallow, couldn't think. In that frozen moment, Tobias clipped my head and everything swam.

Hands grabbed me, pulling me along. Dane shouted my name again, closer but not close enough, and my instincts took over. I twisted and jerked, but my equilibrium couldn't take it, so I had to give that up. Every noise pounded through my head.

One set of hands dragging me disappeared with a shout, throwing me off-balance. Another yanked me back and then shoved me away with more shouts. I stumbled and caught myself on my hands and knees. After a few blinks, I willed my eyes into focus and looked up.

Dane had reached us, taking on several of the men at once. I'd never actually seen him fight. When he'd pinned me in the shuttle, I hadn't seen anything. When he'd laid Tobias flat on Garam, I'd been busy with Harper.

He moved so fast, like he knew what the men were going to do before they did. Tobias took a swing, but Dane had already ducked, twisted, and pulled one of the other men into the path of Tobias's fist. As one man moved toward me, Dane pulled him back, spun him around, and smashed his nose with an odd forearm strike.

I tried to push myself to my feet so I could help, but then I saw Laisa sprawled on the ground, unmoving. My breath caught for the second time and my legs refused to support me. One of the men near her still had a gun in his hand.

There were too many, even for Dane. Tobias and one of his friends slipped away when Dane was busy with the others, hauling me off the grass and dragging me toward a hover transport with a tree logo painted on it.

I struggled, hoping to slow them down, but Tobias got his arm around my throat and pulled me along. I tried to look anywhere but at Cusser's smoldering shell and instead saw Dane take more hits, making me flinch. A crew of guards raced up the path, but they were too slow, too far away.

I twisted as we neared the vehicle, trying to see how badly Laisa was hurt. Maybe it wasn't that serious. Maybe she'd just been knocked out with a blow to the head.

Please, let that be all.

Dane dropped the man with the burned leg and one of his friends, then finally spotted me as the other two ran for the transport. He moved to follow, but they were already shoving me inside. I was too far away. One of the men fired a wild shot at him that was more than a few sniffs off target, but it was enough to stop my heart.

The door closed, and no amount of shoving or kicking could keep Tobias from speeding us away. Two of the men pinned me to the floor while the third bound my hands and feet with polymer bands and gagged me with a strip of cloth tied around my head. He pointed some kind of gadget my way and declared me "clean." At that point, I settled down, conserving my energy for when it could do me more good.

As we sped away, I laughed just a little, causing the men to look at me like I'd come unhinged. It kept me from crying. People thought I was kidnapped eight years ago. Now, for the second time in less than a season, I actually had been.

17

I'D HOPED THE CANDARAN GUARDS would get to a ground transport of their own and quickly catch up, or have some solid way of tracking us. As over an hour passed without a hint of rescue, I gave up that idea. The vehicle Tobias had stolen was common enough. It was certainly authentic, judging by the faint smell of fertilizer and grass clippings lingering throughout the interior. The Garamites were good with tech, so they'd probably disabled any identifying tags or locating signals.

After some initial protests about leaving the other two men behind, which Tobias vehemently shut down, the Garamites kept quiet. With the gag, I couldn't ask questions or make demands. They kept me on the floor in the back, so I couldn't see where we were going. The best I could do was twist around to change the position of my legs once in a while and try not to rub my wrists on their too-tight bindings.

Despite my efforts, my legs cramped and my wrists became

sore with threatening blisters. That's when dark thoughts crept into my mind. What if the Exiles couldn't find me? What if Tobias had a way to get me off Candara? What if I couldn't keep them from starting a war with Thanda?

When I closed my eyes, I saw Dane's as he tried to reach me, knowing he'd be too late.

That knot behind my ribs was back, and it had nothing to do with the hits I'd taken.

He'd find me.

Meanwhile, there was something very familiar about the homicidal feelings rising in my gut. The same feelings I'd had when Dane first abducted me.

I was much less conflicted about directing them toward Tobias and his friends.

Right when I thought my legs would fall off and my wrists would explode, the transport stopped moving. The men got out, opened the hatch in the back, unfastened my foot restraints, and dragged me from the vehicle.

Tobias had stopped the transport in a cave, but we didn't stay inside. My legs didn't want to cooperate, feeling as gelatinous as the harri-harra sludge down in the mines. Two of the other men supported me by the arms, hauling me from the cave to a grove of trees. I took in everything as quickly as I could.

The city had disappeared. Not a sign of it anywhere. The sun dipped toward the horizon, and I couldn't see any other source of light.

I had no idea which direction we'd gone from Gakoa, how

close we were to any other cities, whether there might be rural settlements nearby, whether we'd left the populated province altogether. Nothing. For all I knew, we were in one of the quake-heavy regions with a sparkling name like Gaping Chasm of Death. Not an inspiring thought.

As the men deposited me at the base of a tree and refastened the restraints, I felt something jostle against my leg.

My wrist transmitter. Dane had given it back days ago with an apology for breaking the fastener. I'd been too busy to fix it and had just carried it in my pocket. The Garamites' signal scan when they took me hadn't picked it up, since it wasn't broad-casting. Or maybe just because Thandan junk-tech was beneath their notice. If I could activate it, someone might be able to trace the signal.

It wouldn't happen anytime soon with my hands bound. And if I wasn't careful, Tobias and the others might hear Dim-wit's response—I couldn't exactly count on the drone to be dis-creet. And Cusser...Cusser was beyond hearing me.

No tears, Essie. Not now.

Step one was to get the restraints off.

The men set up a camp with bags they brought from the transport. Blankets and meal-packs and I didn't know what else. A well-put-together kidnapping if ever I'd seen one, and it only got worse when Tobias sat next to me.

"Oh, don't look at me like that, Essie," he said. "We should be friends. I suppose in the spirit of friendliness, we can take this off." He pulled the gag away from my mouth.

"What in blazes are you thinking?" I said, annoyed at the slight rasp in my voice. "The Candarans won't just let you go."

"I'm sure you're right. Here I thought I was just coming to

collect an unpaid debt, but then I get here and find our friend Essie-the-Thandan isn't a Thandan at all. You're worth a lot more than some shuttle repairs, aren't you?"

Tobias was on a roll. First he wanted to use me to start a war with Thanda, and now he knew who I was. Maybe I was going to get traded to Windsong like a case of merinium after all.

No, because you're going to get out of this. We'd stopped for the night because the transport wasn't equipped to navigate without roads, so it was too dangerous to travel in the dark. That gave me some time. Hopefully enough.

"You must be hungry," Tobias said. "Here."

He held something like the nutri-bars we had on Thanda to my mouth, and I took a bite. A bit stale, but nothing wrong with it, so I took a second bite as well.

"It'd be easier if I could hold it myself," I said.

"Oh, I'm afraid our friendship hasn't reached that level of trust just yet. We'll see how it goes."

I finished the nutri-bar without comment. *Wait for the right moment, Essie. And that's not when your temper's charging up.*

Dusk turned to full night with small talk about a game called morpek that meant nothing to me. Candara had no moons, so night in the wild was very dark. The Garamites had some portable electronic lights, but they didn't cut the blackness by much. I liked the wretched situation even less when I couldn't keep an eye on my surroundings. One by one, the other men tucked in nearby with their blankets, but Tobias stayed on watch.

The darkness pressed in on me, not knowing what was out there, what unknown Candaran creatures might come for me in the night. My skin crawled. Now was the time, before my panic made it impossible.

"Tobias, I can't feel my hands, and I have to go."

"You're not going anywhere," he said.

"Have you blazing Garamites innovated yourselves out of the need for biological functions? I mean I need to *go*."

He sighed and may have rolled his eyes. I couldn't see. After a second, he leaned forward and fiddled with my bindings, setting my feet free. He stood and pulled me up, activating a hand-held light.

"Move, come on."

We walked deeper into the trees, to an area with some scrubby bushes, and he removed my wrist restraints before shoving me to my knees. "I'll be right over by those trees, so don't think I won't hear if you try to sneak off."

I knelt there while he walked away, counting his footsteps as I rubbed my tender wrists and flexed my hands, trying to get the blood flowing. Thirteen. I could barely see his light if I peered over the shrub between us. Hopefully that was far enough.

My arms ached from my shoulders to my throbbing fingertips. I reached into my pocket and carefully drew out the wrist transmitter.

"Dimwit, no verbal response," I whispered. "Tell Dane to track this signal to find me. Two beeps to confirm."

By the time the beeps came through, I'd covered the device with my hands, muffling the sound. Now I needed to keep the signal going as long as I could. It had an open-transmission setting, but that particular model always slipped back to receptive mode eventually. The good transmitter had gone for a swim in the sinkhole with me. I switched it to the open mode and tucked it back into my pocket, hoping it would hold long enough for Dane to locate.

I rustled around in the undergrowth a bit, stood, and took a few steps toward Tobias. He met me halfway.

"Feeling better?" he said as he put the restraints back on my hands—in the front this time, and not as tight.

"Much."

We got back to the camp, and I watched where Tobias settled before picking a tree to sit against.

"If you're waiting for me to fall asleep so you can take off, you'll be waiting a long time," he said.

"No, I'm not waiting for any such thing."

He stayed quiet, and I huddled against the tree trunk. Knowing I'd possibly set things in motion let me shake off worries of the dark and doze a bit. A reserve of energy had to be a good thing.

Dozing only worked so well. The night grew cold, and the wrist restraints still cut painfully into my skin, like a year's worth of blisters piled up all at once. Light tremors rumbled through the ground at least twice, waking me and putting my nerves back on edge.

Tobias did sleep eventually, but only after waking one of the others to take a shift. When I couldn't even doze anymore, I kept myself busy imagining how I'd beat the smirk off Tobias's face, every hit and dodge.

Night didn't last forever, and compared to Thandan nights, Candara's were brief. I looked up through the trees as the stars faded, and minutes later the first bird chirps filled the air.

Then another chirp.

"Dane Essie find Essie."

That blazing heap of—

I didn't get to finish the thought. Tobias knocked me over,

pawing at me until he found the transmitter. He threw it down, crushed it under his boot, and hauled me roughly to my feet.

"Get to the transport," he barked at the others. "Go! We're getting out of here."

We got through one clump of trees before light flooded the area, blinding me. The other men shouted in surprise, but Tobias pulled me close with one arm around my waist. My feet were free—I could kick him or break his toes—but I froze when something cold touched my temple with a high-pitched whine of energy charging. His gun. I blinked through the light, which came from distinct points around us. I could make out just enough to determine they were mounted to guns.

Way too many guns.

"Let her go, Tobias!" Dane's voice, coming from the second light left of center.

"No, I think I'll hold on to her for a bit longer. I wasn't far off the mark on why you brought her from Thanda, was I?"

The cockiness of Tobias's words couldn't hide the panic lacing his voice. His plans had just come unraveled and he was taking it hard. That didn't bode well for the girl with a gun to her head.

He'd made a mistake, holding me at the waist. I had some range of movement, but the timing had to be right. I couldn't see beyond the lights, but I knew Dane would be watching me, leaving the other men to the rest of the guards. I looked directly at the second light left of center and mouthed the word *three*.

"I'll tell you what you're going to do," Tobias said.

One.

"You're going to back away and let us pass."

Two.

"Or I'm going to put a hole in this pretty royal head of hers."

Three.

I ducked.

Tobias's arm tightened on my waist, so I kicked with one foot as I twisted to break his grip. Charges sizzled through the air above me and to either side. My maneuver left me off-balance, and I fell to my knees.

The lights changed to a more diffuse setting, and I blinked away the afterimages. By the time I could see clearly, Dane was kneeling with me.

"Are you okay? Are you hurt?"

"My wrists are blazing killing me."

He looked down at the rough polymer restraints and pulled a knife from his boot, cutting me free. My wrists throbbed, then tingled as he held them, his thumb brushing across my old scar. I couldn't drag my eyes away from his hands, trying to figure why they were different from any other hands I'd known.

"Thanks."

"You're welcome."

I finally raised my eyes to his. "They found out who I am."

Dane nodded, relinquishing my hands. "I noticed. We'll make sure they haven't told anyone else. Come on, our transports are this way."

"Wait, I need to get something."

I stood and turned around. Tobias lay crumpled on the ground, groaning as the guards trussed up him and his friends.

At least the smirk was gone.

Resisting the urge to kick him in the teeth anyway, I walked back through the trees and found the transmitter where Tobias had left it. His boot had smashed it into the dirt more than crushed it. I could stitch it up. When I turned, Dane was right there.

"Ready to go?"

"Definitely."

Dane had brought much speedier transports than the utility vehicle. They would get us back to Gakoa before the sun cleared the mountains. I finally got a clearer look at Dane's condition. Particularly the purpling bruise around his left eye, which made my gut twist.

"What's that?"

"What? Oh, in the park," he explained, "one of Tobias's friends got a lucky shot in."

"And you didn't bother treating it because . . . ?"

"We've been busy. They landed in another city a few days ago, and I didn't find out until an assistant told Lunak about a stolen utility vehicle. I'm sorry, Essie, I should've told Kip what happened on Garam."

I gestured to one of the guards to hand me a medical kit. The supplies were unfamiliar to me, but Dane pointed out the transdermal rejuvenator. I activated the device and worked it over the bruise, watching it slowly fade, trying to tell myself it was no different from treating the gash on his head when the shuttle crashed.

But it was completely different.

Avoiding his eyes was impossible, especially when they stayed locked on me. They set something jittering under my skin. I felt other eyes, too. Some of the guards, but they turned away when Dane glared. I needed a distraction, and the medical kit in my lap reminded me of a question plaguing my mind.

"Laisa . . . Is she all right?"

"I don't know. I had her taken to a hospital and made sure the best doctors would see to her. But then we left, and I've been looking for you since."

He didn't say so, but if they had to send Laisa to the hospital, she hadn't just been knocked out. I pushed the possibilities out of my head, but that left a question I likewise didn't want to ask.

"And Cusser?"

He shifted, taking the kit from me. "You saw him. I think he can be repaired—I'm sure he can—but it'll take some time."

Silence fell as he healed my wrists, and I made no attempt to break it. I had no words left.

We arrived at the governing complex. Dane insisted I get some rest while he filled in the council and got a report from the hospital. Regardless of his insistence, I had better things to do than sleep or deal with the bickering old leaders.

I went to the spare lab where Cusser had been stowed.

My drone with the dirty vocabulary, downgraded to a pile of scrap metal. The blast had decimated several core components. There wasn't enough left to even run diagnostics. And it would need major body reconstruction. Maybe Cusser could be repaired, but I couldn't do it alone—I needed the rest of the drones. Clank could do the welding, and Clunk could fabricate components with absolute precision. Replacement parts, recoding . . . Whirligig had backups of all the drones' programs. Ticktock knew better than I did how all the processors, power supplies, and relays fit together. Zippy would salvage every possible bit from the damaged originals. . . .

But they were behind me, planets away. The wrong direction. Even if it worked, there was no guarantee Cusser would be the same again.

I should've made it stay at the complex. I should've designed the defense program better, knowing the kinds of weapons people like Tobias used. I should've paid more attention.

I shouldn't have gone to see Laisa at all.

The door opened behind me less than an hour later.

"Laisa?" I knew the answer just by looking at Dane's face, but I had to hear it anyway.

"She died. At such close range, the damage..."

Everything spun, but I kept my feet. I remembered being in her head, being *her*. "She had family. A husband, children."

"Yes."

Dead. My mother's friend, a mother herself, was dead because she talked to me. Because she dared to get in the way. Because death had failed to claim me eight years ago and now mocked my survival.

Dead because I wasn't where I was supposed to be.

Do what needs doing.

I traced my fingers along the edge of the blast hole in Cusser. There would be no repairing it. It wasn't what needed doing.

"Get everything ready," I told Dane. "We're leaving for Windsong."

18

LESS THAN A DAY LATER, the shuttle launched. And not Dane's shuttle. We took Tobias's—now that he was in lockup, he wouldn't need it. The shuttle had a similar design but was larger, with four side compartments—two to each side—and a heftier engine. Besides, Tobias had already done the hard work of giving it a generic, untraceable registry.

We even had permission to do it. Since Garam had no centralized government, the council talked to Brand as a senior member of Tobias's colony. The Garamites weren't thrilled with the way Dane and I had left, but Brand said Tobias had acted without forethought. Killing a bystander disgusted him, so we should take whatever advantage we could from the tragedy. What Brand called "lack of forethought" I called being outright unhinged, but the result was the same. On the positive side, some subtle questions confirmed that no one in Brand's colony thought I was anything other than Thandan.

Kip didn't want us to leave so soon, or at least not without him. He knew coming along was impossible, though. Olivia knew his face. Besides, he'd be needed with the fleet waiting for us.

So it was just Dane and me, pointing a shuttle back toward Garam. We'd give the planet a wide berth, but going that way meant that from Windsong's perspective, we could be coming from either Garam or Thanda. Not from Candara.

Just the pair of us—I should've been used to it, but I wasn't. Not anymore. The journey to Windsong would take twenty-seven days. Alone with a boy who'd kissed me, plus Dimwit... but as usual, I didn't count the drone. Its presence only reminded me that I'd wanted Cusser to come along, and why it couldn't.

"All right, come on," Dane said after locking in the course. He stood from his chair and looked at me expectantly.

"Come on and what?"

"Twenty-seven days is plenty of time for you to learn how to fight better."

I couldn't help it—I bristled and glared. My fighting skills had done me pretty well so far... most of the time.

He smirked, which annoyed me even more. "Yes, you're very good for a self-taught fighter. But you know the people we'll be up against there, and you know the restrictions."

Right. Palace guards would be highly trained, and the whole capital was under an interference field that rendered certain types of tech useless, particularly energy weapons. The palace told the public that Olivia's powers couldn't abide "violent energy signatures." Really just a clever way to make assassination that much harder, and to give guards an excuse to carry swords and knives.

If there was one thing Olivia and my father loved, it was mixing the appearance of an old-fashioned royal court with splashes of the new.

Learning to fight like Dane wasn't a half-bad idea, even if it rankled a bit, so I followed him to one of the side compartments. He'd completely cleared it out before we left, except for some shock-absorbing mats on the floor. Hopefully that meant neither of us would break anything.

At least I'm dressed for the occasion. The satin and silk had stayed on Candara, but so had my old Thandan rags. Dane and I both wore something in-between, the kind of clothes you could get on any planet, functional and ordinary.

We stood in the center of the room, facing each other. "All right, try to hit me," he said.

It felt like someone had asked me to run new optic lines in the drones using only my feet. A foreign and awkward task. All he got back from me was a stare.

"What?"

"One, I already know I can't hit you unless you let me. Two, every time I've fought there've either been shares on the line or someone trying to hurt me. Fighting like this isn't natural."

"I can make you mad if that'd help."

"Aye, I'm sure you could."

His expression shifted to a reproachful frown. "You need to stop saying 'aye,' Essie. And watch the accent. You're not supposed to sound like you've spent years among miners."

"Aye—ugh. *Yes.* Yes, I know."

"Come on, then. Take your best shot."

So I did. As expected, he blocked it like he was swatting a fly, his eyes never leaving mine.

"Again, with a follow-up."

I did. Nothing.

"Again. Don't always lead right. Try to surprise me."

Pointless as it was, I did. Over and over. I even tried tossing in a kick or a backhand to throw him off, but he batted everything down.

A growl of frustration finally slipped out. "This is useless, Dane."

"No, it isn't," he insisted. "You're smart. You can learn it."

I didn't know whether to believe his confidence. He'd lied to me too well before. That fact niggled and gnawed, refusing to be brushed aside. I needed to hear some truth, and I figured the place to start was the question I'd been avoiding. "Tell me something first. What are you?"

His stance relaxed. "What?"

"You heard me. Dane isn't a Candaran name. Blazes, Kip isn't a Candaran name, either. But you obviously *are* Candaran, and you're important to the council, so what exactly are you?"

He hesitated, like he had to decide whether it was worth telling me. "Kip's name is Keppes. Mine is Kadei, but my father called me Dane so I'd blend in more."

I took a half step back. "Kadei? That's an old royal name."

"Yes, it means *storm*. So we were both named after the weather. I guess you *do* know a few things about Candarans."

"Mostly from lessons about the 'evil' empire my father's family overthrew two centuries ago, so no telling how accurate it is. I didn't think the old royal family was still around. That's why the council treats you like they do?"

His eyes darkened. "My father should be leading our people. The next in line always has a choice—serve with the council, or take over as ruler of Candara. With my father imprisoned, I'm one year away from making my decision, so Kip holds my place on the council."

A choice. To be a king or part of a committee. Nothing like the rules of succession on Windsong. The question of which he'd choose half formed on my lips, but Dane spoke first.

"Come on, let's try again."

I took one swing—easily blocked—and stopped. "Wait. You're not playing both sides of this fight, are you?"

He immediately caught that I meant Transitioning for an advantage, and he froze. "Essie, I would never do that to you. Ever."

Shame crept through me for even asking. "Sorry."

"That reminds me, though. When we get to Windsong, you should practice Transitioning to non-Candarans. Try to stay grounded in your own self while you do it, use both perspectives."

Just as quickly, the shame shifted to disbelief. "You're the one always talking about the law, about proving Exiles can be trusted."

"Between the law and you taking every advantage you can to protect yourself, I choose your life."

"And who should I practice on? Olivia? How about my father?"

As rinked off as I was getting, Dane remained irritatingly calm. "Strangers would be better to start with. Easier to keep your attention separated."

"That's even worse!"

He tipped his head to one side. "Enough stalling. Now that you're mad, try blocking me."

He came at me, and I tried. Really, I tried. It did feel more like the cage, but it didn't help. I hated being so bad at fighting compared to him. He didn't go anywhere near full-force, and good thing, too. I couldn't begin to stop him. The contact was nothing more than a tap, but each felt like a message tattooed on my skull.

You're. Not. That. Good. Essie.

"Tank it! I can't do it, all right?"

"Why not?" he countered.

"I just can't. Where'd you learn to fight like this, anyway?"

A slight shift in his posture said the answer wasn't as simple as the question. "I was born in enemy territory, and my father wanted to make sure I could protect myself. After he sent me away and he was arrested . . . let's just say I had some anger that needed directing."

A cold pulse ran through my chest. That anger was my fault.

"Now, come on," he continued. "What am I doing that's so different from what you're used to?"

"You're too blazing fast."

"What does fast mean? I've seen you run, I've seen your reflexes. You're fast, too. Why am I faster at this?"

I didn't have an answer, so I kept my mouth shut.

"No wasted movement, Essie," he began. "Movement takes time, so don't waste it on anything unnecessary. It's like I tried to tell you before the VT fight: every action lives in its own moment, nothing longer than it needs."

I wanted to ask what that was supposed to mean, but figured he'd only answer with something even more abstract and nonsensical.

We went at it again, but the incessant taps started unhinging me. My shoulder, my cheek, my back—I couldn't even figure how he'd reached my back. Instinct took over, and amidst the blocking, I tried to counterstrike.

Still, nothing got through.

I took another approach, trying to maneuver and get an armlock.

He turned the hold around and twisted, throwing me flat on my back. The mat took the worst of it, but it still knocked the wind from my lungs. Dane just stood over me and offered a hand.

It's going to be a long trip.

Training had an upside; it kept us busy enough not to notice the monotony of the journey. It also had downsides, most of which showed up as pains in my backside.

For days, it seemed just as pointless as it had at the start. Dane said I was improving. I didn't believe him but kept quiet. Then finally, after a thousand attempts, I hit him, not hard, but right across the jaw. I thought he must have let me, to give me confidence, but he was just as startled as I was. And he laughed.

I'd never seen him laugh before—not a real, unrestrained laugh—but once he did, it seemed so natural. Like something he was always waiting to do.

I wished he had reason to do it more.

We worked even harder after that, refining my sloppy technique, adding more complex moves, and working a little with weapons. I found I had some skill at knife-throwing, which helped my confidence. Everything he'd said about wasted

movement started to click. Each strike started with the end in mind. He was still far better than I was, but I could tell it took more effort to stop me now.

As I improved, we also worked on slipping and breaking holds, which brought another obstacle. Little taps while sparring were one thing, but I'd never liked being confined in a hold. Getting caught in one had been my least favorite part of the cage fights. This was different. Half of me wanted to break free and hit him harder. The other half didn't want to fight Dane at all, even in training, because there was something about letting him hold me. Something almost nice.

Dane didn't mention practicing my Transitioning again, although I knew the subject wasn't closed. I couldn't help noticing he hadn't suggested I practice with him. Even besides his claim that strangers and non-Candarans would be better, he likely didn't want me in his head any more than I wanted to delve into it. He didn't try to make me angry during training bouts again, either, which was a good thing. I picked up his techniques better when I stayed calm.

Fortunately, we didn't spend all our time fighting. My aching muscles needed a break now and then, and I almost always spent it in the engine area with Dimwit. The tech it ran on would likely be fine in the interference field that blocked weapons, but I wanted to work on shielding some of the more delicate components just in case. The old bucket was unpredictable enough as it was. For the same reason, I'd also rigged a new control to let us mute its voice when needed. I should've thought of it years ago.

"Here," Dane said one day, drawing my attention from shielding Dimwit's auditory processor. "For your knee."

I glanced at the offered rejuvenator patch before turning back to Dimwit. "Right, just as soon as I'm done here."

Dane had other ideas. He sat next to me, pulled up my pant leg, and applied the patch to the purpling bruise himself.

"Sorry again about that." He rubbed the patch lightly, sending a tingle through my leg that was half the rejuvenator and half his touch.

My first instinct was to jerk away. I steered that urge into a shrug instead. "No, I should've realized I'd gotten close to the bulkhead."

He sat back against the wall and watched me as I stitched. As much as it used to bother me, I'd gotten used to it. Being around Dane had become almost comfortable, something I'd never thought I'd be around anyone who didn't have four metal legs.

Except when he did things like touch my knee. That wasn't comfortable, but I couldn't decide what it *was*. My hit reflex had eased up almost to the point of disappearing. And he never tried anything else—definitely nothing like kissing me again. I didn't know why not. I didn't know much about what went on in his head.

I couldn't figure him on my own, and Transitioning was out of the question. Maybe it was time to ask.

"Dane, why are you here?"

"There's not much else to do on a ship flying a set course. If I'm bothering you, I can go somewhere else."

"No, I mean why are you coming with me at all? You're important to your people. There's a good chance we'll both die before pulling this off, and no guarantee that we'll get your father and the others out first. Your plan to trade me was probably the better one."

The muscles around his mouth tightened. "I told you, I couldn't do that once I knew the truth."

"I don't see why not. If someone said I could trade a stranger's life to get my mother back...I'd have a right hard time saying no."

"Well, there's the first problem. You're not a stranger. The Candaran royal family is allowed choices, and this is my choice. Besides, as much as I hate a lot of your plan, it's better. *When* we pull it off, it'll do more than free my father. It'll free your people...and you."

I glanced up and saw how he looked at me. Really *saw* it. Not the way men like Moray did, like they only wanted to take from me. Not the way Kip did, full of regret. Not even like Petey did, with his admonitions to bundle up for a cold one. Dane's way was different, had been for ages—as if he didn't want anything from me, yet wanted everything.

My stitches wouldn't come, no matter how I tried to focus on the work. "Dane, that time when you woke me and...you know..."

"When I kissed you and you didn't hit me," he provided.

"Aye—yes, that. Did you...well...Have you changed your mind since then?"

His eyes warmed with a smile. I'd seen that smile more lately. It was a nice one. "Definitely not."

Men who wanted me didn't back off until I caused enough pain to get the message through. That was how it always worked. "But you haven't tried to since. I don't understand."

"Not that complicated. I think I'm in love with you, Essie. But I also think you're not ready. I shouldn't have sprung it on you like that, so I decided to take it at your speed."

A sudden rush of heat made me wonder if the engine had malfunctioned. No, I was just blushing. Instinct told me to run away from something so foreign, but I had nowhere to go. The whole reason I was going to Windsong was to stop running. I focused on Dimwit's innards.

"And how exactly are we to know when I'm 'ready'?"

"I'm not sure. Probably when you figure out why you didn't hit me. You've cracked men's kneecaps for doing less than I did."

True, I had. My instincts usually made pretty solid sense to me, but they should have prompted me to rip out Dane's throat. They hadn't. Instinct failure on all fronts.

I knew one reason I hadn't: Dane and I were friends again. I liked that.

That left me with another puzzle. I had no blazing idea what my speed *was*.

Days passed. We trained and prepared. The closer we got to Windsong, the quieter I got. Even when Dimwit rattled on about "Fly Essie shuttle Essie Dane shuttle fly," Dane was the one to tell the drone to shut it. I hardly spoke, but I also couldn't stop watching Dane. Couldn't stop thinking about what he'd said.

I think I'm in love with you.

He'd followed me out of love. Deep down, I'd let him come because I was selfish and wanted to keep him with me—wanted one person I could trust at my side. But I'd created a very big problem.

One of the side compartments had a bolted-down table and bench. I often sat there and lost myself in my number puzzles when I wasn't training or fiddling with Dimwit. The day we would cross into range of Windsong's sensors, Dane entered the compartment and slid in next to me, his arm brushing against mine.

I scooted away.

"Essie?"

I looked up from my slate and saw the pain in his eyes. It had been ages since I'd moved away from him like that.

"They can't find out, Dane," I said.

"Find out what?"

"Who you are. *What* you are. They'll kill you."

"That's why we have the story. We covered all that. Essie, they won't know."

His hand had crept back toward mine. I let my fingers graze his before pulling away again. "That's not part of the story. I'm supposed to be above you. If they find out I care..."

Something lit in his eyes with the shade of a smile. "Does that mean you *do* care?"

A ping sounding throughout the shuttle spared me from answering. I hurried out to the command compartment, Dane right behind me. Windsong had become a discernable blue disk on the viewer. The ping signaled an incoming communication.

"Garamite vessel, you are entering the sovereign space of Windsong, realm of the Supreme Crown, King Matthias. Please state your business and cargo."

Dane turned to me. "Are you ready for this?"

"No, but don't let that stop you. You're the one who has to deal with this part. Remember the security phrase."

He took a breath and touched a panel on the console. "Our business is to enjoy the splendors of the Royal City. We prefer not to declare our cargo over an open channel, but have heard the Supreme Crown prefers blue skies over fields of snow." A phrase meant to evoke my eye and hair color, and my name besides. At least, it had been eight years ago.

A pause. "Please hold your current course until you receive further instructions."

We waited in silence. Five minutes, then ten, on into twenty before Dane spoke.

"Are you sure they'll know what that means?"

"If they go high enough, yes. Don't worry. Taking a long time is a good thing."

Less than five minutes later, another ping with a different voice. "Garamite vessel, we are transmitting a course to the Royal City. Be advised that a squadron will be deployed to escort you shortly. This is for your own protection from Exile forces occupying the war zone on the far side of our planet. Please do not deviate from the transmitted course."

"Understood. Initiating course change." He deactivated the communication system and grunted. "Exile forces on the far side."

"He's convinced the general population for eight years. We'll have to pretend to believe it, too."

Six new blips appeared on the tactical display, coming toward us from Windsong. With my hand shaking slightly, I checked the registry signatures. The Golden Sword—the king's guard.

My father knew I was coming home.

19

NOTHING IN THE ROYAL CITY HAD CHANGED.
Water everywhere, in fountains and in canals with glittering granite bridges spanning them. Planters lined the causeways with the finest flowers, rainbow orchids pointing the way to the palace. Citizens walking through the city made as much a rainbow as the flowers did, with hair of every color, including some as white as mine. When I was a child, everyone had worn bright patterns. Now, the clothes were bold colors with flared hems, decorative collars, and jeweled accents. The fashion of Windsong was alive and well. Like Candara, the buildings were stone, but much more intricate, with carved pillars and statuary, or inlaid with gleaming, smooth marble.

As we passed lower over the city, people looked up and pointed. They saw the emblem of the Golden Sword on the escort fighters and they cheered.

It was a good thing. They might not have known yet that I'd returned, but they knew *something* had happened. A full escort wasn't something they saw every day. There would be gossip and questions everywhere. All I had to do was make sure a few palace servants saw me, and news would spread quickly.

The fighters guided us to the military spaceport at the edge of the city, and Dane landed the shuttle smoothly. A contingent of Golden Sword guards and a single woman—not in uniform—approached right away. Just from the purpose in her walk, the pride in how she carried herself, and the way the guards followed her, I knew she had to be important.

Dane and I got up and went to the hatch. "Remember your role," I said. "Don't slip."

"Same to you, Princess. Come on, Dimwit."

Dane walked out of the shuttle first, and I followed only when he turned back and nodded. Once out, I faced the assembled group. I recognized the red-and-gold trim on the woman's sleeve—a senior aide. Not one I remembered, but that didn't mean anything. My father had no tolerance for mistakes from his aides, so they changed often. She looked me over, one eyebrow slightly raised, but was careful to keep the rest of her face expressionless.

"Please follow me," she said. "We will take you to the palace."

No questions or introductions. Another good sign. I'd enjoy them while they lasted.

We followed to an armored transport—Dimwit managed not to lag behind—and formed a convoy to the palace. The sun hovered at the horizon, bathing the city in an orange-red glow.

Seeing the walls, turrets, and towers, the gardens and fountains, caused a pounding in my chest that echoed through my head. It was real. I was back. My father and Olivia were somewhere within those walls, and I would face them within minutes.

You can do it, Essie. Just like Mother.

Mother had faced them both almost every day—her husband and the woman he used as his tool to control the masses. She'd never shown fear. I wouldn't, either.

The aide led us through the entrance hall and into the confusing maze of corridors I could map in my sleep. Dane kept a step behind me—always behind, but never more than the one step. Dimwit trailed along, its metallic feet clicking against the tile.

As I'd hoped, servants peeked at us from rooms and hallways as we passed. When they were in pairs, I heard faint whispers behind us. I just hoped those whispers spread quickly beyond the palace walls.

I knew the path, winding around behind the throne room to the private chamber where more delicate matters were discussed. My heartbeat doubled as we approached, tripled when the door opened, and quadrupled when we entered.

My father stood behind a desk, leaning against the mantle of a large fireplace. As tall and broad-shouldered as I remembered, but with more gray in his hair and beard. He didn't look over even when the door closed and locked behind us.

"Is it she?" he asked.

The aide stepped forward. "We need to verify your identity."

I'd expected this, so I turned my back to her and pulled my sleeve down over my shoulder. She took a small black light from one pocket and a high-dose injector from the other. Dane seemed to move a sniff or two closer, but there was nothing he could do. If the aide declared me an imposter, I'd be dead before the words reached my father's ears. She ran the black light over the tattoo, and I held very still. A slight gasp escaped her throat.

"It is, Sire."

"Then you are dismissed, Margaret."

The aide left. The door closed and locked again. My father finally looked at me. A string of emotions flashed through his eyes—shock, then hunger, fear, and warmth. Only when they settled on the last did he speak.

"Snowflake?"

"Father."

My voice trembled, but the emotion causing it was nebulous enough to bring him across the room, his arms outstretched.

"Darling, you're home!"

Every muscle wanted to tense; I wanted to back away, to run, to hit him. I couldn't do any of it. Instead, I had to step forward. He enfolded me, pulled me close, kissed the top of my head.

Touching me... too close...

Breathe, Essie. Pretend he's someone else. Anyone else. Everyone you're doing this for.

I defied every instinct I had and returned his embrace.

A memory crashed in. *Father tucking me into bed, telling me stories.*

Blazes, where had that come from?

After a torturous eternity, he pulled away, taking my face in his hands so his eyes could more easily devour it. "My little girl. We've searched for you, the whole system."

"I'm sorry. I'm sorry, Father. I thought I'd never get home."

Before we said anything else, a hidden door to one side opened, admitting Olivia to the room, and Father finally released me.

Unlike him, Olivia didn't appear to have aged a bit in the

past eight years. If anything, she looked younger, likely thanks to the revita-tech she always pushed the Garamite doctors in the Royal City to improve. Dark hair pulled back in a sleek, complicated twist; a fitted burgundy gown with a vaguely militaristic cut, its luxurious fabric offset by a chain looped about her waist and the metal latticework of her heeled boots and headpiece; everything meticulously in place. None of the opulence mattered, as my eyes were drawn to her face.

Olivia had as many masks as she had gowns, but her eyes couldn't hide the truth. Those eyes set the public quailing even as they shed tears of gratitude for her miraculous "healings" as royal theurgist. Those same eyes pierced into me, demanding to know how I dared remain alive.

I couldn't breathe. Nothing had changed.

"Snow! I didn't dare believe Margaret was telling the truth. Let's look at you." She took my hands, holding them out so she could take me in. "So grown-up. I just can't— What magic has returned you to us?"

Magic. Right.

"Yes, tell us everything," Father said. "I must know how you were kept from us so long. The last we knew, one of Olivia's guards escorted you as planned to the orchid festival."

Time to weave a tale as intricate as any code I'd ever written. I cast my mind back to that day eight years ago, reaching for a few details to bring truth to the lies.

"It was so confusing. We barely made it into the festival, just enough to see an arrangement of crimson orchids. Then the crowd went mad—I think some people were fighting—and I was separated from the guard. I thought it would be okay; I'd disguised myself like you always told me to. But before I could find him, someone held something to my face, and I blacked out. When I woke, I was on a shuttle bound for Thanda."

My father didn't bother to hide his surprise. "Thanda? Who would take you there?"

"A band of Thandans and Garamites who fancied themselves separatists. Once on the planet, infighting over how to ransom me broke out, and I took the chance to escape."

"The guard who lost you," Olivia said, her eyes shrewd, "he wasn't part of the plot?"

I put on my best look of surprise. "No. I never saw him again. He didn't return here to alert you?"

"No, he did not."

I shook my head, helpless and confused. "Perhaps he ran, fearing punishment."

"Darling, if you escaped so early," Father began, "what kept you from us?"

"My own fear. I couldn't trust anyone on Thanda, so I didn't dare tell anyone who I was. I tried hiding among the peasants in the Bands, but then they became dangerous. So I wandered north to the wild territories beyond the mines and found the Umbergild Ascetics. They took me in, and eventually I trusted them, but of course, they couldn't do anything to help me return home. I'm sorry, Father. I should have been braver and more clever."

Father hummed thoughtfully at my story. "Little wonder the Midnight Blade we sent didn't find her."

The Midnight Blade. If Olivia's guards handled the search, it explained why they'd never found me in Forty-Two. I was certain there'd been no search at all.

Even if there had been a search, my father was right—they couldn't have found me among the Umbergild Ascetics. It had been sharp of Dane to think of looking for me there, but succeeding would've been tricky. For one, the Ascetics were isolationists, forbidding any tech that could communicate beyond their borders, or anything allowing them to travel faster than a man could run. For another, they were notorious liars to outsiders. Thus the trick of our story, holding a sniff of truth. I'd come across the Ascetics just before settling in Forty-Two, and their leader had been friendly with me due to my age. But if either my father or Olivia went to the trouble to send someone out to the Ascetics to verify my story now, Gildon would acknowledge knowing someone of my description, tell them three different stories, and advise them to pick whichever they liked best.

"What happened then?" Father asked.

"This boy, Dane." He'd been so quiet and unassuming, Father and Olivia had ignored him—standard behavior toward a servant. Even Dimwit kept still in the corner. "He and his sister escaped a terrible life on Garam, crashing their shuttle near the Umbergild settlement. The Ascetics had their beliefs, but I couldn't leave any possible survivors, so I went and pulled both of them out before a fire reached them. For saving his sister, Dane swore to protect my life to the end of his days. Once I knew he was trustworthy, I told him my identity. He set to work repairing his shuttle to help bring me home."

"But the craft you arrived in seemed in excellent condition," Olivia said.

"Dane's shuttle couldn't have made the journey here from Thanda's current position, and I didn't want to wait anymore—it had been so long already—so we stopped on Garam. I admit, I'd stolen some merinium from a shipment on Thanda. A Garamite named Brand traded us for the better shuttle."

I checked their eyes. Father was convinced. Even Olivia seemed to find it plausible enough for the moment. When Father smiled, I knew the first obstacle was behind us.

"Young man, you wish to serve my daughter?"

Dane kept his eyes lowered, as subservient as the king could want, the act inscrutable. "Yes, Sire. My only desire is to ensure no harm comes to the princess ever again."

"Excellent. Her absence has delayed the formation of her personal guard. You shall be the first member of the Silver Dagger."

"I'm honored, Sire."

"You alone will protect her until other worthy guards can be found. And this contraption?" he asked, waving toward Dimwit.

At my gesture, it skittered to my side. "One of the Thandan mining drones. It malfunctioned and wandered to Umbergild. Life in the settlement could be boring, so I applied Tutor Benedict's lessons, tinkering with its programming. It's become something of a pet."

Father gave Dimwit a once-over and let out a booming laugh that made my throat close up. "You always did like your odd little toys. I imagine it will bring new life and charm to our halls, just as you will. It calls for celebration—a ball! My queen, the realm must share in our joy, don't you think?"

"I will set to work immediately," Olivia said. "The performers and musicians . . . all will be arranged."

"You must be tired from your journey. We will begin tomorrow." He clapped his hands twice, and a servant appeared at yet another hidden door. "Garrick, escort Princess Snow and her personal guard to the suite I ordered prepared. Darling"—one more hug and a kiss to my cheek—"I am so happy you've returned."

I squeezed him back before he let me go. Dane bowed, and we left the room through the secret door. My hands wanted to shake. I told them to wait.

I maintained my composure as Dane, Dimwit, and I followed the footman across to the residential portion of the palace. He was young and eager to please, chattering about how wonderful it was to have me back, how the king and queen must be beyond joy.

They were beyond something, right enough.

"Here we are. Your suite, Your Highness. Plenty of room for your guard as well in the quarters through to the left," he added, nodding to Dane. "Your belongings are inside. Do you need me to show you around?"

"No, thank you, Garrick," I replied. "It's been a while, but I remember every speck of this palace very well."

"Of course."

Garrick gestured for me to enter, but Dane shoved past, going in first. Before I could panic that he'd forgotten the careful act we had to follow, I realized he hadn't. A personal guard wouldn't let his charge enter a room without first ensuring it was safe. It had been too long since I'd had anyone treat me like that, and the young footman was as startled as I was.

"You'll have to forgive him," I said. "He knows I was kidnapped from my own city. Imagines assassins everywhere. He does take his honor oath seriously."

At that, Garrick relaxed and smiled. "I'm sure Their Majesties will be gratified to know of his devotion to duty."

Dane returned after a few minutes, his face like stone as he gave me a sharp nod.

"Very good," Garrick concluded. "If you need anything further, you need only call. Sleep well, Highness."

I entered the suite with Dane, closing the door behind us. The main room was larger than it had any right to be, traditional and gaudy, very much in my stepmother's taste. Dimwit found a spot to recharge and went on standby. I noted the two doors that would lead to my quarters and Dane's, ignoring everything else, and turned to him.

"You checked?"

He nodded, holding up the slate from his pocket. "No monitoring devices."

Finally, I let go, collapsing against the wall as every muscle rebelled, trembling as violently as I had when I fell through the ice. Dane sat with me and took my hands in his, so warm and steady.

"You did great, Essie. Every bit a princess."

"You—you saw, didn't you? How she still wants me dead?"

"It doesn't matter. She won't get a chance to hurt you, I swear it." There was something in his voice, and I raised my eyes to his. They darkened as his jaw set. "I also saw your father . . . how he *doesn't* want you dead. How he wants something else. You're not to be alone with him under any circumstances—do you understand?"

It hadn't taken him long to figure that. Did that mean everyone had always known and let it happen anyway?

"Even full-blooded Exiles—Candarans—can't force anyone to do anything, right?" I asked Dane.

"Yes, Tipping is the closest we come, and that only works when the person we Transition to is already considering something. The rumors that we could do more than that started because some Candarans broke the law and compelled people by threatening to expose their secrets. Why do you ask?"

I shivered again. "Because I always thought I should've been able to stop the bastard, but I couldn't."

He held my hands tighter. "You should have told me. I never would have gone along with this."

"All the more reason *not* to have told you."

His sigh was the only answer to that. "You're going to make me regret this ten times over before we're through, aren't you, Essie?"

"Maybe. But I'm glad you're here so I don't have to be called Snow *all* the time. The sound of that name . . . I've always hated it."

"Even when your mother said it?" he prompted gently.

"She didn't. Not when we were alone. *Snow* is my father's vanity. My mother gave me a real name."

"I told you mine. Will you tell me yours?"

"Elurra."

Dane squeezed my hands before finally releasing them. "A Candaran name. So it had to be secret, just between the two of you."

I shook my head. "No, she found a way to make it real, right under my father's nose." Twisting to turn my back toward him, I pulled my sleeve down off my shoulder, revealing the royal mark. "Look carefully at the filigree surrounding the *S*. Do you see it?"

His fingers suddenly on my skin, lightly tracing around the tattoo, sent a very different shiver through me. I reminded myself to breathe.

"There it is," he said. "*Elurra.* Only if you know to look for it. How did she manage?"

I pulled the sleeve back into place. "She drew the design herself. She was an incredible artist, everything simple on the surface, with amazing complexity in the details."

"There's just one thing I don't understand. Why would your mother do it? Why would she agree to put her child through what you endured?"

"I don't know everything. I was so young when she died. The bad things didn't start until after she was gone, so I don't think it was anything she ever imagined. Still, I know why.... She would whisper it in my ear every night. 'Windsong needs you to give them better than they have.' It's what she believed in, making things better for people. A naive idealist, maybe."

"You miss her."

Those three words did the impossible, drawing tears to the surface. I would not cry, though. Not in front of Dane. Not in front of anyone.

"She was the only person who cared what happened to me."

Dane didn't say anything at first, just wrapped his arms around me. It was nothing like the holds I broke in training. Still strong, but the strength was more than physical. I leaned into his heat, like the sun I'd missed all those years on Thanda.

"She's not the only one, Essie," he whispered in my ear. "Not anymore."

20

NIGHTMARES INTERRUPTED my sleep nearly every hour. Always knives. Kip holding the knife, concluding I wasn't worth keeping alive after all. Tobias with a knife to my throat, slashing it before Dane could take the shot. Moray with a knife. Father and Olivia. Through my heart, in the back, it didn't matter—always enough to kill me.

When morning came and I met Dane in the main room, he held out a knife to me. I jumped back.

"In your boot, remember?"

I cursed my edginess. He'd offered the handle, not the blade, so what was I worried about?

"Are you okay?"

"Rough night," I muttered, slipping the knife into the side of my boot. "I doubt the day will be much better."

"One thing at a time. First, you have to survive breakfast."

"What about you?"

"Already ate."

Of course. To everyone else in the palace, Dane was an underling, nowhere near my level. If I ever forgot to act like I was above him, they'd send him away, or worse.

As if things aren't botched enough.

"Dimwit, stay here unless we call. Dane, you've got the transmitter, right?"

Dane held up his hand, showing the device strapped to his wrist. No one would notice a well-worn accessory on him like they would on me.

After enjoying one last moment of peace, I led the way to the breakfast room—not to be confused with the dining room, which in turn wasn't the same as the banquet hall. Father and Olivia were already seated inside, too many servants to count at the ready. Olivia took a calculated look at both Dane and me while Father's eyes flashed with another torrent of emotions before he smiled.

"And there's my Snowflake!" he said. "I worried I'd imagined it."

I smiled as genuinely as I could. "It *is* hard to believe I'm finally home, Father."

His expression softened, his eyes settling again. "You'll get used to it soon enough. It's where you belong."

True, but not for the reasons he thought.

A servant pulled out my chair, and I sat. Dane stood far enough behind me for decorum, but close enough to be there if anyone thought to come after me with a butter knife.

I'd forgotten how much I hated royal meals. Servants to pour my juice, offer my napkin, add salt to my eggs . . . I wanted to slap them all and tell them to find something better to do. When I was little and Father was away, Mother would arrange picnics

instead. Sometimes in the garden, or sometimes in her chambers where we'd build tents out of blankets. My favorite was when I'd eat strawberries and she didn't mind if I made a mess.

Remembering kept me from lashing out at the servants. They didn't have a choice.

I itched for my scanner, wondering what the chances were that Olivia had poisoned the food. No, she wouldn't do anything where my father could see. Even when she'd ordered Kip to kill me, she waited until Father was away inducting a new governor in Greenside Province. She would never risk his finding out she'd acted against him. My toast should be safe.

"There is much to do," Father said as the plates were taken away. "The whole kingdom will want to meet their princess at last, but we mustn't send you out looking so common. Olivia?"

"Yes, Snow has a full schedule today, first and foremost with the tailors. Something for your guard, as well."

Hours with the royal tailors, poking me with pins and fussing over lengths of gaudy fabric.

Why doesn't she just kill me and get it over with?

Dane did not like being separated from me, but he had to be fitted with a uniform. Other than the pin-poking, I knew the tailors wouldn't hurt anyone, so I gave him a look that said not to argue. He remembered his "place" and relented, but he whispered one word as he passed me.

"Practice."

Just when I thought maybe he'd forgotten. I didn't want to, but I knew why he suggested it then. Fittings meant lots of time I was expected to stand still, so if I couldn't keep half my attention in place, no one would notice. It was also one time I could expect people to touch me. Made perfect sense, but made me look forward to the rest of the morning less than I already had been.

It wasn't as bad as I'd feared, but close. The tailors had a full studio within the palace. They swarmed immediately, inspecting me like a freshly manufactured shuttle component.

"This figure! We can work with this."

"The hair and complexion, though. We must bring in color."

"Colors that will bring out her eyes!"

"Oh, dear, this unfortunate scar," one of the tailors said, grabbing my wrist. "We'll have to draw attention from it until the doctors can see to it."

I yanked my hand back. The doctors could remove all the scars I'd gotten from fights—I didn't care—but they couldn't touch the one on my wrist. Not the one from Cusser.

The tailors were too busy with their plans to notice my disapproval. They measured me, put me in outfit after outfit, and poked me as expected. It didn't take long for them to notice an unfashionable accessory—the knife in my boot.

"I was taken once," I said. "I won't be taken so easily again. You'll need to find a place for that in whatever you dress me in."

They accepted it in stride, as I'd expected. I was certain Olivia kept a number of small weapons hidden on her person, and the uniforms for all the royal guards included hidden sheaths and pockets.

The tailors moved quickly, flitting from one task to the next, so it was difficult to find an opportunity to Transition. Finally, one stopped to hold my arm out perfectly horizontal while another experimented with a draping sleeve. I focused on the contact of her hand on my elbow and looked for the pull, straining to find it as I hadn't had to with Laisa. At the same time, I tried to do what Dane said and stay grounded in myself. Without being sure what that meant, I imagined heavy weights in my shoes, holding me down, but still the pull came.

I straighten the princess's arm—it dipped slightly, and if Celia can't get this sleeve perfect, she'll go on about it for days. At least the princess doesn't give orders like the queen. My head is throbbing already.

But I still feel my own body, the ache in my arm from being held up for so long. It's like a phantom ache, coming from outside this tailor. Maybe if I try moving—

The tailor released my arm, snapping me back to myself, and I stumbled.

Every tailor was immediately at my side with "Oh, Your Highness, are you all right?" and "Would you like to sit down?"

"No, I'm fine," I insisted. "Just still getting used to all this. Please, continue."

The Transition hadn't been perfect, but it was something. I tried not to show the fatigue it left behind.

With all the fussing, I did get one pleasant surprise. The clothes didn't include as many gowns as I'd feared. Just a few, especially one for the upcoming ball, but otherwise I'd be allowed to wear pants. As each garment was fitted and pinned, one of the women helped remove it and fed it through the automated tailoring system.

I stitched machines, and here was a machine that actually stitched.

My sudden laughter didn't make sense to the tailors, but I didn't care.

The speed of the machine impressed me, a basic garment with pins and marks going in one end, a finished item with trims and details coming out minutes later. I still preferred my version of stitching, though. Making up code as I went, even if it meant a few mistakes along the way.

My father held to such strange parts of the past, archaic traditions and ceremonies, leaving others behind in favor of technology. All part of an elaborate show to distract the populace and maintain control. All part of the man I'd never managed to understand.

"What are you doing here?" one of the tailors burst out. "You can't—Oh, my apologies, sir."

The commotion started when I was behind the changing screen, so I peeked over the top. It seemed Dane had finished with the uniform fitting and wouldn't leave me unprotected a moment longer.

As much as I hated the princess-and-her-guard act we had to follow, the black uniform suited him. Sharply cut to make him look even taller, with silver trim matching the emblem of the Silver Dagger—the princess's guard—over his heart. I glanced down and spotted a knife tucked into each boot, and I suspected another was concealed in his belt buckle.

Not one Thandan miner had ever looked like *that*. Staring at him suddenly seemed like the best way to spend the afternoon.

"Are you almost finished with the princess?" he asked. "She has an appointment in an hour."

The chief tailor sighed. "I suppose we have enough for a start. What is her appointment?"

"A reception with the territorial governors."

"And what have you got there, Garrick?"

I'd been too busy staring at Dane in his new uniform to notice the footman standing with him. He held two flat cases, each no larger than his hand.

"His Majesty sent me with these for the princess," Garrick said, opening the boxes. Each held a necklace. "This is a gift from Queen Olivia, and I believe the locket belonged to the late Queen Alaina."

I hardly glanced at Olivia's gift—a ruby-studded pendant in the shape of an apple I remembered her wearing a few times. My eyes were only for my mother's silver locket. She'd worn it every day, and I knew what I'd find inside. Images of my grandparents. Only now I knew they probably weren't even my *real* grandparents—just part of the false history provided by the Candaran council.

When the chief tailor asked which I'd like to wear to meet the governors, I didn't hesitate. "The locket, please."

"Very good. Antiques are quite the fashion right now. Let's see. . . . Ah! The green dress."

No fewer than three of the tailors wrangled me into the dress, pulling the bindings so tight, I had to assure Dane they weren't torturing me. Not in a way that required his intervention, anyway. At least they hadn't forgotten my stipulation—a sheath for my knife was strapped to my leg—and they fastened the locket around my neck.

A problem presented itself immediately: I'd never worn heeled shoes in my life. They seemed the most inane, inefficient type of footwear ever devised. After standing in them for the past few hours so the tailors could get the dress lengths right, I could balance pretty well...as long as I didn't move. Walking demanded a lot more concentration. Not easy when the Transition earlier had taken half my strength.

When they finished binding me in and fussing with my hair, I half tiptoed out from behind the screen. Everything felt wrong—my arms and neck too bare, my legs confused by the folds of fabric draping and swishing around them. I looked to Dane, ready to roll my eyes, and saw him slip. For a second, he wasn't the young guard devoted to duty. He looked at me like the Candaran boy who'd said seven confounding words: *I think I'm in love with you.*

If I blushed, there'd be no hiding it, so I walked to the door as quickly as the ridiculous shoes would let me, knowing he would follow.

"Don't do that," I whispered once we were alone.

"Do what?"

"Look at me like that. Someone will notice."

He laughed—quietly at least, but I still glared at him.

"No one looks at me when you're in the room, Princess."

"Stop talking that way!"

"Why?"

I didn't get a chance to explain, because my ankle finally rebelled, toppling me sideways. He caught me by the arm—his warm hand on my skin—and held on as I regained my balance. His touch was both gentle and strong...and too tempting when someone could see us any minute.

I jerked away. "I only have an hour to learn to walk in these things. Let me concentrate."

His tone, unlike his hand, was cold. "Of course, Your Highness."

Territorial governors. Men and women who'd gotten a taste of power and more than a taste of wealth by enforcing my father's rule throughout Windsong. Sycophants and cowards when it came down to it.

No one I wanted to spend an afternoon with, but they were very excited to see me.

"Princess Snow, wonderful to finally meet you."

"We're so relieved you've returned unharmed."

"And such a beauty, like your mother."

I battled to keep my composure, especially at the mention of my mother. Each governor greeted me with a traditional kiss of my fingertips. It made me want to scrub my hands. The well-greased words they offered me and each other made me want to scrub everything else.

I missed the simple dust and grime of Thanda.

Once they finished greeting me, the governors chatted idly about life in their territories as we waited for my father to arrive. The weather, the state of agri-tech . . . the resistance of some citizens when they learned they'd been recruited into the war effort. When I picked that up, I edged closer to the governor who'd said it, trying to eavesdrop more.

"I understand it's a daunting thing," the man said. "But I tell them, would they rather be with the king's army on the far side of the system? Cut off from their homes in the miserable wastes of Candara, the ground shaking beneath them every other day and fighting for their very sanity against the worst of the enemy? That's generally enough to give them some perspective."

I glanced at Dane, who shook his head minutely. This talk of troops fighting on Candara was news to him, too.

"Indeed," said a woman. "The militia's efforts have kept the war to the outlands. Can you imagine if those hideous people breached the territories?"

Hideous people, meaning Exiles. Did the governors really think Candarans were involved in the outland battles? As the upper echelon of planetary leaders, I'd thought they would know the truth. I kept my expression blank, giving nothing away.

"Snow, this dress is lovely. The tailors did excellent work."

A blank expression wouldn't do for Olivia, so I forced a smile instead as I turned to greet her. "They did. Thank you for instructing them so well. I wouldn't have known where to start."

Her eyes darted down briefly. "And your mother's necklace suits you. Though I admit, I'd hoped to see you wearing mine."

I scrambled for an excuse. "That one's such a special piece, I thought I'd save it for the ball."

She returned my smile. It looked as genuine as mine felt. "I look forward to it. If you'll excuse me, I have some business to attend to."

Once she walked away, I hunted for another conversation that might reveal something, particularly mention of the Candaran prisoners. I wasn't supposed to know about them, so I couldn't ask. But no one wanted to talk to me about anything other than how I looked or how happy they were I was alive.

After several minutes, a set of doors opened, and everyone turned to bow as my father entered the room. I felt Dane move closer to me.

"Governors!" Father said. "So happy you could join us in welcoming my daughter safely home after all these years. At last, the realm of the Supreme Crown has its heir, so I may rest easier knowing the kingdom will be led long after my days."

"May your days be long indeed, Sire," said one of the governors.

Father started to cross the room toward me. I braced myself to maintain the most difficult part of the act, but he was stopped by his aide, Margaret, less than halfway. She whispered to him for a long moment, and his expression darkened.

"My friends, I have terrible news. The Exiles have launched a strike on the Third Regiment, advancing at least twenty links. Catastrophic losses to the Third."

The governors erupted, heaping abuse on the Exiles, swearing vengeance would be brought tenfold. I had no question anymore. These men and women thoroughly believed war raged between Candarans and the militia of Windsong, at least in the outlands, and possibly they believed the king's army fought on Candara. They'd been as duped as the public. I couldn't blame them. Father lied so well, even *I* almost believed him.

I risked a glance at Dane. Whatever he felt, he didn't let it show, but I knew he was thinking the same thing I was. If we could prove to the governors how my father had lied to them for years, the first layer of his control would collapse.

To do that, we needed evidence. We had a lot of work to do.

21

AFTER MEETING WITH the governors, Father asked me to join him for a round of Taktik. I remembered what Dane had said about not being alone with him, but it turned out not to be a problem. Both Dane and Father's personal guard from the Golden Sword stationed themselves at the edge of the study—ostensibly to protect us from any external threats.

Childhood memories rushed into my mind as Father set things up. He would lay the board out on a table, the antique wooden pieces looking so fragile, I couldn't believe they represented a hundred troops at a time. He'd begun teaching me just before Mother died. I remembered the hours of play, never daring to tell him I was bored. The way his eyes gleamed when he decimated another of my armies. The way he mocked me when I suggested treaties or asked why our armies were fighting in the first place.

I wouldn't make those mistakes again.

"Let's see how rusty your skills are, shall we, Snow?"

"I'll try not to disappoint you," I replied.

His opening move signaled a bold attack, but I knew better. I feigned a defensive strategy that maneuvered my troops exactly where he *thought* he wanted them, then cut in with an early offensive.

After an hour of play, I had the advantage, and he knew it. Rather than fume, he laughed.

"Not afraid of sacrifice anymore, are you? Years away, and you're still your father's daughter."

Was I? A shiver charged through me. They were just wooden pawns. I didn't think of them as real.

Then I saw the warm pride in his eyes. I remembered that, too, how a part of me had always craved it. How I glowed when he said I'd done well. He may have been right. Kip and Dane and even Laisa said they saw my mother in me; I'd always feared my father was my stronger reflection.

Talk about something else, Essie.

"I've always wondered, Father. Why does the Taktik board use a fictional map instead of one of Windsong or Candara? Wouldn't using a real world be better practice for commanding armies?"

"Very astute, Snowflake. But this isn't fictional. It's based on maps of the world our ancestors came from a thousand years ago. We use it because it's good to remember the past, where we came from."

Some details must have gotten botched over the generations. One of the continents had a peninsula that looked impossibly similar to the heeled boots the tailors had made me try on.

Father remained silent for a moment as he fussed with one of the pawns. "In the past, I know I wasn't perfect," he said, his voice too low to carry to Dane and the guard.

I didn't know what he meant. I could barely hear him above my heart pulsing a panicked heat through my body. An imperfect ruler? An imperfect father? An imperfect human being? I didn't want to talk about any of it. Forcing my demeanor into light neutrality took every ounce of my nerves.

"No one's perfect," I said. "We all do the best we can."

His eyes flashed momentarily before he relaxed. "Yes, of course we do. But our family must hold to the highest standard. You have some catching up to do," he continued. "Things to learn, to prepare you to lead this world someday. All the years you've been missing, I was so afraid. I didn't know what would happen when I'm gone. I couldn't entrust the throne to anyone else."

My instincts told me he meant it, and the facts supported that—in eight years, he'd never named another successor. "You'll be around for a long while yet."

"I hope so. And I know the people will realize how lucky they are to have you for their future queen. You'll see at the ball—many things will change."

Father and the Candarans wanted the exact same thing, but on a very different timetable. I said nothing, just smiled and wiped out the army occupying the boot-shaped peninsula.

<hr />

The days leading up to the ball made me wish I'd taken Dane up on his offer to return me to Mining Settlement Forty-Two. I met more dignitaries than I could ever possibly remember. I'd never realized so many "important" people lived on all of Windsong. Of course, as a child, I'd spent most of my time tucked away in private areas of the palace, not yet beginning any official work as princess.

When I wasn't busy with the chancellor of this or the magistrate of that, Dane and I gently cracked into the Windsong computer networks. It was tricky work, covering our tracks, and that limited how deep we could dig. Our first check was for information about the Candaran prisoners, but there was nothing, which had to frustrate Dane. Next we researched each governor, looking for a weak point, one who might be more open to listening to us. No luck there. All the governors were either wholehearted supporters of my father or very careful to never leave any clue that they weren't.

We looked into the war, too. Not much to find there, either, but we found some brief recordings of battles supposedly taking place on Candara. Dane said the landscape was too generic to identify, but it easily could've been staged on Windsong. We just had no way to prove it.

So I kept meeting dignitaries and prepared for the ball.

I had no choice but to get used to the heels. The tailors had sent at least fifteen different pairs of shoes to my room. Some were dainty—with heels. Some were opulent—with heels. Even most of the boots had heels. I managed to walk without tripping anymore, but my feet felt like the drones had mistaken them for a chunk of merinium they needed to chisel off the wall.

"Are you sure you don't want me to call one of the tailors?" Dane asked from outside my room.

"Yes, I am sure," I replied. It came out as more of a grunt

as I struggled with my ball gown. "I've put up with the Royal Hairdresser and the Royal Blazing-Makeup-Fusser today, and I will dress *myself*, thank you."

"Essie, you need to act the part."

"I know! Why do you think I'm getting it out of my system *now*?"

I could have sworn I heard him laugh. "Let me have it, then."

"Argh. I know it's part of the act, but it's so pointless. We should be digging deeper in the computers. There have to be more secure networks we haven't found. I have codes that can get us around some of the lockouts."

"You never know what you'll hear at a royal ball. Think of it that way. Hey, Dimwit, where've you been?"

"Dimwit bumble Dimwit."

I froze. Dimwit had been working on a special task, but its voice was supposed to be off.

"Did you turn its voice on, Dane?" I asked.

"Yeah, when he came in. He's setting up to recharge now."

I relaxed and returned to my battle against ballroom fashion. Finally, I got everything in place . . . mostly. There was no way I could contort myself enough to tie the last ribbon at the back of the gown. I opened the door and went out into the main room.

"Don't gawp at me like that again, Dane. This is how they have me looking all the time—you should be used to it." True, the sapphire-blue ball gown with its silver embroidery and diamond accents was extravagant even by the royal tailors' standards, but still. I turned my back toward him. "Can you get that last one for me, please?"

His fingers brushed my skin as he worked the tie. I bit my lip to restrain my instinctive shiver. "Got it."

I turned around. "How much did I botch my hair in that little wrestling match?"

He carefully adjusted the delicate silver circlet on my head. My hair was wound around and through it so tight, dislodging it was probably impossible. At least I'd talked Father into letting me wear it rather than a more formal crown.

"You didn't," Dane said. "You look perfect. For the record, though, I liked how you looked on Thanda just fine."

His sincerity set off a blossom of warmth in my chest. But the more he talked like that when we were alone, the harder it was for me to act like he was two sniffs from nothing once we left the suite, so I shrugged it off.

"Of course. Grimy and bruised and bleeding. What's not to like? Oh, wait, the necklace!" I'd promised Olivia I'd wear her gift to the ball, so I was stuck with it. Once I retrieved the ruby pendant from its case, Dane helped fasten it around my neck, and I was finally ready.

Without further comment, he opened the door, checked the hall, and let me through. We walked in silence until we heard the music faintly filtering from the ballroom.

"I should have asked earlier," he said quietly. "Do you know how to dance?"

"Unfortunately. Olivia made me take lessons as a child. I'll step on a few toes, but I'll try to be charming about it."

As we approached the private entrance to the ballroom, Father waited outside. He smiled when he saw me. Dane's steady breaths suddenly shortened.

"Ah, Snowflake!" Father greeted me, taking my hands in his. "Beautiful as can be. Ready for your grand entrance?"

Never will be in a million lifetimes. Aloud, I said, "Yes, Father."

He kept one hand and gestured for the attendant to open the door. Another attendant inside rapped a golden staff loudly on the floor.

"Matthias, Supreme Crown of the Realm, and Her Highness, Princess Snow."

We walked through the door, and my eyes instantly hurt. I'd never seen so much color and glitter in one place in my life. Girls in gowns nearly as extravagant as mine, some with hair altered to garishly coordinating colors, and men in what looked to be right cumbersome suits all crowded the floor at the bottom of a wide staircase. I could hardly find anywhere in the room itself that wasn't touched with gold or silver, from the elaborate columns to the musicians' stage to the chandeliers. Raised platforms held contortionists, and acrobats climbed and leaped from one to another.

Every eye was on me.

Do not trip, Essie.

As I held Father's hand and carefully made my way down the stairs, I glimpsed the glint of light off lenses in the crowd. Image recorders. Thanks to all the dignitaries I'd met, everyone on Windsong already knew about my return. Now they would all see me as well. Olivia's opportunities to quietly dispose of me were long past. She'd have to be cleverer.

Unfortunately, she was likely as clever as I was.

Once at the bottom of the stairs, an aide introduced me to Somebody, son of One-Aristocrat-or-Another, who bowed, took my hand, and swept me onto the dance floor.

I'd known it was coming, but I hadn't realized how much it would twitch me out to have a stranger touching me, his hand on my back. I couldn't show it. I had to smile. When I inevitably stepped on his toes, he insisted it was his fault.

Well, naturally. I'd spent the last few years debugging sub-routines and breaking ribs. Of *course* my poor dancing skills were his fault.

The rest of the evening was the same. One dance after another with sons and grandsons of everyone I'd met over the past several days. All of them my age or a bit older. All of them much too interested. *Blazes, is Father trying to marry me off?*

These boys didn't look at me anything like Dane did. With Dane, I knew he *saw* me. The looks from the Windsong boys made me want to bring Petey in from Thanda to rig a spur, right there in the ballroom.

I figured with the excuse of prolonged contact, Dane would want me to practice Transitioning. I tried it once—leading to another set of bruised toes—but the head I found myself in was too self-absorbed to bear, and my dance partner threatened to fetch a doctor.

No more practice in a crowded, overheated ballroom, Essie, or you'll pass out.

Once in a while, I caught sight of Dane at the edge of the crowd. Close enough to keep an eye on me, but far enough to escape notice. I indulged myself several times, imagining I was dancing with him instead. His hand on my back, mine on his shoulder, losing myself in the warmth of his eyes. The fantasy curbed the temptation to dismantle my actual dance partners and was a much more pleasant way to spend the evening.

Another pair of eyes caught my attention more than once. Olivia didn't just watch me—she glared. The kingdom knew she was always a bit stern, so no one was likely to notice, but I saw the words behind her expression. *You're unwanted. You're in the way.*

"Princess, is something wrong with your guard?"

I started, looking up at my dance partner. Aston? Alastair? One of the governors' sons. Unnaturally dark hair slicked back, and entirely too pleased with himself. He resembled his father that way. I followed his gaze to Dane and saw what I'd missed before. Dane's stoic expression was almost perfect, but a shadow of something slipped through.

I wasn't the only one who wanted to dismantle my dance partners.

A cold spike drove through me. Olivia's chances of killing me were still very high. She was sharp enough to pull it off. And if she recognized what I'd just seen, she'd make sure to kill Dane, too. I couldn't let that happen.

Enough people had died because of me.

"Princess?"

"Sorry," I finally said. "No, my guard is fine. He's just new to palace life."

"Ah. If I may say, your thoughts seemed as far away as the Thandan mines just now." Before I could rig an acceptable response, he continued. "Yes, my father told me the tale of your recent years. Trapped on Thanda with those bizarre Ascetics."

"They were kind to me. It wasn't bad."

"Of course they were. How could anyone be unkind to someone like you?"

Oh, people found ways. "If you say so," I said with a polite smile.

"It must be such a relief to be back home where you belong. Back among the right type of people."

My hand itched to form a fist. What did this overwrought

excuse of aesthetic waste know about the "right type" of people? Petey was the right type. So was Kip. Even Brand on Garam.

Laisa—an Exile—was the right type of person.

The boy made a move, the slightest increase in pressure on my back, pulling me a sniff closer. Another one like that and I'd break his windpipe.

Out of nowhere, Dane stood at his shoulder, muttering something in his ear. Aston, Alastair, whatever his name was, shifted his gaze across the ballroom. I couldn't follow without being too obvious, so I tried to read Dane's expression. It had returned to stone, as a personal guard's should be.

The pressure on my back eased, and the boy's smile looked much more forced. "A pleasure to meet you, Princess. Until next time."

He kissed my hand as the music ended and walked away, leaving Dane to escort me from the dance floor. I didn't say anything, just raised a questioning eyebrow at him.

"His Highness seemed to disapprove of something," he muttered, barely loud enough for me to hear.

I looked around and found my father. Everything seemed fine now, and he smiled at me. Whatever disapproval he'd shown didn't make me feel better, but it had kept me from losing control and causing a scene. I couldn't thank Dane in front of everyone, so I hoped he caught it in my eyes.

Before another dance could be arranged, a crash and shout erupted at the public entrance. Dane stepped between me and the commotion, keeping me behind him. He'd certainly gotten the bodyguard routine down quickly. I peered over his shoulder to see what was going on.

Someone barreled into the ballroom with a pair of guards chasing after him. The guests made no attempt to help, just dove out of the way, a few girls screaming. The intruder made it to the center of the room before the guards caught up. A desperate voice broke over all the other noise.

"Please! No, please! The queen is my last hope!"

Olivia stood on a dais with Father, so she was easy to spot as she stepped down.

"Guards, wait."

I laid a hand on Dane's back and whispered in his ear. "Move closer."

His muscles tensed and flexed under my hand, but he did as I said, edging toward the disturbance. Most of the other guests were torn between morbid curiosity and their desire to get far away from anyone with such bad manners. We easily got to a place where I could see what was happening.

A man knelt on the floor, cradling a small child. The man was thin, his face drawn and gray; the child looked the same, but worse. Her clothes hung loosely from her rail-like frame, and even from a distance I could see what hard work it was just for her to breathe.

Olivia stood with a large space between her and the pair, and the crowd made a circle around them. "What's happened, citizen?"

"We live in Goodland Province, on the outland border. A plague has struck us. The doctors can't do anything; they say it may be a weapon released by the Exiles." Dane tensed again but didn't move as the man continued. "My Lucia was the first to fall ill, and she's grown so weak. Please, Your Grace, we traveled nonstop to reach you. This may be beyond all understanding, but I can only hope it is not beyond you, for my daughter's sake."

"Come closer, and I'll do what I can."

The man crawled forward on his knees until he could lay his daughter at the queen's feet. Olivia slowly raised her arms in front of her.

Then everything came unhinged.

The lights flickered and dimmed. Something shuddered through the air, rattling the chandeliers—low-frequency sound, felt more than heard, I imagined. It left behind a persistent buzz in my ears. Olivia made elaborate gestures, seeming to gather something from the air. My eyes had to be malfunctioning, because a sort of aura appeared around her.

Hologram. That's why she made him come to her. The projectors are set for that spot.

Doors slammed at the front of the ballroom, and everyone shouted and turned. Everyone except Dane and me. A wave of dizziness rushed over me—that Transition attempt earlier had been a bad idea—but I kept my eyes locked on Olivia, every movement, every detail.

When the doors slammed, Olivia twisted one of the enormous rings she wore. Then she very distinctly waved that hand in the direction of the man and his child. The ring had to contain an airborne antidote, probably with some kind of pressurized release mechanism. Very clever.

As the lights steadied and the rattling faded, Olivia dramatically collapsed into Father's waiting arms.

I shifted my gaze to the girl. Hard to tell, but it looked like she breathed a bit easier.

Cheers erupted among the guests, praising the power of Queen Olivia and cursing the Exile scum, until Father gestured for silence.

"Take this man and his daughter to the hospital," he said to his aides. "Keep us updated on their condition. My friends, I regret to cut our festivities short, but the queen and I must travel to Goodland Province immediately to remedy this evil."

The dismissal sparked excited whispers as the crowd drifted toward the public doors, marveling at what they'd just witnessed. They were too busy prattling to see Father and Olivia exchange a knowing glance. Dane steered me in the opposite direction, to one of the private exits that would get us more directly to the residential wing. My feet felt disconnected from my body, and the buzzing remained in my ears.

"Quite a show the queen put on," Dane said once we were in our rooms. "Are you okay?"

I was pacing to keep myself from tearing my gown to shreds, just for the sake of destroying something. The buzzing had moved to my hands as well, like I could feel sound through them. "No, I'm not okay. Did you see that little girl? One more day with that poison inside her and she might have died."

"I don't mean that. I mean you. Are you feeling all right?"

"What?" Everything blurred at the edges, including my wits. One little Transition shouldn't have worn me that much. I pushed through it. "I'm fine, I just—I need to think. We need to *do* something."

Dane moved to stop my pacing, but I just changed my route to check the room's temperature controls. They had to be botched, because it was much warmer than they indicated.

"We *will* do something. Can you just slow down?"

His words clicked together in my head. It made sense. "That's the problem! We're going too slow." I raised my skirt enough to pull the knife strapped to my leg. "We should kill them both now, before they leave for Goodland."

Pieces of the blurry world snapped back into focus—too much focus and not enough, if such a thing were possible—as Dane intercepted me. Except it wasn't Dane. It was someone else. I couldn't see past the cruel edges of his face.

An intruder...a spy.

I tried to back away, but the man grabbed my wrist and squeezed a pressure point. The bolt of pain forced me to drop the knife.

Instinct took over. I swung my free hand at him, but he caught it easily.

"What did you do to Dane? Let me go!"

He didn't. He spoke in a guttural language I couldn't understand.

Something locked around my knees, immobilizing me before I could give the intruder's shins a sharp kick. The man's gaze shifted several sniffs below my eyes, giving me another reason to glare. He released my hands and reached around my neck.

"Don't touch me!" I tried to shove him back, but my arms had turned to sludge sometime in the last ten seconds. When my strength failed me, I went to my final weapon, unleashing obscenities like I hadn't since Dane first kidnapped me.

The man made no response other than a tightening of his jaw. Then he closed a fist on the apple pendant I wore and yanked so hard, I thought my neck would break before the chain did.

More words failed to make sense as the man disappeared into the blur surrounding me. Then a familiar electronic voice mimicked the words.

That explained what was holding my knees.

"Dimwit, you useless blazing scrap-heap! Is there anyone you *won't* let reprogram you?" The buzzing in my ears got so loud, I could barely hear myself.

The man returned with an injector in his hand.

I struggled so hard, I overbalanced Dimwit. My knee, hip, and elbow slammed against the floor. The intruder stood over me, blocking the light.

A shadow standing over me, the shadow that makes my heart stop . . . I couldn't breathe. My cheeks were wet. I didn't want to die. When he knelt by me, I lashed out again, hitting and scratching and doing anything I could to make him back off.

"I won't let you!" I screamed.

Never trust Olivia.

Mother's voice. It made no sense. I didn't trust Olivia, but that hadn't stopped her guard from lying in wait to assassinate me.

Find the truth.

"Essie, please! It was the necklace."

That broke through. The necklace. Olivia's gift.

She'd poisoned me.

22

EVERY INSTINCT SAID TO FIGHT, but the tiny corner of my mind that whispered "poison" forced the rest back long enough for the injector to touch my neck.

Then fire. The buzzing throughout my body turned into a jittering flame in every vein, every pore. I might have screamed. I might have died. Then just as quickly as the fire had come, it was gone. Left in its place was a vague feeling that I might be sick.

"Essie, I'm sorry. Dimwit, move, let's get her up."

It was Dane. It always had been Dane, not some shadowy Midnight Blade assassin. I couldn't help holding tight as he moved me to a chair, reassuring myself that he was solid and real. Once my head cleared, though, I glared at the injector on the floor.

"What was that supposed to do, kill me before the poison did?"

His hand rested on my knee. Definitely real. "No, that poison wouldn't have killed you. It just makes you behave erratically. The antitoxin is uncomfortable, but it works fast."

Uncomfortable didn't begin to describe it, but I latched on to the more important information. "How did you know? Olivia has her poisons concocted in the labs, and you didn't even know about them until I told you."

"She didn't concoct this one. Kip told me about it. It's old. Extract of the river lily. Back around the War of Exile, your ancestors used it on people to make them think they'd been controlled by Candarans."

The War of Exile. What we called the Liberation on Windsong. I touched my neck, feeling the emerging bruise left by the necklace. "Why wouldn't Olivia use a deadly poison, then?"

Dane heaved a tense sigh. "If I had to guess, I'd say she wanted the strange behavior to discredit you, making it easier to kill you without making your father suspicious."

"Lovely. Can't wait to see what she comes up with next."

"You should rest. Do you need help getting to bed?"

I pushed myself to my feet. A little wobbly, but kicking off my shoes helped with that. "No, I can manage. Dimwit, come here." I flipped the switch to deactivate the drone's voice. "Get back to work, you."

"Back to work with what?" Dane asked.

"What do you mean, what? The plan."

"What does Dimwit have to do with the plan?"

My head was still foggy from the clash of poison and antitoxin, but I could've sworn I'd told him. Maybe I'd forgotten. Thinking about it made my head hurt, and I groaned. "Tell you later, when I don't feel like I've been wrestling a harri-harra."

"All right. And Essie?" he called after me. "No more gifts from Olivia."

"Agreed."

Olivia and Father were away in Goodland Province for several days. Reports came through the networks that the queen's presence alone had eased the plague, and all the victims were recovering. After they finished, they set about inspecting the outland border defenses.

Their absence put Dane and me at a standstill, even after two days of post-poison recovery. Father had left instructions for me to keep busy approving plans to renovate the royal quarters to replace the current suite and other such drudgery. Dane was supposed to review applications for additional guards in the Silver Dagger. We had better things to do, but we were too far from the Candaran fleet to make our move on high-security areas of the palace, we hadn't made any inroads with the governors, and we'd confirmed we couldn't get any useful information from the main computer networks.

I needed to move, to do something. Olivia had proved she wasn't wasting time, so I couldn't afford to, either. Otherwise, she'd kill me before I could make a difference.

"We have to get out of here," I said on the thirteenth day. Looking at the floor plans from the royal architect gave me a royal headache. "If we want evidence, we're going to have to go out and find it. Talk to people or something."

"I know. But we need your father's permission to go anywhere, and he won't be back for three more days."

"Maybe once he's back, I can get him to tell me the truth himself. I've been playing along. If he thinks I'm going to follow his example, maybe he'll tell me how things really work around here."

"Maybe." It wasn't hard to see how much Dane *didn't* like any idea that meant more time in my father's company. "What we really need is a contingency plan."

"Contingency plan for what?"

"The queen."

I instinctively touched my mother's locket. I'd been wearing it every day since the ball, as soon as Dane and I verified it hadn't been tampered with. "Dimwit's on it."

"That secret project of his? You never did fill me in."

I sat next to where the drone stood fiddling with some fabric swatches I'd left out, and flipped the switch to turn its voice back on. "Dimwit, how's your bumbling going?"

"Dimwit bumble Dimwit."

"How are people reacting?"

"People smile yell people. Dimwit dumb-drones kick Dimwit."

It must have run into some of the cleaning drones. "Anyone try to stop you?"

The drone beeped three times. "Dimwit lost Dimwit people help."

I turned to Dane. "I've told it to bumble around the palace whenever we don't need it for anything else, get people used to seeing it as my unhinged-but-harmless pet."

His eyes turned suspicious. "Why?"

"So when it wanders into the queen's wardrobe, anyone who catches it will think it's just lost as usual."

"And what's he going to do in the queen's wardrobe?"

"Spray everything with thederol."

He sat in the chair opposite me. "Why? That'll wash off easily enough."

"Not from the metalwork on all her shoes and the accents on everything else. Thederol binds to metal. And I'll be carrying this." I pulled a pressurized cylinder from my pocket. "Do you know what happens when thederol is exposed to varitane gas?"

Dane's eyes widened. "Essie, if you're too close when it ignites—"

"That's why it's a last resort. Only if she gets me cornered and you're not around."

"And why didn't you tell me about this plan before?"

The sudden accusation in his voice startled me. "I meant to tell you—honestly, I thought I had, but I guess things got so busy with receptions and meetings, then everything that happened at the ball. What does it matter anyway? I'm telling you now."

"The one part of this that isn't an act is that my job is to protect you. I watched Tobias take you away. I couldn't stop him and I didn't know if I could get you back. But when I did, I swore I'd do everything I could to make sure no one else would hurt you."

The fire in his eyes was back. So was the knot in my chest. I ignored it. "You can't stop life from happening. Life is pain."

"Self-destructive ideas like that are exactly why I need to know everything."

Everything. The word was too big, sparking a fire of my own that reached too far into the dark corners. Dane had no business in those corners.

"Keeping secrets kept me alive."

"When the secret involves combustible chemicals, it can get you killed," he said.

"I didn't mean to keep it a secret! Besides, I know more about those chemicals than you do. The drones use them all the time in the mines."

"You know a thing or two about being reckless, too, don't you?"

I was on my feet without consciously deciding to stand. "Says the boy who *kidnapped me*."

Dane flinched but didn't back down. "Is that it? You still don't trust me?"

I did. I knew I did, but I was too annoyed to tell him so. "You haven't exactly made it easy to know what to believe."

He stood as well, which meant I had to look up. "I think you're just making excuses."

"Of course I am. That's what royals are best at." I scooped up the slate with the idiotic floor plans and stalked off to my room. "Turn Dimwit's voice off and send it back to its bumbling."

"Absolutely, Your Highness."

Your Highness. The cool metal of my mother's locket beneath my shirt seemed to pulse a mild rebuke, reminding me exactly how fake the implied superiority was.

The sooner we could get going with this coup, the better.

⊶▦⊷
⊶▨⊷

After days of twiddling my algorithms, Margaret-the-aide told me Father was back. The sharp edge between Dane and me had dulled enough that I was glad he insisted on coming along for my afternoon meeting. Arguing or not, I felt less jittery with him around.

"Snowflake!" Father greeted me when we entered the private chamber behind the throne room. "I'm sorry I've been so busy. These new developments in the war . . . The Exiles will never let me rest, it seems."

"I wanted to talk to you about that," I said. "I'd like to visit the outlands."

"Out of the question. It's too dangerous."

I'd expected that. "I don't mean the front lines, Father. There must be areas where the militia commanders make decisions, take care of the wounded, and all that. Maybe if I see it for myself, I can think of some way to help." When he opened his mouth to protest again, I cut him off. "I'm not *that* delicate. I did survive eight years on Thanda. Besides, military service is among my duties as princess-to-the-crown, isn't it?"

He hesitated, rapping his fingers on his desk. "It is. Are you certain that's what you want? You could stay here, arrange more social events."

"That's not the kind of princess I want to be. I want to be one that's of use to you and Windsong and the entire realm. Like you said, learn how to lead someday."

Another glimmer of pride lit his eyes. "Yes, you always liked to keep busy with something useful. And nothing can replace experience. When you return, we can discuss your thoughts."

"Return from where?" Olivia had slipped in through one of the secret doors again. I caught a half-second glare at my mother's locket and took a slow breath to keep my face impassive.

"Snow wishes to visit the outlands, see if she can be of some use."

Olivia's glare shifted to Dane. He stood too close, and suspicion lit in her eyes. I shot him a fierce glare of my own. Too fierce, maybe—I saw a flash of surprise before he took a half step back.

"Very dangerous in the outlands," Olivia said smoothly. "Is that wise? She's so young."

"When I was her age, I led a battalion in my father's defeat of the rebel movement on Garam. And she's strong. Yes, I think it will do her good. I'll make arrangements," he said. "You'll be able to leave this evening."

I called to mind the feeling of my first successful upgrade on Whirligig so my smile would be genuine. "Thank you, Father."

Olivia smiled as well. A very different smile. "Let's leave your father to coordinate that, Snow. Come walk with me in the garden."

Any excuse to refuse would look flimsy and weak, so I followed her out to the rose garden, Dane on my heels. Olivia's own guard from the Midnight Blade followed as well. Once we were on the footpath, decorum demanded the guards drop back out of earshot. I would bet all my Thandan shares that Dane's hand didn't move more than a sniff from his best throwing dagger.

"Snow, dear, are you sure this is what you want? The war has made the outlands an unpleasant place."

"I can handle it."

She looked sidelong at me. I tried to read her eyes, but all I got was the usual suspicion and distaste. "Can you? Thanda is one thing, and the Ascetics' home is hardly a war zone."

No, it wasn't. And I couldn't tell Olivia about the mining injuries I'd seen and the fights I'd been in, so I stayed silent.

"Do you know what Exiles are like?"

"I know a bit. And that's part of why I'm going, to understand the situation better." I decided to try a little dig. "The kingdom will be mine one day. I need to learn all I can before then."

"First you must prove you're fit to lead," she said sharply.

"I think I might surprise you."

"I think you're a lot like your mother."

"Thank you. Quite the compliment."

Olivia stepped a little closer. I focused on a bush of delicate tricolor roses to keep from tensing up. "Do you know the one thing that makes us vulnerable to the Exiles?" she asked. "Lack of conviction. And I think you'll find I don't suffer from that in the slightest. Without that to prey on, they're weak."

Any response I might've had caught on her last words. Was she saying she thought I *did* lack conviction? That I'd never be a proper queen because of it? Or was she hinting she'd known what my mother was?

And what I was?

Getting out of the palace for a while sounded better than ever.

The trip to the outlands meant no heels. That was a positive. The possibility of rooting out some evidence against my father was another. I tried to focus on those. Father insisted on a long route by hover transport to the other side of Windsong, saying both armies used far too much antiaircraft weaponry to risk me in a shuttle. He did let us use the fastest transport available—so it could have been worse—and sent one of his Golden Sword guards to pilot it.

When Dane and I arrived at the transport hub, the guard stood waiting at attention. Then he snapped a salute at me. I just stared until Dane subtly kicked my foot, reminding me to give the most regal nod I could muster.

"Your Highness," the guard said to me. "Sir," he added to Dane.

That got Dane to stare. I considered kicking *his* foot, but decided against it.

"You're the senior officer of the Silver Dagger," the guard explained. "That means you outrank me."

He had to be ten standard years older than either of us, but he didn't seem to mind being outranked. If anything, he seemed happy to be accompanying us.

"What's your name?" I asked as we climbed in.

"Theo, Your Highness."

"Well, Theo, call me Princess if you must, but hearing 'Your Highness' endlessly might unhinge me."

He smiled shyly, turning his attention to the predeparture checklist. "If you say so, Princess."

I didn't like hearing *Princess* that much more, but I could live with it.

We left before dusk, and the journey would take almost a full day. Because we were going to the other side of Windsong, though, it would only be the next morning. We stayed awake as long as we could, preparing for the time adjustment. Dane fell asleep first, convinced enough that Theo wouldn't try to kill me mid-journey, while I remained fixated on my slate.

The guard glanced over his shoulder before speaking up quietly. "If I may ask, Princess, what is that you've been working on?"

"Just a bit of programming. I fiddle with tech when I have the time."

"Nothing *but* time on this trip, I suppose. The sun will be back around to us soon, though, so at least you'll have something to look at besides the inside of this thing."

I looked at the comfortable seats and sleek control panels, with plenty of room to walk around. "It's not that bad. I'm not exactly used to palace opulence anymore."

"Yes, I heard. The Ascetics on Thanda, was it? Tragic that you were kept from your family, of course, but it does sound like you had an interesting time of it."

"That's one word for it."

Theo glanced back again and smiled. "Most things in life are a bit of good with the bad, aren't they? Just the same, I'm sure we're all glad you're back, and helping His Majesty like this, too."

This man wasn't what I'd expect of one of my father's guards. Friendly, open, even kind. Then again, Kip hadn't been what one would expect of Olivia's guards, either. But Kip had been my mother's guard first and had just put on an act for Olivia so he could stay on after Mother's death.

"Could I ask, Theo, why did you join the Golden Sword?"

"Oh, you don't want to hear a silly story like that one, Princess."

"Actually, I do. Unless it's too personal."

With just the light coming off the console, I could still see a slight blush. "I remember your mother, you see. Queen Alaina. She visited my school and talked about the citizens of Windsong, the things she felt we stood for...honesty, hard work, trust. The same things my parents always taught me. She had

such a presence, a way of making you believe things were possible if she said they were." He caught himself. "Forgive me,
Princess. It's not my place to speak of her."

"No, please, go on."

It took him a moment, but he continued. "That day she visited, I decided I wanted to join the Midnight Blade, to protect
her and fight for what she believed in. She died not long after
that, and I swear, you could see the whole planet grow darker
as we mourned her. Then with the betrayals of the Exiles...I
decided to join the Golden Sword instead, help your father bring
peace back to this world and to keep your mother's memory. So
that's why."

I wanted to say something kind or comforting, something to
let him know my mother would have been happy to have him
in her guard. The words refused to come.

Words like that didn't live inside me.

Instead, all I could identify was rage. This was a good man,
who believed in doing the right thing, and my father had him
completely duped. For several minutes, I considered telling him
the truth. Maybe Dane and I could use an ally.

Not yet. I'd just met him—not nearly enough time to trust
him with what we were doing. My first impressions could be
off...though they usually weren't. I'd known Petey wouldn't
wrong me almost as soon as I met him. I'd definitely been right
about Tobias.

And Dane...My impressions had changed several times
since I pulled him from the shuttle and thought he was terrifying. Maybe I'd managed to be both right *and* wrong on that one.

Theo would have to stay in the dark for a while yet. But if
we overthrew my father, the existing members of the Golden

Sword would have the option to serve the new leader. Men like Theo would serve well.

One more thing to do before I got myself killed: make sure Theo got the chance to fulfill the dream my mother inspired, improving the world rather than serving a tyrant.

Something touched the back of my hand, and I glanced down. Dane. I wondered how long he'd been awake. Given the way he looked at me in the dim light of the cabin, long enough to know I was thinking about my mother.

I turned my hand to let him take it in his, and a tightness clenched at my throat. For a few moments, I indulged in the thought that my whole universe was nothing more than Dane holding my hand.

That wasn't true, though. Theo could turn and notice. I pulled my hand back and curled up on my seat to get some sleep.

Not a good time to get emotional, Essie.

Plenty of time to cry when I'm dead.

23

TRAVELING THROUGH THE provinces of Windsong proved bittersweet. I'd nearly forgotten the beauty of my home planet. Maybe I hadn't wanted to remember. After years of Thanda's dim, dingy grays and bleak landscapes, the color and variety kept my eyes locked on the windows. Mountains, valleys, plains... Windsong had everything. We passed near the whistling canyons, though not close enough to hear the music the wind made through the stone formations.

Theo offered to detour and stop briefly. I told him my business in the war zone was too important, and suggested he put the transport on autopilot so he could get some sleep.

Hours more came and went, until even machine code and animated logic puzzles couldn't keep the deadening grip of boredom off my brain. Dane and I didn't dare say anything important while we could be overheard, and small talk only went so far with a princess and two guards, one of whom was the clandestine prince of the other's supposed mortal enemy.

Then I noticed the view changing, even in the dark. The lights were dimmer here. More sparse.

My bones chilled with the phantom memory of Thanda and the mining settlements. The lights were the same. Cheap and barely sufficient. Theo answered the question before I asked.

"We're crossing into the outlands, Princess. Sir, if you would keep an extra eye on the tactical scanners. We're steering well clear of the known Exile encampments, but I don't want any surprises just the same."

Exiles wouldn't be a problem, but Theo didn't know that, so we had to keep up the act. The silence in the transport over the last few hours of the journey was anything but boring. Dane resolutely watched his scanners and everything else he could see. I asked Theo for schematics of the transport so I could get familiar with its inner workings, in case we suffered damage in an attack that wouldn't happen.

All an act, yet I still managed to get most of the schematics memorized. It was something to do. No real Exiles hid in the outlands waiting to ambush us. The only enemy was my father's army of imposters. We weren't in any real danger.

As the sun peeked up again over a range of mountains, I saw just how real it was for everyone else.

Weapons. Big ones, and lots of them.

I didn't know much about weapons, not the way I knew about drones and computer codes. The palace had nothing more advanced than a blade, and Thanda's weapon of choice was a solid fist. The most I knew about guns was that I didn't like Tobias pointing one at me. The weapons here were levels beyond that. Devices that looked cannonlike sat at regular intervals around the settlement alongside towers bristling with antenna arrays.

Our destination lay in a wide valley that must have once been farmland. A cluster of buildings was nestled along the bank of a river. Most were prefabricated, bare and functional, like the shacks on Thanda, but a few buildings stood out as predating the "war." A farmhouse complete with expansive porch and old-fashioned shutters on the windows sat at the center. A few shacks away, a massive barn dwarfed the smaller structures around it, its green paint peeling and faded.

A light on Theo's console blinked and beeped twice. "That's just the perimeter guard acknowledging that we're friendly, Princess," he explained.

He piloted us smoothly between the cannons and towers, approaching the buildings. I spotted men in faded uniforms going from one to another, some giving orders, others taking them. One waved us toward the barn, with the door already opening to allow the transport inside.

"Here we are, Princess. Fort Saddlewood. I'm sure I don't need to tell you to keep your wits while we're here."

No, he didn't, but I appreciated the sentiment.

I checked that I had the gear I wanted—mostly a scanner and a slate—and exited the transport. Three soldiers stood waiting and immediately bowed.

"Princess Snow, I'm Larsen, fort captain," said the one in the center, a man old enough to have hair peppered with gray, but young enough to handle himself in a Thandan bar. "It's an honor to receive your visit."

Try to look regal, Essie. "No, it's my honor, Captain."

"The message from Command didn't say much, Your Highness. Is there anything particular you want to see?"

"Only everything. The whole operation and anything you can tell me about it. I'm here to find a way to make some real progress in this war, see if we can end it before our grandchildren are in your position."

It sounded like a good line, at least in my head. The captain must have thought so, too, because he snapped to attention. "Yes, ma'am—er, Your Highness. My apologies."

"Ma'am is fine." *Anything's better than my not-so-"Highness."*

We began the tour with the captain's command post, Dane and Theo keeping in step behind me. A wall-size screen displayed a map of the outlands, with certain areas glowing red. Areas controlled by the pseudo-Exiles. Too many of them, and too large. Green icons indicated militia bases like Saddlewood, and smaller blue icons represented troop encampments.

One look and I knew what the next move should be from either side. It was just like a game of Taktik. I could see the pawns, see the strategies. It was still all a game to my father, but even knowing it was fake, a piece of the picture didn't make sense. It was a piece too obvious for the militia to miss.

"Captain, what do you think the Exiles' goal is? They push deeper into the outlands when they could put pressure on the provinces here and here."

"I don't claim to understand them. Maybe they want a strong foothold here before braving the tighter defenses at the border. Or maybe they think the prisoners are being held somewhere out here. Though if they were, I can't believe they wouldn't have found them in eight years now."

Finally! "Prisoners?" I prompted.

Larsen shifted uncomfortably but didn't avoid the question.

"Ah, didn't realize you didn't know, ma'am. When you were taken, the Exiles in the Royal City launched the first strike. Most were captured."

I nodded in what I hoped was a thoughtful way. Inside, I was ready to turn around and make the day-long journey back to the palace with the excuse I needed to ask about the prisoners. Dane had to feel the same way, far more than I did. We still needed to finish the tour, though. Hopefully we'd get more information, making the delay worthwhile.

We left the command post, and Larsen led the way past several shacks, mostly used for storage, toward the largest building there.

"We're a little different from the other forts, as we receive many of the injured here," he said. "Originally that was because we were back far enough from the front lines, though as you saw on the map, that's not the case anymore. But our perimeter defenses have held, and we have some good medics. Transporting the injured out of the war zone is nearly impossible."

But we'd gotten into the war zone easily enough. How much harder could it be to get out? "Why is that?" I asked.

"Those bastard Exiles target medical transports in particular. Pardon my language, ma'am."

Dane's sharp intake of breath echoed in my ears. Hopefully the others took it as horror that anyone could be so cold rather than fury at my father.

We walked into the large building, which functioned as the infirmary.

I wanted to turn and run, but Dane and Theo blocked me in.

Rows of cots ran the length of the building, every one of them occupied. Based on the noise coming down the stairway to our right, the second level had plenty of patients as well. The noises... soft moaning, an occasional cry of pain. And no wonder. From where I stood, I saw blood-soaked bandages, burnt flesh, and wrapped stumps where limbs should have been. Some turned to look at us, but most were too consumed by their misery. The air choked me with a smell I'd never experienced, cheap antiseptic mingling with wounds that festered despite the medics' best efforts. Open windows allowed a hint of a fresh breeze. It didn't help that much.

Hospitals like those in the Royal City had the tech and resources to treat all of these and more, freeing them of pain, repairing the damage quickly and efficiently. But Father kept the hospitals out of reach. He didn't think these soldiers were worth it. They were just the pawns.

Like Dane's mother. He'd said she died when he was born. No one died in childbirth anymore, not on Windsong. Not without some kind of willful neglect.

My stomach roiled. All those years on Thanda, I'd thought I understood my father's monstrosity. That understanding deepened when the Candarans told me they weren't involved in the war at all. Father put his own rule above everything and everyone—even his own people. Confronted with these soldiers, dead and dying due to Father's actions, it reached a new level of reality for me.

But the same man had told me bedtime stories. Had shed tears when he told me my mother was dead. Had been heartbroken when I was missing and genuinely happy when I returned.

Had done other things.

It wouldn't come together. The pieces jammed into spaces where they didn't fit.

Collect data now, Essie. Process later.

I cleared my throat. "Captain, I don't want to get in the medics' way. Could we see some of your weapons stores?"

"Of course, Princess."

I wanted to drink the fresh air once we were outside, but I restrained myself to more controlled breaths. We didn't go far, just to one of the storage shacks next to the infirmary. Larsen slid open a crate and removed a gun.

"This is our standard field rifle. Range of half a link, variable charge. Steady and reliable, but the Exiles' weapons are a bit better. I've often wondered if they're getting contraband from the brains over on Garam. I haven't any proof, of course, ma'am."

Maybe he had proof of something else. I turned and gave Dane a slight nod.

"May I, Captain?" he said. Larsen handed him the rifle, which he quickly broke down, laying out the components on another crate.

I stepped closer and looked it over, glad for a puzzle to focus on. I didn't know much about weapons, but when I saw the guts of a thing, I could figure it. Charge generator, polarizer, conduits, contact relays . . . Something was off. The scanner from my pocket confirmed it, and I saved the scan file to my slate. With that configuration, the gun would fire bolts that looked pretty good, but didn't do much more than give the target an irritating shock.

It was all true. Nothing but theatrics on the "Exile" side, but the Windsong militia soldiers didn't know that. The injuries, the deaths on their own side, they were all too real.

My mind clicked through the information, stubbornly trying

to make it compute, refusing to wait any longer. The effort distracted me, turning the rest of our tour into a meaningless blur.

When I surfaced, the captain said he had duties to return to and left us in Theo's care to decide what else we wanted to do.

"You can see, Princess, they do the best they can here," the guard said. "It's the same or worse all across the outlands. A bad situation all around."

"War usually is," I murmured. "Theo, would you mind checking in with the medics? Get a list of supplies and tech they need. If we can't get the injured to the hospitals, we should at least get these infirmaries as close to hospital-quality as we can."

"Certainly, Princess."

It was a task that needed doing, but all I really wanted was to get Theo out of the way so I could talk to Dane. The guard left for the infirmary, and I set off in a different direction toward the near edge of the base. Past the shacks with soldiers carrying out their tasks, out into the wild fields overgrown with brush and young trees. My sleeve snagged on a branch, scraping the skin underneath, but I just tugged it free and kept going. Once I knew no one could hear us, I turned to Dane and let the words burst out.

"It doesn't make any sense!"

He stepped back, startled. "What do you mean?"

"I mean none of this adds up. Why is my father carrying on with this now that I'm back, now that it's *acknowledged* that Exiles didn't take me? Why does he insist on convincing this whole planet we're at war with you?"

"Do you know anything about your own history?"

Only what the tutors had told me. Being on Thanda had been

all about running away from the past. I said nothing, but it was answer enough for Dane.

"Kip told me a few things. It's because Matthias's power was slipping, Essie. He's never been able to keep hold of the kingdom like your grandfather could. He doesn't know how, not like a real king. Unrest and uprisings plagued his reign from the beginning. He brought in Olivia as royal theurgist, and that helped for a while, but the people didn't actually like her that much. So he married your mother, and the kingdom was more stable than it had ever been during his rule. When she died, he almost lost the throne."

I flinched. After Mother died, after the wedding to Olivia . . . that was when everything changed.

Dane stepped a little closer, but his eyes held sympathy, not threats. "Then you disappeared, and he took the chance to create a convenient enemy out of people he's already afraid of. Afraid because if we Transition, we can understand anyone from the inside. Afraid because there's no keeping secrets from us. That's what Transitioning is, Essie; it's about understanding people, and to someone like your father, that's *worse* than the fear of possession or mind-control. He chose the kind of leader he'd be years ago, and it was the wrong choice."

I knew what he wasn't saying. I was the right choice. "He's my father. What if you and Kip are wrong? What if there's more of him than my mother in me?"

"We're not wrong."

He reached for my hand. I wanted to let him take it, but I pulled away. "Don't."

"No one's going to see."

No one will see, no one will know, it'll be our secret. . . .

"I said, don't."

The edge in my voice sent him back a step. "Essie, I'm sorry, I—"

"I had a choice, too, Dane," I cut in. "Fight for the right to live quietly on Candara with you or come to Windsong, where the odds say I won't survive the year, but hopefully I'll take my father and Olivia down with me. My choice wasn't supposed to include you coming along and getting killed, too, and when I'm probably going to die anyway, you shouldn't waste your feelings on me."

Dane shook his head. "You're brilliant, Essie, but you're still dim on a few things. Feelings can't be wasted. Knowing they're real for however long they last makes them worth having."

Something wrenched inside me. "You're wrong. Feelings can be real without being worth anything at all."

"Why's that?"

"Because somewhere inside me is the little girl who loved her father, and in his twisted black heart, he *does* love me. After all he's done, what's *that* worth?"

Dane had no answer, and neither did I. His eyes said he wanted to blank it out for me, make it so it had never happened, but we both knew that was impossible.

The silence hung, and in the end, neither of us got a chance to break it.

A screeching buzz, like a wasp the size of Dimwit, tore through the air above us. We spun just in time to see a crackling ball of energy hit the infirmary, enveloping it in a net of lightning.

Then we heard the screams.

I launched myself toward the building and nearly tore my arm off. Dane had grabbed hold and was pulling me another way.

"What are you doing? We have to get in there, we have to help them!"

"No, we have to get out of here right now!"

"What kind of blazing coward are you?"

Another building was hit—maybe by a different weapon, because it just exploded, the shock wave knocking us down. Dane lost his grip on my arm, so I pulled myself up and started running. As usual, he was too fast, tackling me hard to the ground. I tasted blood. I swung my elbow back and made contact with something, maybe his ear. Enough to weasel out from under him, but not enough to get very far.

"Theo is in there!" I protested, trying to break his hold around my waist. *I sent him in there.*

Another shot, another building consumed by electricity.

"I'm sorry, Essie, but it's too late for them. Come *on!*"

He was right. The screams from the infirmary had stopped. A sudden cold flooded me; a piece of me died. I wanted to go home, even if home meant the palace. I stopped fighting Dane and let him pull me into a run.

Men scattered all over the base, ignoring us as they shouted at each other to repair the perimeter defense, to launch countermeasures. Some just ran for their lives. One passed near a shack when it got hit. Then he was gone.

Just gone.

Anything left was unrecognizable as ever having been human.

The shock left me stunned enough for Dane to drag me to

the barn and shove me into the transport. He took the pilot's seat and swore.

"The controls have a security lockout. Can you bypass it?"

The schematics I'd studied flashed in my mind. No time for code-breaking. I had to fool the computer into forgetting it needed a code at all. I grabbed some gear, pulled my slate, got on my back underneath the console, and yanked off the access panel. Each conduit was a thread, and I traced them through the fabric of the control system. Everything disappeared but the puzzle. One thread stood out, then another. A few stitches, a few twists and knots.

Finally stitching again. A smile flitted across my lips, but fell away just as quickly. Theo was dead, and I was happy because I didn't have to act like a princess for a moment.

I wanted to throw up.

"Essie, I hate to rush you, but could you hurry?"

The anxiety in his voice told me not to ask why, just work faster. "Almost got it. C'mon, you botched little—there!"

The engines came to life, the transport lifted off the ground, and we surged forward so quickly that I slid, jamming my leg against one of the seats. I hauled myself up into the chair and checked the rear display on the console.

Flames engulfed the barn. That explained Dane's anxiety. Buildings smoldered and sparked all around us, smoke obscuring everything. Another explosion bucked the transport, throwing me against the side console.

"Your turn to hurry, Dane."

"Working on it."

He slammed the accelerator and jerked the lateral controls, narrowly missing a chunk of metal that had torn from a wall.

For a second, I thought he'd gotten turned around and we were going the wrong way, but then I saw the river. He was taking the shortest route out of the wreckage.

The burning ruin that had been a militia base minutes ago disappeared in a mass of smoke and debris behind us. Another fire lit inside me, replacing the chill I'd felt earlier.

"I'm done. I can't do it anymore. No more games and pretending. I'm just going to kill him."

Dane could only afford a quick glance away from the controls, but it was like a laser drilling into me. "No, you won't. We stick to the plan."

"Why?"

"Because we're too far from Kip and the fleet, and we're not ready."

"What does it matter? I can't look him in the eye and be the dutiful daughter and pretend I don't know that he just killed those men, and his own guard, too. I can't do it!"

"Yes, you can. Because your father didn't do that."

Minutes ago, he'd been lecturing me on my father's machinations. The words caught in my chest and took a second try to get out. "What?"

"He knew you'd be at Saddlewood. He never would have launched that attack today."

"Then who?" The answer struck me as soon as I'd asked the question.

"Olivia must have access to the army posing as Exiles. She just took another shot at killing you, and in case you missed it, she almost succeeded."

24

WE BYPASSED THE SAFETY LIMITS of the transport, trimming a few hours from our return trip. Dane and I remained silent most of the time. I busied myself with small tasks, ensuring the royal identification code broadcasted cleanly so the defenses at the outland borders would let us through, and transferring the gun scan to a small data-chip I tucked safely inside my locket.

A message came from the palace when they got word of the attack, stating an escort would be sent. Dane refused, claiming he didn't want any more attention brought to our location. Then he had me disable the transport's locator. Simple enough.

"Do you really think I'm a coward?" Dane asked.

I refused to look up from my slate. "Isn't that what you call it when something bad happens and you run the other way?"

"You don't get it, do you?"

"Get what?"

"Why I'm here."

I tapped out a few ideas for a self-modulating subroutine. Maybe someday I could send it to Petey and someone could see if it fixed Zippy's timing issues. Petey . . . I still hadn't gotten word to him. "No, I get that. To save your father, clear the name of Candarans everywhere. Good reasons."

"Look at me, Essie!"

His voice was so sharp, so full of an emotion I couldn't define, that I couldn't help turning. Anger. That was part of it. And something else.

"I told you, protecting you isn't an act. So when the attack started, my first instinct wasn't to run away. It was to get *you* safe. And not just because of how I feel about you—because you're this planet's best chance at a real future."

"What do you care what happens to Windsong?"

Dane refused to release my gaze, and it was harder than ever for me to break away from his. "Candara isn't my home. It never has been. *Windsong* is where my parents fell in love, where I was born, where my mother died. This will always be home to me."

The locked room overlooking Gakoa flashed in my mind, the mountains and river, the peace of being separate from everything but taking it all in. The place of a king watching his kingdom, holding the weight of his world. Dane clearly hadn't wanted any part of it.

"You don't plan on claiming the Candaran throne, do you?"

"When we rescue my father, it'll be his to take, if he wants it."

"I saw how the people there looked at you. Kids like Tatsa. How they love you."

His hand twitched on the controls. "Maybe. But they don't need me. Not like your people need you."

He was so wrong. Not about what the people of Windsong

needed, but about how this was going to play out. I couldn't sit there and listen to him anymore. I stood, thinking I'd get some sleep on one of the bunks at the rear of the transport.

"There's something *you* don't get, Dane," I said. "I'm just a pawn in this. Sometimes a pawn can set things in motion, but they rarely make it to the endgame. Not with the power we're up against."

After I slept, I took a turn keeping an eye on things so Dane could rest. When he woke up, we went back to not talking. The closer we got to the Royal City, the tighter I gripped my knees, my nails digging into them.

"We have a problem," I said. "I wasn't exaggerating before. I can't be near my father and pretend I don't know what he's doing. Not after that. Not after seeing those men. It doesn't matter that he didn't order the attack. He's ordered others. How can I be in the same room and not tear him apart?"

"The same way I've managed to be on this planet without anyone finding out what I am. You're going to take that anger and use it to fool everyone. You're going to make your father think you hate the Exiles just as much as he does, and you're going to find a way to turn that against him."

It made sense, turning my anger that way. But I knew it would be the hardest thing I'd ever done.

The Exiles did this. The Exiles killed Theo. The Exiles blew that man apart right in front of me. Over and over, I repeated it to myself, asking what the next step would be if it were true.

Guiding the transport into the city with an escort of armed

skimmers, I saw the soldiers in the infirmary. Walking from the transport into the palace with a phalanx of Golden Sword guards surrounding me, I saw the man who had simply disappeared, his eyes in the moment before he was gone. Entering the throne room to face my father and Olivia, I saw Theo, blushing as he remembered my mother.

Father looked both relieved and furious upon seeing me. Olivia just looked furious. I wondered what lie she'd told him to make the attack a mistake. A botched set of orders. The wrong coordinates. A rogue lieutenant acting on his own.

I didn't care. I could guarantee I was more furious than both of them together. Father approached, arms out to embrace me. No way could I take that without trying to rip his throat out, so I cut him off, letting the fire fly through my voice.

"Where are the prisoners?"

As hoped, that stopped him. "What?"

"The captain at Saddlewood told me how this started, how the Exiles took advantage of my kidnapping to launch this war. You stopped the first attack and took prisoners from their embassy. I want to know where they are."

Father's expression shifted again. "Snowflake, you don't need to worry. Those prisoners are secure. They won't be able to hurt you."

"I don't doubt that, but if I'm to lead this world someday, I need to face our enemies. I want to look in their eyes and assure them they will *never* see freedom while I live, that their people will not frighten me into a corner. I want to see their faces as I snatch any shred of hope they have left in them."

I hated every word as it left my mouth, but pride glowed in Father's face. Pride that someday I'd be exactly the kind of ruler he was. The expression brought back the roiling nausea. "If that is what you wish, Daughter, you shall have it."

"I will see to it," Olivia said. "My guards do watch the prison, after all."

That was a problem—her first two attacks hadn't worked out, and I knew she'd try harder this time—but I refused to let her see my fear.

"Make it soon," I snapped, turning to leave before she could respond.

The servants read my mood, practically diving out of the way as I stalked to the residential wing. As soon as we were in the suite, the mask fell, and I began to hyperventilate.

"Essie breathe Essie."

For the first time in my life, I couldn't tell the drone to shut it.

"Essie, slow down," Dane said, taking hold of my shoulders.

I jerked away. Hurt flashed across Dane's eyes, but it had just been a reflex. "I'm sorry, I just— What I said, I didn't even think. If the prison's guarded by the Midnight Blade, and you won't be with me—"

"Wait, what?" he cut in. "Of course I'll be with you."

"You can't be, Dane. Even if one of the prisoners weren't your father, someone will recognize you."

"They'll see I'm with you. They won't give me away."

"*You* will give you away. Seeing them and your father, how can you—"

"Let me worry about that. I'm not letting you go alone. Besides, if I didn't go, the queen would be suspicious."

That was true, but every cell in my body rebelled against the idea. The fear coalesced to something I could identify.

"Olivia's too determined to kill me—you've seen what she

can do," I said. "All I'm doing is buying time. And if my father finds out what I'm doing, he'll kill me himself. But they *can't* kill you, Dane. They just can't. You have to see it through. You have to finish what my mother started. Promise me."

He hesitated before putting a hand to my cheek. This time I let him, even though the warmth of his skin only added to the burning terror in my heart. "I can't promise that, Essie. I can't, because if they're going to kill you, they'll have to kill me first."

The terror bubbled into panic. "Then what good is any of this? What if we both die before accomplishing anything and your people can't get through the defenses? We fail. My father wins, and nothing changes."

"It's simple. We won't fail. *If* they kill us, we make sure it's after we've done too much damage to reverse, and Kip will see it through. But I have no intention of letting that happen. So here's what I'll promise: I promise your father won't win."

He was so confident. Maybe confident enough for both of us. I lingered in his touch one more moment before turning away. "Tell me when Olivia sends word about the arrangements."

"Are you going to get some rest?" Dane asked.

"No, I'm going to contact Theo's family."

I didn't know whether it would help, getting a message from the princess-to-the-crown, telling them how sorry I was about his death. But it was all I could offer.

Life was so much easier back when I was selfish.

⚬━▦▦▦━⚬
⚬━▨▨━⚬

Before we left for the prison, I told Dimwit to move on the plan to bumble into Olivia's wardrobe and spray down everything with thederol. It would be better if he made the attempt while I wasn't around. Of course, if I didn't come back from the prison, it wouldn't matter if he got the thederol on Olivia's things or not. In that case, I hoped Dimwit would be sharp enough to just wander away before someone decided to scrap him.

Father came to see us off, stating Olivia was otherwise occupied. Just as well. The two Midnight Blade guards who would be accompanying us made me uneasy enough.

"You do what you said, Snow," Father said. "Face the enemy, show them you aren't afraid, that they'll never defeat us."

"What about the Exiles' body-hopping?" I asked. "Do I need to guard myself against it somehow, to keep them from turning me into their puppet?"

"We've already accounted for that. You have nothing to fear."

I couldn't imagine what that meant, and the words brought anything but relief. The only way to keep *me* from Transitioning was to make sure I didn't touch anyone, but I knew that wouldn't stop a full Candaran.

The journey to the prison was much shorter than the last, but felt longer. I didn't bother asking the guards' names. They didn't look like types I wanted to get to know.

We traveled out of the city, across the border to the next province, and wound into a canyon cutting through the Ridgecrest Mountains. Deeper and deeper, dipping into a side canyon with barely enough space for the transport in some places. Finally we stopped in front of a building butting up against the rock face.

Building was an overstatement, though. It was hardly bigger than my shack on Thanda, nowhere near large enough for any kind of prison. Dane and I followed the other two men inside.

It wasn't the prison. It was the guard station. The guards

who'd brought us just nodded at those on duty. They knew to expect us. A tunnel had been cut into the mountain through a heavy door at the rear of the guard station.

It turned out my father's love of the traditional—to the point of archaic—had gone too far.

He didn't have a prison. He had a dungeon.

I'd never been in the actual mine on Thanda, but it had to feel very similar. Dark and cold and damp, moisture gathering on every surface. A mingled stench of mold and filth set off an urge to gag—the Station back on Thanda was the royal rose garden by comparison. The only light came from flickering sconces spaced along the wall. Dane followed so close, I could hear a slight raggedness in his breath, but he stayed in control.

The first cell came on our right. No door. No barrier of any kind. Just a cave with a stone ledge covered in threadbare blankets, a corroded toilet, a stone basin with water trickling in continuously...and a woman with a heavy chain manacled to one leg.

At least, I was pretty sure it was a woman. She huddled on the ledge, wearing little more than rags, her long straggly hair obscuring her face.

"This is the most arrogant of them," one of the guards said. "It can't even be beaten out of her."

His words made her look up. There was still life in her eyes as she glared at the guard, then an extra spark as she glanced at me. Before I could come up with a response to the guard's declaration, the light flickered brighter, and I saw.

Scars across her throat.

They took her voice.

It didn't make sense. She didn't need her voice to Transition.

Even for Dane, Transitioning took *some* effort, so in her physical state, I doubted this woman could muster the strength to do it anyway. Now I understood what my father meant. Olivia knew how to stay invulnerable to Tipping; she would've told her guards in the early years. Then the willful neglect had taken away any threat left in the Candarans. So what was the point of the mutilation?

Faint noises of moving chains in other cells triggered the answer. Without voices, the only way the prisoners could communicate or even know the others were still alive was to Transition to each other. And they were too weak.

They were alone.

Keep the face on, Essie. Keep up the act. Twitch out later.

I took the cold of the cave and put it into my voice, never taking my eyes off the woman. "Leave us. Perhaps I can get through to her."

Maybe they thought I would beat her. Maybe my royal authority was enough for them. Whatever it was, the guards left. I waited until I heard the heavy door close at the head of the tunnel, but even then I didn't drop the act, and I didn't let Dane move. An image recorder was bolted into the rock face, taking in the entire cell. I'd expected that, though. I had one hand in my pocket and flipped a switch on a tiny signal emitter I'd stitched. It wouldn't block the recorders, but it would interfere with any microphones. No one would hear as long as I kept my voice down.

I strode across the cell and grabbed her chin, putting my face right in hers. I hoped it looked intimidating on the guards' display. For her part, the woman looked like she wasn't sure what to think.

"Do you know who I am?" I whispered. "Do you know who my mother was?"

She nodded, now glancing back and forth between me and Dane, who hovered protectively next to me.

"Then you know I'm not part of this. We'll try to get you out, but it might take a little while longer." Her eyes kept lingering on Dane's, then darting back to me. "You know him, too. His father?"

"Darrak," she whispered, barely. With the damage to her vocal cords, I had to lean closer and watch her lips to understand.

"Where is he?" Dane pressed. "Which cell is he in?"

She shivered, and her eyes glistened with tears. The chill in the air cut even deeper.

"He's not. He's dead."

25

"HOW?" Dane's question was more rasp than whisper.

"Infection. Seven years ago. When we still had the strength to Transition to each other. His last thoughts were of you and your mother."

He stood so close, his arm against my shoulder, that I felt his reaction. A microscopic hint of physical collapse before he regained his posture. He'd stopped breathing.

So had I. *Too late, too late, too late.* Seven years too late. Dead before I'd even left the Bands, when I still jumped at every approaching shadow. Dead before I knew how to fight. Dead before Dane and I had any blazing chance of doing anything about it.

There were others, though. I couldn't fall apart now, and I couldn't let Dane, either. I gripped the woman's chin more tightly, as if she wasn't giving me what I wanted.

"How many others are still alive?"

"Not sure. I—I see them carry out the bodies sometimes. Ten? Maybe more."

"Can you hold on a little longer?"

"No," Dane cut in. "We can't leave them here. We have to get them out now."

I was afraid he'd say something like that. I gave the woman a little shake, hoping it still looked right. "Did you bring an army in your pocket, Dane?"

"There are only five of them."

"You think we can take out all five before anyone alerts the palace? And then what?"

Before Dane could continue arguing, the woman cut in. "Kadei, you mustn't endanger yourselves. We can wait. Princess, please, be careful. The queen's guards, they talk. They'll do anything to keep her in power, even go against the king, but you can't trust him, either."

Nothing I didn't know. After one more shove, I backed away, letting the disgust I felt for the guards show on my face as I looked at her. I didn't say another word, just stalked out into the tunnel and checked the remaining cells. More than twenty, fewer than half of them occupied. None of the other prisoners looked up when I entered and crossed over to them. Not until I whispered in their ears, "Soon." Then they met my eyes and saw that it was a promise rather than a threat.

I had no idea whether I'd be able to keep that promise.

When I'd seen the last one—an old man who looked like gravity alone should have broken him—I returned to the head of the tunnel and pounded on the door. Dane had done nothing but follow me in silence, glaring the whole time. He still didn't want to leave them. I wondered if he'd forgive me.

The door opened, bringing a warm draft of fresh air. Mostly fresh, with an undertone of onions. The prison's three guards were eating lunch.

"Done what you came to do, then?" asked one of the men who'd accompanied us.

Dane kicked the back of my heel. It took me half a gasp to figure why. The guard hadn't shown the proper respect.

I crossed the room to where he lounged at a console, using a knife to pick scum from under his fingernails. "Did you address me, *guard*?"

He took his time replacing the knife in its sheath. "Forgive me... *Your Highness*. Do you wish to return to the palace now?"

"I do."

I didn't wait, going straight to the transport with Dane right behind me. The pair of guards followed after delaying just long enough to make it clear they didn't feel I was in any position to order them. Dane refused to look at me as the craft lifted into a hover and moved away from the prison.

Away from the prison, but not back the way we'd come.

"Guard, where are we going?" I demanded.

"Don't worry yourself, *Highness*. We need to check the perimeter outpost before making the return trip."

Plausible enough, but all I heard in my head was Dimwit's electronic voice. *Wrong way wrong way.*

I kept a sharp eye on the scenery. Overgrown trees and shrubs, scarcely enough room for the transport to pass, and nothing resembling a path to follow. That didn't necessarily mean anything. The route to and from a secret prison wasn't likely to have markers and signs at every turn.

Neither was a route to a secluded area perfect for killing an unwanted princess. My hand drifted to the top of my boot, reassuring myself that my knife was securely in place.

After several minutes, though, an antenna assembly came into view. It probably detected anyone who wandered too close to the prison. The transport came to a stop, and the guards turned.

"If you don't mind, Princess, you're handy with tech like that drone-pet of yours, and we could use some help checking the relays," one said.

Dane's eyes said no, absolutely not. But the tight confines of the transport pressed on me in sudden claustrophobia.

"Anything to speed it up," I said.

They made an "after you" gesture. Turning my back on them sounded like a truly bad idea, but I didn't dare put up a fuss. Dane stepped in right behind me. Didn't matter that he was mad at me. No one could get to me without going through him first.

I didn't like that any better.

My back prickled with three sets of eyes watching it. Every instinct said to forget appearances and just run. Two steps away from the transport, I surrendered to panic and spun around.

Good thing, too. Dane sidestepped the guard behind him, pivoting at the same time to smash his fist in the man's face. But the second guard already had a gun out, pointed straight at my head.

His finger wasn't on the trigger yet. Idiot thought the gun alone would be enough to scare me.

I moved like Dane taught me, knocking the gun from the guard's hand before he had time to blink. He blocked my second strike, his eyes shifting, taking me seriously.

Round one.

The gun was lost in the undergrowth, but the good news ended there. I attacked; he blocked. He attacked; I dodged. We each got some glancing contact in, but nothing to make any real progress.

Then he stopped playing around.

A fist to my gut knocked the wind from me. An elbow to the side of my head sent sparks across my vision.

Back up, Essie, get some space, some room to breathe.

Too slow. He had a grip on my wrist. A flash of sunlight glinted off silver.

Knife!

"Essie, get down!"

I dropped to a crouch, nearly falling forward. The hand released my wrist, and the knife plunged into the ground just a few sniffs in front of me. I lifted my eyes. The black and pewter handle of another Midnight Blade weapon stuck out from the guard's neck, his eyes glassy with surprise. He swayed and fell. I turned to see Dane standing with his hands on his knees, breathing hard. The other guard lay on the ground nearby, unmoving. I watched his chest. *Really* unmoving.

Dane had killed to save me. He'd ended two lives.

I hadn't even thought to pull my own knife. Maybe the habits of cage fighting. Maybe I was too afraid of using such deadly force. I wanted to vomit, cry, or curl up and go to sleep forever. Instead, I stayed still, wishing the wobbly world would do the same.

"Are you hurt?" Dane asked between gasps.

"I'm fine. You?"

He didn't answer. He turned and walked several steps away, both hands gripping his hair. His shoulders shook, and he fell to his knees.

 279

Then a noise like nothing I'd ever heard. A cry, a howl, a roar. All of those. None of them.

It had nothing to do with Olivia's guards and killing them. The horrible sound that tore through my ears was the pain he'd held in since the prison, since learning his father was long dead.

I knew I should go to him, comfort him, but I didn't know how.

Then figure it.

The dizziness had faded enough that I could push myself to my feet. He was only a few steps away, but it felt like a hundred links. When I got there, I still wasn't sure what to do. I started with resting a hand on his shoulder, trying to steady its shaking. He reached up and closed his hand over mine, squeezing it tight. Something warm passed through me, burning through fissures in my heart.

It hurt.

All I know is pain running through every nerve, every vein. My ribs ache, but it's not the bruises of the fight with the guard—

—the guard I killed—

—the blood—

—dead—

—Father dead all these years. I'll never see him again. Never—

I yanked my hand away. "I—I didn't mean to, Dane, I'm—"

"I didn't stop you," he said, his voice rough. He stood and returned to the transport. "We need to get out of here."

For two heartbeats, I just stared at my hand. I'd Transitioned for the first time since the ball, but aside from the effects of the fight, I felt fine physically.

It had been easy. Like with Mother.

I kept my mouth shut and boarded the transport. Disabling the security lockout so Dane could pilot it was easy enough. He hesitated before engaging the engines.

"There are only three of them at the prison now," he said.

I couldn't stand what I was about to say, but the words came out just the same. "We can't, Dane. There's not enough room for all of them, they need doctors, and we're too far from the fleet—it's not time. All we'd do is get them and ourselves killed. We need to find a way back to the palace without passing the prison again."

"Whatever you say, Princess."

He got the transport moving, picking a route that would take us in the right general direction. I could only let the silence hang for a few minutes.

"Dane . . . I'm sorry about your father."

"It's not your fault."

Those words felt like a gyro-compressor squeezing my chest. "But it *is* my fault."

"Essie, don't," he said sharply, his eyes fastened to the controls. "It isn't."

But it is.

26

ARRIVING AT THE PALACE was nothing like the last time. No escorts at battle-readiness. No concerned father waiting anxiously. As far as anyone knew, we were expected and on schedule. Only one person would realize how false that was.

Dane maneuvered the transport into its dock but didn't move to get out yet, his hands still resting on the controls. We'd been silent for most of the journey, but now he turned to me.

"You could tell your father what happened, but I'm not sure you should."

Tell Father that his wife had made ongoing efforts to kill me? "I don't know, either."

"Would he believe you?"

That was the question without an answer. "He might. Or he might not. Either way, it would be too easy for Olivia to turn it around on us, especially when we're standing on so many lies. Better not risk it."

Dane nodded. "What about Olivia?"

That would be tricky. "I'll handle her. Alone."

"No. Not alone, Essie."

I slipped the cylinder of varitane gas out of my pocket. We'd given Dimwit over eight hours to get his job done, and Olivia typically changed outfits at least three times a day. "I have this if I need it. You go back to the suite and I'll meet you there." He opened his mouth to continue his protests, but I cut him off. "Don't argue, Dane. Do as I say."

I pressed a hand to my mouth, but it was too late to catch the words. The look he gave made me feel like my insides were full of baby harri-harra maggots. I'd spoken to him like a princess to her guard, only there wasn't anyone around to justify the act.

An apology lodged in my throat. *Those* words wouldn't come out. Instead, I walked away.

Once inside the palace, I asked the first servant I saw where I could find the queen. I was directed to one of the libraries. Olivia stood at a full-desk computer display, but I couldn't see what was on it. Nothing good, certainly. She looked up when I entered, and for once, her masks failed her completely.

Fury. Pure and clear.

I kept one hand in my pocket, lightly holding the canister. "Good evening, Olivia. I'm afraid there was an incident at the prison, and your guards were unable to return with us. Thought you should know."

She still had the option of making up a story to tell Father, something to turn him against me. It all depended on how confident she was in her ability to convince him.

Slowly, carefully, her mask of indifferent benevolence reasserted itself. "Terrible shame to lose good guards. I'll have to make sure they're better trained next time."

Translation: Eventually I'll succeed.

I knew she would. But she hadn't managed it yet. At that rate, I had a pretty good chance of surviving long enough to make my murder the last thing she did as queen of Windsong.

That would be worth it.

"I'm sure you will," I said. "Thank you for arranging my visit to the prison. I know who my enemies are now. Good night."

I walked out of the library, half expecting a knife in my back before I reached the door. Too messy for her, though, and no convenient Exiles to blame for my death in a prison riot.

Back in the suite, Dimwit sat alone in the corner. "Did you get the job done?" I asked.

Two beeps. Done, yes. Whether or not it had been botched . . . only one way to find out.

With the drone stationary and muted, silence wove through the air. The door to Dane's room was closed. I thought about checking on him. Maybe apologizing. Definitely apologizing.

But I left him alone.

＊＊＊

Days of nothing passed.

I kept busy enough. I recorded a video message to use when the Candaran fleet launched the attack. It took fifteen tries before I was satisfied, and the message got added to the data-chip with the gun scan tucked safely in my locket.

Meanwhile, Dane and I attended meetings with Father and militia commanders where I offered suggestions for a counteroffensive in the outlands. My ideas were heard, thoughtfully considered, and added to a list of things that would never happen because Father controlled both sides. Still I went, showing all the passion and hatred of the Exiles that he wanted to see, hoping he would give me more information. Sometimes I thought I saw a hint in his eyes that he would let me in on the secret soon. But not yet.

The social events didn't let up, either. I visited military academies where recruits for the various royal guards trained. I visited women's clubs where ladies with nothing better to do discussed projects for the betterment of the Royal City, such as rearranging the flowers lining the causeways. Everywhere Princess Snow went, the people were thrilled to see her.

Almost everywhere.

Dane and I kept up our act when in public. When we were alone, we rarely talked at all. He grieved for his father. Thanks to my Transitioning slipup, I knew exactly how much it hurt, and I didn't know how to help. How could I help, when the man would've been alive if not for me?

I kept a chart in my head, counting down the days until we'd be close enough to the fleet to set things in motion. The count proceeded with equal parts dread and anticipation. Whatever Dane and I did, I might not survive it. But it would be over.

Twelve days...nine...five. The last few passed in a blur of more military strategizing and smiling for image-captures.

"The queen would prefer you wear one of the dresses for the school visit," Dane said when he saw me on the morning of Day Zero. "Says a good impression is particularly important right now."

I entertained the idea of turning around and changing into a dress for about half a nanosecond. Then I finished pulling my boots on. "I don't take orders from Olivia. Children don't need to see a fancified princess in a gown, do they?"

"Whatever you say—you're the princess."

He'd said that a lot over the last several days. So much that my ears hurt when I heard it. This was one time too many, and the pain snapped something inside.

"Didn't exactly ask to be a princess, did I? Didn't ask to be chased off to Thanda or taken away again or any blazing thing except to come here and stitch this mess, and I'm doing the best I can."

"Your accent, Ess—"

"Oh, shut it, Dane, I know!"

I tried to move past him to the door, but he blocked me. "I know you're anxious about today. I heard Theo tell you about how your mother—"

"If I want your advice, I'll ask for it."

He froze. I'd done it again, treated him like he was something less, like his words weren't worthy of me . . . like he wasn't the only person on the planet I knew I could count on.

I didn't mean it. He had to know I didn't, that everything inside me was coming unraveled and it just came out around him because it couldn't anywhere else.

When I tried again, I kept my voice softer, imploring. "Dane, please. Just don't. I can't think about it."

His posture eased, just a little. "All right. Let's get going."

The school visit redefined agony. Dane had known exactly what he was talking about. The visit reminded me too much of

Theo's story of meeting my mother. I couldn't inspire anyone like she had.

The children, however, didn't know that. I'd insisted the visit be less formal, no rehearsed speeches from me—like I'd know what kind of speech to give. Instead, I visited individual classrooms. The older children were polite, clearly doing exactly what their teacher had told them to. The last classroom was a very young group, though. The children crowded around, so excited, asking more questions than I'd ever heard in my life, never waiting for a response before moving to the next.

"What's it like living in the palace?"

"Do you really have a swimming pool made of merinium?"

"What's the queen like? What's the king like?"

"Did you really live on Thanda? Is it awful there?"

"Geoffrey," the teacher cut in at the last. "Remember what we said about manners."

"It's all right," I insisted. "Yes, I lived on Thanda since I was a little older than you. It's very different from Windsong. Much colder and darker. But not everything was awful."

"What was your favorite thing there?" a girl asked.

I'd never thought about it before, so I considered the question. "Walking at night, when it was quiet and felt like there was no one around for ten links."

"Ugh, I hate the dark."

Her reaction made me laugh. So simple and honest, not caring that she was disagreeing with royalty. Why should she?

The teacher asked the children to show me some art projects they'd recently finished. Paintings of everything from the palace to family pets to an imagined creature that lurked in shadows under desks and sucked out children's brains when they were supposed to be doing their assignments. The teacher's smile became much more forced as the little girl responsible for that painting told me about the brain-suckers in vivid detail, but I liked the story.

As the others told me about their paintings, I didn't have to do much other than smile and nod. My mind began to wander, thinking what it would have been like to attend school with other children, to make creative excuses for not doing my work, to play in a park like the children on Candara.

It had never been an option, and it was too late now.

A boy who'd already shyly shown me a picture of his family approached Dane. His little voice just carried over the latest painting narration. "You're the princess's guard, right? Part of the Silver Dagger?"

"Yes, that's right," Dane said.

"How do you get that job?"

Dane cleared his throat slightly. "Well, my situation was a little different. But to be a guard you have to work hard and be willing to always protect the princess, no matter what."

I stared harder at a painting of the whistling canyons in front of me. I refused to turn away from it, sensing that if I did I would find Dane's eyes on me.

"Do you have to do *everything* she says?" the little boy asked.

"Pretty much."

I will not look.

"I guess that's not so bad. Not as bad as when my sister gets all bossy, at least. Yeah, I think that's what I'll do."

"What is?"

"Join the Silver Dagger when I'm old enough. I want to protect the princess, too."

My insides froze and exploded simultaneously. I couldn't breathe and breathed too much.

Just like Theo. I hadn't said anything inspiring, anything to make that boy think I was worth protecting, but he wanted to anyway. Wanted to serve. Wanted to get himself killed.

My eyes finally darted to Dane's. He saw my reaction and smiled kindly at the boy before approaching the teacher.

"We should be going," he said. "The princess has another appointment to prepare for this evening."

It was the truth—I had to have dinner with the "young ladies of the court," when I'd rather have my eyeballs soaked in acid—but it was more than that. It was Dane saving me in another way, by getting me out before I came apart. The children said their goodbyes and I tried to smile, but I didn't feel it. Finally, we escaped the classroom.

"Essie, it's all right," he began.

"I told you, just don't," I snapped. Again. "Please . . . take me home and I'll get ready for that blazing dinner."

He shook his head and sighed. "Whatever you say, Princess."

27

MY DINNER WITH the young ladies of the court was exactly what I'd expected: giggling girls trying to win my favor with compliments and agreeing with anything I said. The very opposite of the children I'd spent the afternoon with.

I considered saying something about the Exiles, or something distasteful, or just something unhinged and ridiculous to see how they'd respond. That at least would have been amusing. If I thought any of them had a single interesting thing to say, I'd have made her the Royal Best Friend on the spot. No such luck, and my thoughts wandered again.

While we ate dainty hors d'oeuvres, the Candaran prisoners languished in the filth of their decrepit cells, unable to even cry out to each other in their misery. While we feasted on more food than three times our number could eat, citizens of Windsong bled and died in the outland fields, having no idea their enemy was the crown itself. And while the girls picked at rich cakes, fretting about what they would do to their figures, Queen Olivia plotted new schemes to end my life.

I didn't talk about any of that. Instead I smiled and nodded and laughed when I was supposed to. Every bit the princess my father wanted me to be. Strong but pleasant, agreeable yet authoritative. Still, each giggle and excited squeal I heard made me sick.

One thing helped me keep the mask on. We'd reached the Candaran fleet. Dane and I would make our move within the next few days. We'd take down the defenses, broadcast the truth to the world, and one way or another, it'd all be over.

After hours of nonsense, I made my exit with Iris, an aide charged with accompanying me back to my suite. Walking through the palace without Dane felt strange, but the dinner had been very traditional—no men allowed. Iris led the way in complete silence, which suited me well enough after all the giggling. The quiet corridors felt refreshingly peaceful. At least, they did until the hairs on my arms started prickling. Olivia wouldn't try anything in the palace with my father around. I knew she wouldn't, but my nerves wouldn't listen. I focused on the extra weight of the knife in my boot—helpful if I ever had the wits to use it—and the pressurized cylinder tucked safely in my pocket.

Nothing happened all the way to my suite in the residential wing, and I cursed myself for being a skittish sparrow before bidding Iris good night. With the door closed behind me, I relaxed, pulling my boots off and tossing them aside. Not very princesslike. I didn't care.

"Dane?"

No response. It was late, so he must have already turned in. I had to stop lashing out at him. Appearances weren't important anymore, and stress had taken the habit too far. I'd apologize in the morning, and we'd plot out the timeline for the end of the world.

I went to my room and pulled the fastener from my hair, shaking it loose. A swish signaled the door in the front room opening. Apparently, Dane *hadn't* already turned in.

"Dane? Where'd you go?" I called.

"I sent him and your pet on an errand."

Not Dane's voice. I spun around. My father's body filled the doorway, and lightning exploded in my heart.

You're not to be alone with him under any circumstances. There I was, alone. All these days and days with nothing, I'd thought maybe that one thing had stayed in the dark past where it belonged. That at least one part of him would be better.

The look in his eyes was familiar. Nothing good ever came from that look.

"What do you want, Father?"

He stepped toward me. I stepped back. "You were always such a comfort to me. I need it again."

Despite the panic, a hard strength pulsed through me. "That wasn't comfort. And you need to leave."

"It's all right, Snowflake. No one will know."

He closed the distance—I had nowhere else to go—but I'd spent years lashing out at men in the cage . . . men who reminded me of him. With the real thing in front of me, I didn't hesitate.

I pushed him away and hit him, bringing shock to his eyes—I'd never dared strike him before.

The shock quickly shifted to anger.

He came back more forcefully, too quickly. He was so much larger than anyone I'd ever fought. I got a few more hits in, but a bruise over his eye and blood trickling from his lip did nothing to stop him. He caught my arms, resisting my efforts to twist away.

Then he squeezed.

Squeezing, pressing . . . bruises to hide in the morning . . .

Memories flooded my mind, pushing out what Dane taught me. It was all the opening Father needed, shoving me back onto the bed.

Too heavy, holding me down, can't breathe.

I was stronger now. Strong enough to hold him off, but not for long. Knowing it was useless, knowing it had never worked before, I still tried. Maybe he had doubts, a voice in the corner I could use to Tip his will. I focused my awareness, shifting it to his.

I adjust my grip, hold her tighter—

I snapped back to my own mind, feeling like I'd bathed in mine-sludge. I couldn't. I couldn't bear to see through his eyes. To feel what he felt. I couldn't be him.

He smiled . . . the smile that haunted me every night as I went to sleep, every time I stepped into the cage. The smile that said he didn't care about anything except what he wanted. His eyes mirrored me, a dark reflection of my fear.

"So much of your mother in you."

A surge of strength bought me a space, a breath, and the will to spit in his face. "That's right, because I'm nothing like you."

Father's face contorted as he lurched forward, his full weight smothering me. But his grip on my arms released. Then he rolled off, and I was pulled to my feet. Dane, his face as pale as mine, a knife in his free hand . . . a knife covered in blood.

I instinctively looked back at the bed.

Once I did, I couldn't look away.

My father lay there, his eyes wide, his mouth moving soundlessly, a pool of blood blooming beneath him.

"Are you okay?" Dane asked.

I said nothing, just kept watching. Father's eyes locked with mine. *I won't let you win*, they seemed to say.

"Too late," I whispered.

"Essie?"

Father's body shuddered, and then went still, his eyes frozen forever. The mirrors were empty.

"Essie, we have to go!"

"What?"

Dane forced me back around. His hand went to my cheek as his eyes sought mine. "I'm sorry, I came back as soon as I realized the message wasn't from you. But we have to go. Now. Once they know the king's dead, they'll lock down the palace. We have to signal the fleet."

The fleet. The plan. And no time to do it delicately. We had to get to the command terminal and clear the planetary defenses.

"Right. Okay. Right."

He pushed me out of the bedroom but didn't follow right away. I tidied my clothes, finding no blood on them. Then I twisted my hair back up and pulled my boots on. If only I hadn't taken them off so quickly, I'd have had my knife.

I could've done it myself.

When Dane came out, his knife was clean, and he slid it back into its sheath. He crossed the room and put his hands on my shoulders. I didn't realize how shaky I was until he steadied me.

"I need you to tell me you're all right."

"Aye, I'm fine. I—I'm sorry, Dane."

"For what?"

"For how I keep snapping at you when you're all I've got. And for making you do that."

He said nothing, but the way he gently squeezed my shoulders told me the first was forgiven, and he didn't want an apology for the second.

I put the scene in the bedroom out of my mind, focusing on details, the plan. My gear kit was inside a cabinet built into a decorative end table. I broke away from Dane to retrieve it and strap it on.

"Ready?" I asked.

"Definitely. You have the data-chip?"

I pulled the locket from beneath my shirt and checked. The chip containing the video message and the data from the war zone was nestled securely inside between the images of my maybe-grandparents. I nodded and led the way out into the corridor.

In my head, I clearly saw my mother's notebook. I'd studied the pages for years on Thanda before destroying those holding secrets, before I was certain the details were committed to memory. Camouflaged among the beautiful but innocent sketches, she'd drawn an intricate map of the palace's underground labyrinth. Labs where poisons and other weapons were developed, vaults holding artifacts and valuables, and most importantly the command terminal—a secure room serving as the nerve center of all the control my father held over the planet.

It wouldn't be easy to get to. The direct route was only accessible to the king or queen. That meant going the long way.

I walked briskly, with purpose, resisting the urge to run. Dane kept to his habitual position one step behind me. The servants we passed dipped into curtsies and bows before ducking out of the way. I didn't worry about them. I worried about the guards.

We left the residential wing, took a shortcut past the kitchens, and arrived at a nondescript door near the strategy rooms where Father usually met with the governors and military leaders. No guard. I wasn't sure if that was usual—maybe it was just because of the late hour—but I wouldn't complain.

The door had an electronic lock, but nothing complicated. Just a numeric keypad. Dane kept an eye on things while I fished a slate and multitool out of my kit. I easily tied into the lock, tracked the connections, and stitched around the code. The door opened, revealing a simple lift. There were no controls inside— only one destination.

The lift took us down for what felt like at least two links. When it finally stopped, the door opened again.

A Golden Sword guard stood facing us. He looked as startled as I felt. Dane didn't hesitate. After a flurry of motion—and some disturbingly loud shouts—the guard lay unconscious on the ground. Dane pulled him into the lift and left him there.

"Another reason to hurry," he said. "No telling when someone will expect him to check in. You know the way?"

I looked at the corridor before us—sterile white walls with no identifying marks anywhere. The map came back to me, as clear as ever. The underground was a maze—intentionally so— and if we got lost, we were tanked.

"Straight ahead a quarter link, left past some labs, right past the bio-storage facility, then down a long corridor to the security hub. It branches off to some vaults, but we just have to go straight through to get to the command terminal."

"Got it. Let's move."

The first turn went smoothly, but the labs were lined with windows. Computers and equipment like I'd never seen covered every surface, and along the back, cages to hold test animals.

And night-shift lab technicians at their stations.

When they looked at us in surprise, I glared sternly, like I had every right to be there and how dare they think otherwise. Most turned back to their work. A few glanced at each other. I didn't know if they worked because of loyalty or some other reason, but we couldn't chance it.

"Someone's going to alert the guards," I muttered to Dane.

"We just have to get through the security hub before lockdown. Keep moving."

I did, but when we turned the next corner, I stopped short.

It was a dead end.

Impossible. I *knew* I had the right path. Every stroke of the map burned in my mind. I looked again.

The wall facing us reflected a brighter white than the others. Newer.

Of course. The map in my head was several years old. Things had changed.

"Think, Essie. There has to be another way around."

Dane's voice drew me back from blind panic. I traced the corridors in my mind like a circuit schematic.

"There is. It's a lot longer, back past the labs."

We returned to the main corridor, ignoring the technicians,

and found a pair of guards coming straight for us. One look at their eyes said it was too late to weave a nice story for them. The man going at Dane was ready for a fight. The one coming my way seemed like he just expected to grab me.

Idiot.

I kept it simple, slamming my fist into his gut. As he doubled over, I kicked one of his knees, hyperextending it, and shoved him headfirst into the wall. Dane took a second longer, but still managed to take his guard down.

Without saying so, we knew there was no use in subtlety at that point, so we ran.

We went farther down the main corridor before turning left, following that branch through an odd set of turns. Another pair of guards greeted us when we rounded the last corner, one of them giving me a harder time than the first had. I got knocked around a little before Dane hauled the man away from me.

Yet another left turn took us down a corridor with a dead end after the last intersection. We'd made it to the other side of the barrier. The right side of the intersection would take us to the security hub.

That side was exactly where a pair of guards emerged before we got there.

"I've got them," Dane said. "You go."

Splitting up sounded like a bad idea. "What?"

"I'll catch up."

I knew what he was saying. The guards slowed us down, and lockdown might be sounded any minute. At least one of us had to get through the hub before then, and I was the one with the data-chip.

Every part of me hated it. *Do what needs doing. . . .*

I aimed for the guard on the right, running full-out and going to my knees at the last second, sliding past him on the smooth floor.

Blazes, I'll feel that later.

The guard tried to follow, but from the sound of things, Dane kept them both busy. I ran down a long, seamless corridor with an open door at the end. As I got closer, I saw another guard standing on the far side of the circular room. Just one. The news of our intrusion must've cleared out all the others. One guard between me and the corridor leading to the command terminal.

Just one, but his black-and-gray uniform loomed like a wall. Every guard so far had been Golden Sword, my father's men. With my father dead, they might shift their loyalty to me. Some might be good men...some might be like Theo. But this man was Midnight Blade, loyal to Olivia to the death.

I didn't slow down, running straight at him, hoping to take him by surprise.

No such luck.

He dodged me, grabbed hold, and spun around, throwing me back the way I'd come. I slammed into the ground, pain jolting through me, but forced myself to roll to my feet and face him.

The guard had a throwing dagger in one hand and too much space for me to stop him. Instead of running at him again, I twisted to one side as the knife flew past. I felt it split the air.

Then I watched it plunge into Dane as he ran up the corridor.

My heart stopped.

His momentum carried him forward, tumbling to the ground. Mine carried me back around to the guard.

The guard whose knife was buried in Dane's gut.

He smiled.

Just like in the cage back on Thanda, instinct guided my body, rage fueling it. Only this time, I had everything Dane taught me. No wasted movement, every action living only in its own moment.

Pain sparked through me and I added it to the fire consuming my body. I attacked. When the guard blocked, I hit harder. When he dodged, I moved faster. My vision blurred, but that didn't slow me down.

Soon a knife stuck out of the guard's chest. My knife. I couldn't remember how it had gotten there. It didn't matter. I had to help Dane.

A siren blasted my ears, echoing off the smooth walls. Lockdown. If we got trapped in that chamber, it was over.

I turned, and my eyes found Dane's. He was still with me. He looked right at me and took a breath.

"GO!"

And I did. I ran to the far side of the hub and slid into a new corridor before the security door slammed down.

I didn't turn back until I heard Dane's muffled cry.

The picture of the room seconds before flashed in my mind. He'd collapsed right on the threshold. If he hadn't pulled himself all the way in before the door . . .

"Dane!" I screamed, pounding my fist against the steel.

A control panel blinked on the wall, and I ripped the cover off, jamming a link from it to my slate. My eyes scanned the encryption and security protocols, figuring how it was put together. Fifteen minutes. That was how long it would take me to stitch a patch to open the door despite the lockdown. 'Gig could've done it in ten.

We didn't have fifteen minutes.

My mother's voice vibrated in my bones. *Windsong needs you to give them better than they have.*

Echoes of Dane's voice in my mind, yelling at me to go, shattered the ice I kept around my heart.

He might already be dead on the other side of the door. If he wasn't, he would be soon.

The siren kept reminding me: *No time, no time, no time.*

I bit my knuckle until it bled, staring at the door as if I could go back and change the last few minutes.

I couldn't. Every action lived in its own moment.

"I'm sorry, Dane. I'm so sorry."

And I ran again.

28

THE COMMAND TERMINAL held more tech than I'd ever seen in one place in my life. When I thought about all the different things the massive computer system controlled, my hands snapped to my sides, afraid to touch anything. I'd never been afraid to touch a computer in my life.

Shut it, Essie, you'll have to touch it to stitch it.

The blaring screech of the lockdown siren tempted me to find its controls and turn that off first, but everything else was too important. I unloaded several gadgets from my kit, all stitched during spare moments, none guaranteed to help. At the least, I'd have to do plenty of on-the-spot modification now that I knew what I was dealing with.

This was a lot bigger than cracking MineNet just to see if I could.

Step one was to crack a single layer of access so I could burrow my way in and get access to *everything*. A dummy lockpick program distracted the security systems while I opened up a panel to see if I could stitch my way around. First try hit a dead end, but the second weaseled through.

Display screens along the wall scrolled mountains of information. Too many systems, too many subroutines. Chaos. I hated chaos. I had to get my bearings, find order amidst the badly organized madness.

Everything had a category, whether it was marked or not. Water treatment—I cut my way in and looked at the code to see what it did. I found no routines for sanitization checks or purifying cycles or anything else water might actually need. Just for "targeted additives." Another look confirmed it handled releasing the various poisons in different provinces, down to individual houses.

I shut it down completely.

Orbital defense grid. That got shut down, too, clearing a path for the Candaran fleet.

Next, broadcasting. I didn't want to be delicate and selective. I wanted the broadcast frequencies open—all of them.

The communication system seemed to like its privacy, but I'd been dealing with the drones for years. They were more stubborn than this bloated computer would ever be. I got down underneath a console and ripped off another panel.

My hands shook. The right still bled where I'd bitten it.

Dane . . .

A plume of black hopelessness rose up in my core, flooding out to my trembling fingertips. Now I really understood the sound he'd made that day in the mountains in a way I couldn't before. The day his world ended.

The same sound fought its way through my lungs.

I slammed my hand onto the marble floor, focusing on the sting. "Not. Now. Essie," I muttered.

Solve the puzzle.

My first stitch nearly tripped a lockout, but I cut it off with a second. A third convinced the communication system I was the best friend it could ever have.

For the first time in years—my lifetime, at least—communication on Windsong was free and open. I doubted anyone knew it yet. That was about to change.

I got back to my feet and entered several commands on the console, locking in the frequency I'd memorized for the Candaran fleet and opening a channel on the off-planet network.

"This is Snow," I said. "You lot had better be where you're supposed to be."

"Ready and waiting." Kip's voice. The black ache inside swelled again. "What's the situation?"

I swallowed hard so I could get the words out. "Matthias is dead, the defense grid is down, and I'm about to make the broadcast. Start moving in."

I cut off the transmission before he could ask about Dane.

A little more digging revealed a section for outland operations with two subsystems nested inside. The networks each side used to communicate and coordinate their forces. I double-checked which was for the so-called Exiles and killed it. Then I flagged several files, adding to my collection of evidence, skimming the contents as I did.

The operational overviews revealed how my father had kept the deception so secret. The "Exile" army was relatively tiny. Most of the attacks were automated, like the one on Saddlewood.

Just enough troops to stage occasional man-to-man battles. Enough to convince the world. Few enough to be sure of their loyalty.

A lot of blood on those few hands.

Something else in those networks made my brain itch. I looked closer. All the "Exile" operations had Olivia's clearance code tagged on, while the militia's had Father's. Every single one, no exceptions. The networks had been fully isolated from each other until I opened up the whole system. Had Father and Olivia worked as a team, keeping things separate for clarity, or had Olivia been behind the fake war all along, duping Father as much as everyone else?

Had I made a mistake?

Too much oxygen and not enough. Another panic attack. I couldn't focus.

I thought of his expression when he talked about the Exiles and violence in the outlands. He'd lied to me too many times. I didn't know what sincerity looked like on his face.

If he hadn't known...if he'd thought the war was real...had he still deserved to die?

I thought of my bedroom, what Dane had kept from happening. What no one else had ever stopped. Was that enough reason for Father to be dead?

It was for me.

And Dane...

My knees half buckled before I caught myself on the console. The scream of the lockdown siren pushed me back up.

Not yet!

My job was almost finished. I took out my locket and retrieved the data-chip, loading it into a reader. All I had to do was add its files to those I'd just rounded up, compiling them all into one packet, and set up a broadcast for all available channels.

I got halfway through the first part when something slammed into my side, knocking me to the ground.

Instinct rolled me into a crouch, facing the attack, despite the pain radiating through my ribs.

Olivia. She'd slipped in the direct entrance through the royal quarters.

Too slow, Essie! I'd known she'd be on her way. Where else would she have gone?

"What have you done?" she demanded, advancing on me.

I didn't bother with an answer. I was more concerned with the long rod in her hand. The police force in the Bands carried something similar to beat down kids who got in their way. The blazing siren drowned out the sound of her metal-encrusted boots on the hard floor.

She had the rage—that was clear on her face—but I knew she didn't have training or practice. I could handle this.

I dodged her next swing, nearly flattening myself on the ground, then grabbed the weapon before she could change direction. I tried to yank it away, but she pressed something on her end of the rod.

The invisible cage in the VT fight on Garam was nothing but a gentle breeze compared to the pain that charged through me. Every muscle went rigid. I couldn't breathe. I couldn't see. I couldn't even cry out.

Maybe this was death. So close, only to fail at the end.

But the pain stopped, leaving echoes twitching through me. Still a chance, but I'd have to be sharp.

"You stupid, selfish little girl," Olivia said, the rod poised for another strike. "Your father should be here by now. Where is he?"

I pushed myself off the floor, telling my ribs and head to shut it when they screamed. "Dead."

The look in her eyes brought a pulse of satisfaction, dulling the pain. "You lie."

"No. I watched him bleed to death."

Her shriek might have held words, but I didn't waste energy deciphering them. I scooted away from her wild swings, dodging to avoid contact with the weapon.

Just a little space. Just enough room to move. Just enough to get to the console and enter the last few commands. But Olivia had always been driven, and now was no different. I kept from getting hit again but couldn't even find enough time to stand.

Finally I had an opening. I slammed my foot into her knee. She cried out and stumbled back but didn't fall. Still, it broke her rhythm, making her more wary.

She wasn't used to pushing through pain.

I slipped my hand into my pocket, grasping the cylinder. I needed to move back, get just a few sniffs more space. A little stalling should give me time to do it.

"We both know you're going to kill me," I said. "Could you at least tell me why?"

"Because I'm tired of you getting in the way, wretched girl. You're just like your mother, bringing nothing but weakness to your father."

I was in the way because I was in line to the throne, but I saw something else beneath the surface, shining in her eyes. The reason she hated *me*.

She knew what he'd done. She blamed me for that weakness.

I almost threw the canister right then, but I was still too close. Before I could find a way to continue stalling, she did it for me.

"I won't make the same mistakes he did. I'll destroy all the Exiles as we should have years ago. You'll be the first to go."

So she knew that, too. "You mean the second. My mother was the first. Why didn't you just tell my father what she was?"

"Because the fool loved her. He would have made her death too quick. You Exiles deserve to suffer."

Exiles suffering . . . Dane . . .

I couldn't afford the distraction. Not yet.

"Someone taught you that we deserve to suffer," I said. "Who was it?"

The venom in her eyes could have turned a harri-harra in its tracks. "The Exile who killed my parents."

An unexpected flicker of pity moved through me. I understood pain so deep it could steer the whole course of a life, change an identity.

But Theo and the soldiers at Saddlewood shouted the truth in my head. Father may have deserved to die, and whoever killed Olivia's family, too. But *they* didn't deserve it.

My mother didn't.

Dane didn't.

I didn't.

Olivia came at me with the rod again, charged high enough I could see sparks crackling on its surface.

Please, Dimwit, if you've ever done anything right, let this be it.

I pulled the canister from my pocket, flicked the release valve with my thumb, and threw it at her.

The chemicals reacted instantly. Blue flames blossomed around her legs, concentrated on the metalwork of her boots, which began to glow with heat.

Her screams melded with the siren. I rolled out of her path, but the heat followed my right foot. My boot had caught fire where I'd kicked her, picking up some of the thederol. I yanked it off and threw it across the room. My foot still felt like fire, but the burn wasn't bad.

Olivia tried removing her boots as well, but they were too thoroughly engulfed to touch. She hopped in a strange sort of dance, stumbling toward the console.

My breath caught. She couldn't destroy the computer. I braced myself to knock her out of the way if I had to, but she tumbled the other way into a wall.

Then the flames were everywhere.

I wrapped my arms around my head, trying to block out the sound. Nothing could block the smell—the acrid, putrid stench of burning death. I retched.

By the time the fire control system recognized the unusual flame and released its extinguishing spray, it was too late. I tried not to look, but once I did, I couldn't un-see it. *I did that to her.*

If my stomach hadn't already emptied itself, it would have at that moment. Then I remembered the man at Saddlewood who'd been blown apart in front of me.

I didn't know how to feel.

Instead of deciding, I hauled myself off the floor and hobbled to the console, my burned foot screaming every step. My hands couldn't hold a tool steady enough for the sloppiest stitch, but it didn't matter. The stitching was done. I tapped the last commands, and my recorded message was loaded into the communications network, moments away from going worldwide. System-wide.

The job was finished.

Dane...

My head ran the numbers automatically. The knife wound, the rate of blood loss, the time that had passed.

And that assumed he'd gotten clear of the security door.

I didn't bother fighting the tears. There was no one left to hide them from. The siren silenced, and my own voice echoed through the room.

"I am Princess Snow, daughter of King Matthias. Many of you remember my mother, Queen Alaina. When I hear you speak of her, I know how loved she was by her people. But she had a secret. She was not one of you. She was Candaran—an Exile."

I had to get into the security hub. Had to see for myself. But it was still locked.

"Although I was young when she died, I know she regretted the dishonesty. She did it because she believed she could make a difference for this world, for this solar system. Because she knew that my father, King Matthias, is an evil man."

"Aye, he *was*," I muttered, loading command codes onto my slate.

"Included with this broadcast are files detailing the crimes of Matthias and Olivia. I encourage you to examine them closely, confirm that there's been no tampering. Above all else, I am here to inform you that there is no war against the Exiles. The armies slaughtering the militia in the outlands are controlled by the crown. As I speak, the true forces of Candara are moving in to end the bloodshed. Do not fear them."

Fear...every shambling step down the corridor toward the

security hub amplified the fear shuddering through me. But I didn't stop.

"They are not here to take power. They are here for me. My true name is Elurra. I am a daughter of both Windsong and Candara. And I am asserting my right to the throne, but only if the people of Windsong will have me."

Right then I didn't want the throne. I wanted to see the nightmare awaiting me and let the world end.

The message finished, leaving me in silence at the security door. I entered a code from the slate and braced myself, imagining the worst so I couldn't be surprised.

Surprise gave way to confusion.

The guard I'd killed lay just where I'd left him. The door on the opposite side of the hub was already open, a large pool of blood crossing its threshold.

So much blood.

But no body. No Dane. Just some very strange tracks trailing away from the blood.

Tracks that looked suspiciously like those of a four-legged mining drone.

29

I FOLLOWED THE BLOOD TRAIL through the maze of corridors but quickly ran into a problem. The technicians flooded out of their labs and spotted me. I couldn't run—not with one boot and a burned foot on top of what felt like badly bruised ribs and an overall aching body. But their approach didn't seem violent. It seemed more...concerned.

"Princess, you have to get somewhere safe."

What does safe have to do with anything? "Have any of you seen a robot, about this tall?"

"What? They'll know you're down here. Come on."

A couple of them took my arms and hurried me along, taking most of the weight from my injured foot. My brain couldn't process fast enough.

"Who are you talking about?" I asked. "Who'll know I'm here?"

"The king and queen. Your broadcast."

I shook my head. "They're both dead."

The whole group of them paused. Then a man behind me gave a gentle shove. "It doesn't matter. The Exiles have arrived and the Midnight Blade are resisting. Maybe the Golden Sword, too."

"How do you know?"

"The networks are flooding with information now that the locks are off."

But where's Dane?

They didn't know the answer to that, so I went with a different question. "Why are you helping me?"

The woman holding my left arm replied. "We suspected what your father used our poisons for, but those who tried speaking up...nothing good happened."

"And we *do* remember your mother," added the man behind me. "Queen Alaina was a good woman."

"But she was an Exile. I'm half Exile."

Someone in the group laughed. "Well, not doing a very good job possessing us, are you?"

They got me into the lift—no more unconscious guard inside—and things started to blur. Servants and technicians hurrying me to the private chamber behind the throne room. Watching the networks as word spread that the king and queen were dead. A member of the Golden Sword arriving and swearing his loyalty to me, guarding the room.

Waiting. Worrying. *What happened to Dane?*

After hours or days or only a lifetime of minutes, the door opened. I tried to stand, but my body refused.

Half the governing council of Candara entered, Stindu at the head. He wasn't the one I wanted to see. "Where's Kip?" I asked.

"Still seeing to the skirmishes in the outlands," Stindu said.

"The Midnight Blade have stood down, but more fighting of one kind or another could break out any time. You promised us a queen. Time to see if you can deliver."

I couldn't. I'd planned everything up to this moment, but never imagined I'd live long enough to see the other side.

Not alone, anyway.

The door opened again.

"Dimwit! Where's Dane?"

"Dane Dimwit call Dimwit."

The wrist transmitter. Dane had been wearing it. "Report, Dimwit. Tell me what happened."

"Dimwit door open. Dimwit medical protocols. Doctors Dane doctors."

Something inside me exploded, like a ball of light filling me up. "You got him to a hospital? He's alive?"

A long beep. "Doctors critical critical critical! Dimwit Essie find Essie."

The light dimmed but didn't go out. Dane had been alive when Dimwit got to him, but I'd seen the blood. It might have been too late.

Or it might not.

The council erupted around me, demanding to know what had happened, waiting for me to translate Dimwit's broken speech patterns.

I held up my hand. I had to know how bad it was. "Shut it! Dimwit, you said you opened the door. Was it completely closed?"

One beep. That was no.

"What blocked it?"

"Legs...Dane legs."

Claiming the throne should have meant I could do what I wanted, but another lifetime passed before I left the palace and went to the hospital with a pair of Golden Sword guards. Madness ruled the hallways, doctors and medics rushing to treat casualties—some royal guards, some Candarans, and some citizens caught in the middle.

The hospital staff had better things to do than attend to royalty, so I was glad I'd wrapped my hair under a scarf and told the guards to act like we were just there to check on injured friends. It helped that I was there to do exactly that. Dimwit tapped into the computer system to find Dane's room, leaving the doctors to do their healing.

The guards remained stationed in the hall when Dimwit and I went in. I stood just inside the door, motionless except for one hand pulling the scarf off my head. Dane lay on the bed, one arm dangling over the edge. The drone went straight to the medical readouts, but they were beyond me, so I stared at Dane's chest until I saw it move at least twice. He was alive, but so pale. "Major blood loss and trauma." That had been the doctors' reply to the palace's inquiry. "Recovery uncertain. Will continue to monitor."

The sheets were drawn up to cover him, but the shape underneath was unmistakable: one leg intact, the other ending at the knee.

The bed angled to prop him up a little. His arm dangling over the edge like that irked me. Like no one cared that he had precious little blood to spare and could hardly afford to have any of it pooling in his hand. That finally moved me across the room. I took his hand to rest it more comfortably at his side, but once I held it, I found myself not letting go.

I couldn't let go.

I studied his face as I had never dared when he was awake, as I hadn't since pulling him unconscious from his shuttle. The planes and angles, the lines of his jaw and nose that made him look vaguely like his uncle. The curve of his lips, usually so serious, but waiting for a reason to smile.

He was still beautiful.

I was still terrified.

The things that terrified me now were much more complicated and confusing.

His lips continued to draw my eye. I hardly remembered what it had been like when he'd kissed me. Too fast, too sudden, and I'd been too half-asleep. But the reason I hadn't broken his nose was obvious. He was the first person I'd ever *wanted* to kiss.

Maybe it was unhinged. Maybe it was even wrong. But I didn't know whether he'd make it through another hour, and I couldn't risk losing my last chance.

I drew one leg up to half kneel on the edge of his bed, gently resting his hand on his chest. My heart thundered, which only made me wish I could lend some of its strength to him. With the slightest hesitation, my fingers skimmed over those perfect lines of his face—through the brown curls that tickled the edge of his ear, down along his jaw, and over his chin before brushing lightly across his lips.

I leaned forward, my hair falling over my shoulder, so close I discovered he had seven tiny freckles sprinkled across his nose.

Then closer, and I closed my eyes, pressing my lips to his. They were warm, still with life in them.

His lips touching mine, touching me, and I wasn't lashing out or running away. I'd spent my life always doing one of the two, but not anymore. Not when it came to him.

I pulled away enough to whisper, "Don't you dare die. Not when I'm finally ready."

Then I kissed him again just to hold the tears back. He couldn't die. I couldn't lose him.

He shifted beneath me.

Before I could back away, his fingers curled around the back of my neck, holding me in place.

I let them. I'd never let anyone so close before. But I never wanted Dane any farther away from me again.

Then it was a real kiss, his lips moving to find where they fit with mine, exploring and searching. I swore I could read his mind without Transitioning, could feel how he'd ached for this, how long he'd been waiting.

Or maybe that was me.

My fingers wound through his hair, memorizing the gentle curls. His other hand found my waist and pulled me to him, pressing against my bruised ribs, and I winced.

Dane stopped, but kept me close. "You're hurt."

I looked at him like he was unhinged, because he was. "Nowhere near as badly as you are."

His fingers lightly ran up my side, adding pressure until the tingle that stole my breath gave way to another sharp twinge through my rib cage. "That's bad enough."

"I'm fine. Are you in pain? I shouldn't—I'm sorry—"

He silenced me with another brief kiss, sending sparks of electricity down my spine—the kind that definitely didn't hurt—his fingers tangling in my hair. "I feel all right, Essie. I think it has something to do with that thing."

I followed his nod to the device strapped to his upper arm. A med-infuser. Lots of painkillers, probably, and something to prevent infection, especially for his leg.

"Your leg. Dane..."

"It's better than being dead. You can stitch me up a replacement as good as the original, I bet."

That wasn't funny. But I was surprised he knew what I was talking about. "You know what happened?"

"I first woke up a while ago. The doctor explained everything to me. I'm lucky they saved the one."

"No one told me you woke up. It took hours to get them to tell me anything! I didn't know if...I thought you might..."

"Are you saying you wouldn't have kissed me if you knew I'd live?"

"No, just...I was scared."

He gently pulled me down to lie next to him, my head tucked against his shoulder. So close. So unfamiliar. It set my skin buzzing.

Moving away wasn't an option.

"I was scared, too," Dane said. "The doctor couldn't answer all my questions. The prisoners?"

"The council rescued them. They're in a hospital closer to the prison."

"Good. But something's still bothering you. What's wrong?"

A lot of things were bothering me, but when I came to the hospital, it was with one particular question ricocheting in my

head. "When you told me to go, to run, did you Tip me? I don't know how to keep you from Transitioning to me."

"Why do you want to know?"

"Because if you did, I hate you for it. If you didn't, I hate myself for not even hesitating."

"Then I did. Can't have you hating yourself."

"Don't. Tell me the truth."

"Dane truth Dane," Dimwit added.

Dane sighed and immediately winced, the chirp of the medical monitors speeding up. The stab wound. He was in more pain than he'd let on.

"Essie, I told you I would never do that. Not without your permission. But don't hate yourself for it. It was what I *wanted* you to do. And it worked, right? We won."

Won... Was that what we'd done? My mind filled with images—my father bleeding to death, the guard with my knife in his chest, Olivia's body consumed by flames, the council demanding I make decisions, take action, act like the queen I'd promised I'd be.

"I'm scared I'm going to botch this, Dane," I said softly. "The plan was to die fighting and make sure someone who knew how to be a leader stepped in. Someone like you, or Kip. I don't know how to be a queen. Not really. Blazes, we both know what a miserable act the whole princess thing has been."

"What if I could do it with you?"

"How?"

"Every queen has her king."

I twisted around to raise an eyebrow at him. "Oh, I see. You want the Windsong throne instead of Candara's?"

He smiled, so he knew I was teasing. "That's not really it."

"You need to work on your timing. Suggesting I marry you when I've only just gotten used to the idea of kissing you, it's completely—"

He silenced me again with another kiss, one my body relaxed into. I was definitely getting used to it.

His next words weren't teasing at all. "Essie, I don't want you to be alone and scared anymore. That's all. Royal engagements are always long. If you decide you don't need me or my help anymore, you can change your mind."

"Well, that's not likely, is it? I'm a right stubborn mine-rat."

"Essie stubborn Essie."

"See, even Dimwit knows it," I added.

"I think that drone's a bit sharper than you realize," Dane said. "He could make a good nanny someday."

A strange sort of tingle fluttered through me. "First kissing, then an engagement, and now you're talking about kids already? Are all Candarans in such a blazing hurry?"

He closed one hand on mine. I hadn't realized I'd laid it on his chest. "No, it's probably just me."

"You'll be here to help me either way, won't you?"

"Definitely."

Something twisted inside. "What about Candara?"

"That's the beauty of it. Like you said, you're a daughter of both worlds. I'm Candaran, but Windsong is my home. Maybe we can finally bring our people back together somehow. Garamites and Thandans, too. This is where we all started." He fell silent, but something in his hold told me he had more to say. "There's a problem, though," he finally said.

"Only one? I can think of at least ten."

"If we go ahead with it...if you say yes...how do we tell our children that we fell in love after I kidnapped you?"

I thought back to waking up on the shuttle, how angry I'd been, how much I'd wanted to kill Dane when I understood his plans.

It felt like three lifetimes ago.

I slipped my hand away from his so I could touch his cheek, familiarizing myself with the feel of his skin, the slight hint of stubble after what had been a very long day. "If they ask, we'll tell them we met when I saved your life, and then you saved mine."

"What, with the sinkhole? I told you, that was Dimwit, not me."

"Dimwit Essie save Essie."

I laughed—the first laugh in years I'd really felt. "Fine, Dimwit, you can have credit for that one. But my life on Thanda wasn't a life. It was trying to disappear, to exist without existing. You saved me from that, Dane."

"Let's agree on something, then. Your job will be to do what your mother wanted. To give the people better than they've had. And my job will be to make sure you still have time to stitch and weave like you really want to."

That sounded nice. Terrifying, but nice. Maybe we could do it, at least for a few years. Until we undid some of the damage my father's family had inflicted on this system. And maybe as the worlds healed, the people would rig a better way, one that didn't need me to be their queen. I could tinker and fuss with drones and computers, and we could do it in a place that wasn't freezing every single day.

No hiding. No running. That could be a life worth living.

"Dane Essie kiss Essie."

No idea where he'd learned that word.

It was a good idea, though.

30

I STARED AT THE WALL-SCREEN. Newsfeeds from all four planets scrolled in divided sections. More data than one person could absorb, but I tried anyway. When the words started to blur, I tapped some commands on my slate, and the display changed. Much cleaner, less hitting me at once, but the information it held still jammed my headache-throttle to *full*.

The vote had passed overwhelmingly in all the provinces, accepting me as queen of Windsong. The population wanted confirmation that the governors hadn't been complicit in the war before deciding whether they could keep their posts. I agreed, so we were still sorting through files. Until that was settled, all the provinces reported directly to the Royal City.

Thanda was largely behind me as well, thanks to Petey. He had pull on MineNet. I wanted them to have more autonomy, but they needed help to improve living conditions. The Station chiefs—the closest each settlement had to a leader—formed a coalition to work out details.

Garam was another matter. Much more complicated, with many more opinions on how things should be run. Brand served as liaison on that front, keeping me updated.

Then the biggest source of my headaches. A variety of petitions came in from all sides daily, problems for me to fix, puzzles for me to solve. Too many for one person.

Someone entered the office through the door at my back as I switched to another feed. I didn't bother turning. The barely audible click every other step told me who it was long before he wrapped his arms around my waist. I held them there, just in case he thought of letting go.

A sparkle caught my eye. The sight of Dane's mother's ring on my finger still startled me after days and days of wearing it. I pushed the surprise away with the memory of how happy Dane had been when I said yes. How happy I'd been, and still was, especially in moments like this, when we were alone and some of the pressure of being queen drifted away.

"How's the pain?" I asked.

"What pain?"

Every day, I asked; every day, he denied feeling any. It was the only lie I let him get away with. Not like the weight he felt from the blood on his hands. He didn't get to keep that from me. Just like I didn't from him.

But if the pain ever got worse, I'd call him on it.

"I should adjust that actuator on your leg. It might help."

"If you want. Are these the committee logs?"

I sighed and nodded. "I'm not sure they'll ever settle this. How can we make sure Candarans don't abuse their—our— abilities without starting at the assumption that Transitioning is evil? How can anyone trust *me* to be fair about it?"

The warmth of his breath tickled as he whispered in my ear. "Essie. They do. And why shouldn't they trust Elurra, the Supreme Crown?"

"Dane," I admonished him. "Don't call me that. No titles, not between us."

His lips nuzzled along my neck. "My Elurra, my Essie, my brave and clever queen. I'll call you anything you want."

"If I'm brave, it's because I have a good partner. Fifty-one days without system-wide war, but I'm scared it won't last."

"Brave is being scared and doing what needs to be done anyway. Like your mother taught you."

I glanced at the painting above the desk, one of the few things from my childhood I'd kept in the palace when I took the throne. It was of me and Mother—her gaze steady, cradling infant-me in her arms. Calm, but strong. I still wasn't sure how much of her I had in me, but I was learning.

"My bravery cost you a leg," I said. "I hate that."

"Shh. I'm alive and I have you. My leg was a fair price."

Before I could protest more, he turned me around, drew me close, and kissed me. The palace disappeared, and with it all my worries. No more queen of Windsong and prince of Candara. Just Dane and Essie, the only perfect fit I'd ever found in my life.

He pulled back, keeping me firmly in his arms and pressing his lips to my forehead. "You're doing a good job."

"So are you—a good job of distracting me," I teased.

"That's not the only good job I'm doing. I came to tell you how well the conference with the interim provincial leaders went."

"How well *did* it go?"

"I was so charming, they're falling in love with me despite my Candaran status."

"They'd better not," I said, sliding my fingers up the back of his neck so they tangled in his hair. "I'm the only one who gets to fall in love with you."

"I suppose I shouldn't argue with the queen."

I didn't answer, just closed the distance to kiss him again. When I let him go, his smile matched mine.

"Well," he said, "since we've mutually distracted each other, I have a surprise for you. Your engagement gift has arrived."

"I thought we decided not to bother with anything like that."

"I changed my mind. Come see it before you decide whether to be angry. I'll help you go through the logs later."

The data and decisions weren't going anywhere, so I let him guide me out of the office. Dane's stride distracted me as we walked. Anyone who didn't know better would think he just had a limp rather than a prosthetic. I could make it better, though. A new stitch or two, improving the neural-cybernetic interface, and I *would* make it better.

I heard my gift long before I saw it. Chirps and beeps . . . and a few well-chosen expletives.

I turned to Dane, my eyes wide, and he grinned, giving the small of my back a little nudge. With that encouragement, I ran the rest of the way to the entrance hall and saw my ears hadn't lied to me.

Six drones scuttled and skittered, exploring the hall—seven if you counted Dimwit, which I definitely did. Ticktock measured the individual tiles in a wall mosaic, Clank and Clunk argued over which tapestry was older, and Cusser . . . Cusser was patched and whole. Not just whole, but himself again, living up to his name due to Zippy slipping and falling on the marble floor. Whirligig spotted me first and scurried over.

"Instructions, Essie?"

I just stared as Dane caught up, enfolding me in his arms again. "Cusser. How?" I asked. "It would've taken me the better part of a Thandan cycle to repair him."

"Candara has a few things you didn't on Thanda. And once they retrieved the others, 'Gig gave us Cusser's backup programs. He doesn't remember anything after being brought back online, but otherwise should be fine."

I looked around at the seven of them. "But we can't," I protested. "The men in Forty-Two need them. The mine's too dangerous. It isn't fair."

"Mining is on hold. Everyone's working on building up the Bands, and I thought maybe some of the Thandans will want to come settle in the outlands. Your father's merinium reserves are more than enough to keep things going while the rest of the drones are upgraded. They probably won't have the personality of this lot, but that's why I wanted them with you, where they belong. I know you've missed them."

I had. The unpredictable little drones had been my first and only friends until Dane found me. They all looked at me, waiting—even Zippy, who kept trying to get up too fast, which led to more sliding on the floor.

"Remind me which one's Clank," Dane said, so close his breath tickled my ear. I pointed out the drone. "Clank, wasn't there one more thing?"

Clank's storage compartment popped open. He pulled something out and handed it to me.

Mother's notebook. It settled into my hands like a piece of

me, its worn edges ingrained in my memory. I looked up at Dane, unable to find the words to thank him. His smile told me he knew.

"Essie? Instructions?" Whirligig repeated.

I flipped open the notebook, going straight to the sketch of the dragonfly hovering over the orchid.

"Well, I don't know, 'Gig," I said. "Maybe you should download some data files on gardening."

That got them all going again, as Ticktock began listing apple tree varieties and Clank and Clunk debated whether roses or orchids were better in the Royal City's climate. It was noisy and chaotic and disruptive.

It was exactly what the palace needed.

With all that activity, my eye went to the one thing *not* moving. Dimwit stood off to the side, still looking at me.

"Dimwit Essie queen Essie," he said. "Essie mother proud."

And the twitchy malfunction who'd never botched anything he didn't mean to dipped himself into an unmistakable bow.

I didn't fight the tear that slipped down my cheek.

I smiled, and I bowed back.

ACKNOWLEDGMENTS

I WASN'T SUPPOSED TO DO THIS.

I was supposed to be a left-brained math teacher with the extra quirk that I can discuss calculus in sign language. But a whim led to an attempt, an attempt led to an obsession, and several manuscripts later, here we are. Without support and encouragement and challenges from amazing people, I'd still be stuck on that whim.

My gratitude and a touch of idol-worship to my editors, Catherine Onder and Lisa Yoskowitz, who pushed me to know every in and out of my characters and story. Thanks to the genius design team at ilovedust for the amazing cover illustration, and to everyone at Hyperion who helped take this from an idea in my head to a book for real people.

All things are possible because of my agent, Jennifer Laughran. She's a bookseller at heart and a book lover to her core. Thank you for believing in me, for telling it like it is, and for teaching me how to talk on the phone.

Many thanks to the founding members of the Dimwit Fan Club: MarcyKate Connolly, Johanna Quille, Jennie Bates Bozic, Riley Redgate, and Charlee Vale, along with the Kid Crits group at AgentQuery Connect for offering feedback on the early chapters. Special thanks to Mindy McGinnis for being my go-to gal when I needed to stick to my guns, swallow my pride, or get talked off the ledge. Thanks as well to the third leg of the Critecta, Caroline Poissonniez, for getting me to dig into the emotional context of my characters when all I could think about was plot.

Continuing thanks to my students, past and present, for never letting me forget how awesome teenagers are.

To my parents for keeping me well-stocked in books growing up. To my brother for starting my first attempt at writing when we were kids (a tag-team *Star Trek* fan fiction that didn't get very far). To my sister for reading chapters of *Stitching Snow* as I drafted, and keeping the fire lit by demanding, "More. Now. Faster!"

Here's to doing the unexpected.

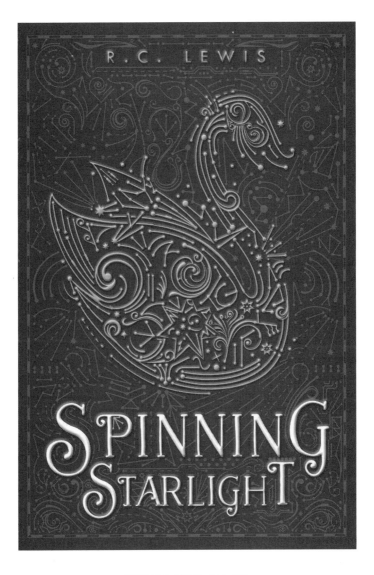

TURN THE PAGE
to start reading R.C. Lewis's next book,
a sci-fi retelling of Hans Christian Andersen's
"The Wild Swans."

1

AFTER SIXTEEN YEARS, you'd think I'd be used to the incessant buzz of vid-cams swarming to chronicle every breath I take. I'm not. Good thing, too, or I might not have noticed when one of the tiny airborne devices slips into the hovercar with me like an errant bumblebee. I shoo it like the pest it is. The lights and hustle of Pinnacle blur by until the city thins, then disappears as I enter the country—or the closest thing to "country" you can find on Sampati. A small river winds through fields and woods extending for several miles, with no sign of any neighbors. The house greets me with a few warm lights along the front path.

As nice as it is to be away from the noise of the city, the two seconds of silence as I open the door press in on me, twist in my ears. I hate the sound of an empty house. It isn't natural.

"Welcome home, Liddi." The disembodied voice breaks silence's hold, the same voice that's greeted me most of my life. Sometimes I wish it weren't the *only* voice greeting me now. "You've returned earlier than scheduled."

"It was like every other party, Dom. Loud music, too much lip gloss, and Reb Vester's existence. I got bored." Bored, and tired of the weight of myriad eyes watching me, manifesting as an ache in my lower back. Or maybe that's just from these shoes. I kick them off and pull the pins from my hair before tapping a touchscreen to activate the wallscreen in the main room. "Pull up those news-vids I was watching earlier. Resume playback."

The first vid loads with a familiar face, sienna-skinned and dark-haired like all us Jantzen kids, and I settle on the couch to watch. I'm not sure why I bother. I could recite these start to finish.

"Among technologists more than twice his age, eleven-year-old Durant Jantzen presented his biometric exercise unit at the Tech Reveal today. Athletes from Pramadam gave the system high praise. . . ."

"Jantzen twins Luko and Vic followed in their big brother's footsteps at this year's Tech Reveal, debuting a customizable pesticide. Ecologists on Erkir have already placed orders for ten thousand units. . . ."

"This year's Tech Reveal brought young Fabin Jantzen and his Domestic Engineer and Itinerary Keeper. . . ." I wonder if Domenik ever feels all meta hearing about his program's debut.

On and on they go. The first year Anton presented at the Reveal, then the triplets. Marek, Ciro, and Emil were only ten, so tiny next to the other technologists and already dubbing themselves the Jantzen Triad. That was the first year after Mom and Dad's accident. The year everything changed.

I watch more years, more Tech Reveals with all my brothers presenting inventions and innovations and upgrades. The narrative changes, though, becoming less about the technology, more about my brothers themselves.

More about me.

"*Durant Jantzen attended the opening of a new art exhibit on Yishu before returning for the Tech Reveal....*"

"*Vic Jantzen presented two different technologies before rushing off to the laserball title match....*"

"*No sign of the Jantzen girl at this year's Tech Reveal....*"

"*Luko, will your sister be presenting this year?*"

"*Emil, when will your sister stop partying and take her place in the family business?*"

"*Fabin, do you think your father made a mistake, leaving the majority of the company to the youngest of you?*"

My brothers answer the same way every time, staunchly supporting me. I don't go to that many parties—it just seems like I do because the media-grubs follow my every move. I'm taking extra time *because* of the responsibility I bear. Our father knew exactly what he was doing, seeing how competitive my brothers were with each other, but how they all doted on me. When I turn eighteen and take control of Jantzen Technology Innovations, the boys will support me. It won't tear the family apart the way it would've if Dad had picked one of them to take his place. They say I'm the best of the Jantzens, that everyone else will realize it soon.

That's been the story since I was six years old. I only believe some of it. Only the parts about my brothers. Somehow I have to make the rest come true.

"Turn it off, Dom."

I get up and go into the adjoining room, the workshop that takes nearly half of the house's first floor. Plenty of space, but I stick to the bench in the corner that's always been mine. This room used to be so noisy and busy, with computers beeping and tools whirring, Dom interrupting to tell us we forgot lunch and that if we didn't eat, he'd cut power to the whole shop.

Used to be, right up until last year when "the Triad" turned eighteen and moved to the city, becoming full-time technologists for JTI like everyone else.

The silence makes me itch.

"Dom, music."

"Genre?"

"Whatever they're saying is the new thing on Yishu. Surprise me."

A syncopated beat fills the room, followed by a point-counterpoint melody on electronic instruments engineered to sound like they're not electronic.

Durant designed some of those. I wonder if this is one of the recordings he's done under a false name. Maybe I'll ask next time I talk to him.

I fiddle with a few of the half-finished projects on my workbench for more than an hour, but it's no use. None of them are any good. Either they won't work, or they're inferior knock-offs of things my brothers came up with when they were half my age.

I can't do it. Not when everyone's watching. Not when my picking the wrong skirt is cause for its own media-cast.

"No Tech Reveal for me this year," I mutter. *"Again."*

The volume of the music cuts in half. "Please repeat, Liddi."

"I wasn't talking to you, Dom. Check my message queue. What have I got?"

He rattles off media-casts of my appearance at tonight's party, requests for interviews, invitations to parties and concerts and fashion shows. I cut him off in the middle of relaying that some senator's daughter from Neta wants me to go shopping with her.

"Nothing from the boys?"

"No."

It's been weeks since I've seen any of them, enough to deepen the ache when everything is quiet. As much as I tell them they don't need to worry about me being on my own, they don't usually believe me for this long at a stretch. Not that it's a big deal. They're busy with the work I'll be part of, if I can ever get my defective neurons to cooperate. Still...

"Dom, send a message to Emil. I'd like to see him." Emil's the youngest other than me. Not only will he drop everything—all my brothers would—but he'll tease me less for asking.

"Message sent. It's getting late. Time for bed?"

"Not yet. Discontinue music."

The house goes silent again as I tidy up my workbench, but I'm not sticking around long enough for it to bother me. I walk out the back door, the grass of the yard cold on my bare feet. Luna Minor is straight overhead, giving plenty of light, and there'll be even more when Luna Major rises in the next half hour. The night phlox is blooming pink and maroon, and the scent of the flowers brings back memories of playing hide-and-seek when we should've been in bed. A time when wondering what we'd have for breakfast tomorrow was my biggest worry about the future. When the scarier future and potential failures were still far enough away to forget sometimes.

I cross the yard into the stand of trees, letting the sound of the river draw me; the grass gives way to smooth pebbles, warming my feet a little with the heat they've retained from the day. It's never silent out here, not even at night. The water rushes along, and nocturnal insects chirp and chitter, the noise wrapping around me. Calming me. A little, anyway.

The Tech Reveal is just fifty-one days away. Hardly enough time to create something groundbreaking when I don't even have an idea yet. My brothers would never say so—they'd never pressure me—but I know everyone worries that I haven't come up with anything to present. Ever. At this rate, I'll be as old as an average technologist at debut. The idea of someone saying the word *average* in the same breath as *Jantzen* and it being my fault makes me shudder. I walk along the river's edge, hoping something will click.

Maybe the ecologists on Erkir could use a less disruptive way to irrigate their agricultural zones.

Maybe there's a way to help data flow more smoothly in the computer networks.

Maybe the tiny moths fluttering by could serve as a model for better vid-cams, with less buzzing.

Bad idea. The annoying buzz lets me know the cams are watching me, which they always are. Everywhere but here, because Luko set up an interference field like a bubble over the property so they can't get through.

Maybe I'll go to some of those events tomorrow so everyone can keep thinking my "busy social schedule" is the real reason I haven't lived up to the Jantzen name.

Domenik was right. It's late, and as nice as it is to walk down the river, it's not helping. I should get some sleep. That means getting back to the house. I've gone farther than I meant to, but at least the return trip means I'll be tired enough to fall right to sleep. Always a bright side.

Except comfortable thoughts of my bed leach away in the

not-silence of the trees and river. Some noises are missing; others don't belong, but I can't place them. A little closer to home, I figure it out.

Voices.

I didn't intend for Emil to drop everything *this* quickly, and he should know better. My feet slip on the bank's wet pebbles as I hurry to tell him off. Really, though, I'm hurrying to see him, so the telling-off will have to be brief. A few steps later, I curl my toes into the rocks.

That's not my brother's voice. None of my brothers sound like that, gruff and sharp-edged, and the voices are too near me, too far from the house.

If the media-grubs have trespassed on the property, my brothers will kill them for crossing that final line, especially in the middle of the night. It's breaking the law. Instinct pulls me into a crouch, then I'm sidling up to the closest tree and straining my ears.

"Team Two, are you in position?"

Not a media-grub. Then another voice, maybe over a live-comm. My pounding heart obscures the words.

"Team Four, hold the perimeter."

I don't like the sound of that. Another tree, a larger one, is nearby and closer to the voice. I creep over to it and peer around its trunk.

Five men all in black stand several yards away. Without the light from Luna Major, I might not see them in the darkness of the woods. They're carrying some kind of equipment and facing the house.

Three options present themselves. I can confront them, I can run, or I can wait and see what happens. Options One and Two are no good. If I heard the voice right, at least three other teams lurk out here. I don't know enough.

Option Three it is.

"All teams, on my mark...go!"

The men race toward the house, dodging the remaining trees before cutting through the yard. It's hard to see but it gets loud quick. A *boom* as they force the door open, maybe breaking it, then gunshots.

Guns.

Charge-bullets flying in my home. Where I should've fallen asleep more than an hour ago.

I brace myself against the trunk and force my legs to straighten out of my crouch. The bark scrapes my palms. Everything shakes.

Boys, what do I do? Why aren't you here? Why couldn't even one of you be here?

A few more shots, then an unmissable shout from somewhere inside the house.

"Find her!"

I'm running before the words fade from my ears.

The other teams could be anywhere—I don't know where their "perimeter" is, the edge of the property or closer in—but I run anyway. I run back along the river, back to where the trees beyond the banks are thicker. Faint sounds follow, then not-so-faint shouts of "This way!" and "Move it!" and "Box her in downriver!"

Boxed in. I picked the wrong direction. The river bends up ahead. If they're positioned right, they'll have me cornered.

The trees to my right block my view of anything useful, but across the river to my left is one of the clearings where the boys and I used to play. Something there catches my eye, and I slow enough to look through the darkness. A lone, shadowy figure stands in the middle of the clearing, waving to me. He's familiar. One of the twins, either Luko or Vic—I can't tell from this distance.

I don't dare call out, and he must not, either, because he just beckons me to him. Across the river. It's small enough, as rivers go, but my brothers always forbade me from setting foot in this part—during the hottest summer days, we swam in a slower stretch upstream.

The gunmen are getting closer, either in my imagination or in reality—doesn't much matter which. I wade in, cold water shocking my feet, the silty bottom squishing under my toes. The force of the current on my ankles, then calves, then knees threatens to push me over and sweep me along, but I fight. As I step toward the middle, the ground drops from beneath me and water rushes up past my chest.

I cry out briefly before clamping my mouth shut. Luko-or-Vic might hear and know I need help, but so might the gunmen. I have no purchase, no traction, and I'm carried several yards downstream. I stop fighting it and just try to make progress toward the opposite bank. A quick glance along the path of the river reveals just what I need—the dark shadow of an old log stretching halfway across. I brace myself and grab hold, the bark cutting into my hands and arms, but I don't lose my grip. It's enough that I can pull myself along the length of it until my feet are under me again.

My soaked skirt and top cling to me as I climb out of the river, the light breeze chilling every inch of my skin. It doesn't matter. I doubt the river is enough to stop the men after me, whoever they are, and I'll warm up soon enough. I force myself up the bank into the clearing and look for my brother.

He's not there.

I blink three times and rub the river water from my eyes. The light of both moons must be combining to play shadow games. But he's still not there.

You imagined him, Liddi. You're scared and wanted one of your big brothers to protect you, so your subconscious pointed the way out of the river-bend trap. And guess what—you're still scared.

The men across the river shout to each other, maybe asking if anyone sees me, if anyone's caught me yet.

I'm alone, and right now I'd give anything for some silence.

The woods continue past the clearing. No roads that way, but I don't need a road to find my way to Pinnacle's edge. The ground is rougher, not smooth pebbles and soft grass like it is on the house side of the river, and I curse my bare feet, but that doesn't matter, either.

I need to get to my brothers, so I run again.

※ — — — ※

I'm pretty sure my feet are bleeding but I can't look. I keep moving. The sight of blood isn't my favorite, and seeing it won't help the pain any. It's been ages since I heard any sign of the gunmen. I keep moving. Between the sweat and the dirt, everything itches, and my body aches. I can't remember which designer sent my latest party outfit. He'll die when he sees what I've done to it, filthy and ragged with a hem torn where it snagged on a branch. Still, I keep moving.

The trees thin, revealing the edge of Pinnacle in the dim

predawn light, and I finally stop. The city means civilization, protection. It means getting to my brothers, making sure we're all safe, and figuring out what in the Abyss is going on. I take a moment to orient myself. Anton's place is closest.

About a million people stand between me and the boys, and at least as many vid-cams. That keeps me frozen at the last tree. I'd had no reason to bring a com-tablet for my walk along the river, but now I would cut off my bleeding feet for one. I could live-comm one of my brothers, they could come get me, and I wouldn't have to walk alone into the city full of watching eyes.

Then again, maybe those eyes are a good thing. The gunmen came out to the house, the one place the vid-cams can't go, and in the middle of the night. Whatever they were planning to do, they wanted to be invisible. Maybe ransom. It would make sense as much as anything.

For once, having every sneeze caught on a vid might be exactly what I want. It might keep me safe long enough to get to my brothers.

Or I might have to run for it again.

If only my feet didn't hurt so much.

It takes ten minutes for the first vid-cam to find me. I'm still on the outskirts of the city, where there wouldn't be much hovercar traffic even if it weren't so early. The cams usually stick to downtown or the trendy entertainment districts, but a few wander the edge of the city, looking for something interesting.

Liddi Jantzen, dirty and bleeding, definitely qualifies as interesting.

One vid-cam turns into two or three, then a swarm buzzing around me. I'm too tired to care, too tired to do anything but force one throbbing foot in front of the other. But not too tired to notice when the buzz turns into voices and the swarm becomes a crowd of people. As the media-casts go out, people backtrace my position and realize I'm in their neighborhood. People who are up early to get ready for work, or insomniacs who haven't been to bed yet—I can tell them apart by whether their clothes are pressed or rumpled—all kinds gather around me. Talking, shouting, jostling . . . It's too much to process when the white-hot fire of my feet demands all my attention. The only other things I feel are the eyes. My rules kick in: never make eye contact. Just keep going.

"Look, I told you it's her—it's Liddi Jantzen!"

"Liddi, what happened? You're hurt."

"Get her off her feet."

"You need to see a doctor."

"More like she needs the police. Someone did this to her."

"She needs both. Get out of the way. Liddi, look at me. Do you remember me?"

I turn, afraid the voice belongs to someone from one of dozens and dozens of parties and clubs I've been to in the past couple of years. Most of those faces disappear from my mind as soon as I leave, so the chance I'll remember isn't good.

But I do recognize this one, and I find myself nodding. A man in his forties, his features slightly rounded and his hair graying. He's familiar, but the name won't come to me.

He must read the question in my eyes. "It's Garrin Walker. I was your father's assistant before . . . well, before. Come on, let's get you some help."

Of course. Walker-Man. That's what I called him when I was

little. He was younger, thinner, but his eyes were the same back when he'd let me play by his desk outside Dad's office. Back when I was the boss's daughter rather than the boss-to-be. Those eyes were sharp and intelligent, but also gentle. They still are. All I have to do is nod again, and he takes charge, guiding me through the crowd and into a waiting hovercar. The chatter and questions are sealed off outside the doors, and Garrin enters a destination in the hovercar's computer before turning to me.

"What did you do, Liddi? Walk all the way from the country estate?"

"Ran, mostly."

"Why? What happened?"

As much as Garrin was kind to me when I was five years old, I can't make the answer form in my mouth. The men breaking into my house. The shouts. The guns. Images flood my eyes, making Garrin less real than the memory.

"I need my brothers," I murmur. I need to know they're safe.

He might restrain a sigh—hard to tell—and nods. "Of course, I'll contact them. First, a doctor for you."

My head's getting too heavy for my neck, and my gaze falls to the floor. "I'm bleeding on your car."

"Don't worry about that."

I don't. Worrying takes too much strength, and I'm using it all thinking about the boys. How Marek would make me laugh, taking my mind off the pain, and how Luko would give me a hug. I need one. I need *them*.

My vision blurs with a combination of tears and exhaustion. I end up in a hospital room, quiet except for the light rush of air sanitizers and the meticulous efforts of the doctor taking care of my feet. His ministrations sting, then cool, then numb, and that final effect seems to spread through most of my body. I break out of the fog when raised voices erupt in the hallway. Loud enough to know it's an argument, but not loud enough to hear what it's about.

"Doctor, have any of my brothers arrived?" I ask.

"I'm not sure, Miss Jantzen. If they haven't, I'm sure they will shortly." He finishes with my feet and raises a scanner to the scrapes on my hands and arms. "You say you got these injuries running to the city from the wilderness preserve?"

It's not a preserve, it's my home, but there's no point in arguing with him. Like everyone else on Sampati, he's strictly a city-dweller, so I nod. "Well, and crossing a river."

His brows knit as he studies my expression. "A river. Why did you do that?"

"To get to the other side."

The doctor doesn't get to press further—thank the Sentinel—because the door to the hospital room bursts open. Two women stride in with Garrin trailing behind them. He's saying something about talking to me alone, but the women ignore him. The younger one wears the dark green uniform of the Sampati Police Force, but with black sleeves. So she's not just any cop—she's here on assignment from the military divisions on Banak. Her tall, muscular build and sleek haircut reinforce that fact, but even her formidable presence can't distract me from the other woman who entered with her.

"Ms. Blake," I greet, habit forcing me to sit up straighter. I may have played by Garrin's desk as a child, but there's no silliness with Ms. Blake, ever. The woman has been managing JTI for most of my life, running day-to-day operations for my brothers. Coordinating the various departments, evaluating which projects have the most promise... doing a lot of the things I'll have to know how to do someday.

"Liddi, are you well? Garrin says you were hurt. I assure you, Doctor, if she's not receiving the absolute best possible care, you'll—"

"I'm fine," I cut in. "Or, fine enough."

Ms. Blake stands right in front of me, her gaze cutting through. "Tell me exactly what happened."

I've been resisting all morning, resisting the words that make it real. My brothers should be the first ones I tell, but with Ms. Blake here, there's no choice. She needs to know.

"Men with guns came to the house. I was outside, walking... thinking. When they realized I wasn't in bed, they came looking, and I ran."

The women are frozen, but Garrin takes a half step forward. "Did they hurt you? Did you get a good look at any of them?"

I shake my head, answering both questions at once. His concern reminds me of my father, which only strengthens my need to see the boys. "Ms. Blake, please, has anyone told my brothers? They should be here. They might be in trouble, too."

Garrin inhales sharply. "That's just the thing," Ms. Blake says. "Liddi, no one's heard from your brothers in at least nine days. We can't find them."